Lady
and
the Beast

by

Gail MacMillan

Lady and the Beast

COPYRIGHT © 2010 by Gail MacMillan

Cover Art by *Tina Lynn*

The Wild Rose Press
PO Box 708
Adams Basin, NY 14410-0706
Visit us at www.thewildrosepress.com

Publishing History
First English Tea Rose Edition, 2010
Print ISBN 1-60154-802-8

Published in the United States of America

Looming over her in ghastly silhouette was a great dark creature whose features were enveloped in a mat of hair. A beast. Some kind of marauding beast come to end what was left of this horrible existence. As it reached to touch her, she opened her mouth to scream and choked.

A gush of vile liquid billowed up her throat. She vomited as the sky above her exploded with a bolt of lightning and roar of thunder. *I'm dying,* she thought. *And this is the grim reaper come for me.*

Then the creature spoke.

"There, there, lassie." Its voice, male and gently lilting with a Scottish burr, startled her. He rolled her onto her side. "Let it come. Ye must have swallowed half the Atlantic. Ye must get it out."

Battered beyond the ability to resist, she continued to belch up great quantities of brine. A feral terrain poked at her throbbing body. She heard waves crashing on a nearby shore. The sound stirred a flicker of memory, a tiny ember in the darkness of her mind. It extinguished as she vomited again.

Finally she choked up the last and lay with her teeth chattering, racked by cold, pain, and horror. Her shuddering brought a fresh agony racing over her. "My ankle!" she cried.

"It's broken, lassie." Again the soft, reassuring voice. "I've put it in a temporary splint. Now, come."

He gathered her in his arms and she couldn't protest. She hurt in every pore, her head hammered with nauseating pain. She moaned. If this half-human creature meant to kill her, it would be a kindness. She could only pray he proved merciful and did it quickly.

Another bolt of lightning rent the sky. In its illumination she caught a fleeting impression of long, curling dark hair and a heavy black beard torn back in the wind. So it was a man, a wild man with a strangely soothing voice and competent hands.

Kudos for Gail MacMillan...

...an award-winning author (*Biography of a Beagle*, 2002; *Ceilidh's Quest*, 2007, both dog stories) as well as author of eleven published romances and two history books. Her short stories and articles have won awards both in Canada and in the USA. She has also written for Reader's Digest Travel Books.

Dedication

To Ron with much love.

Chapter One

Enraged by screaming winds and torrential rain, the maniacal night writhed about as she struggled back to consciousness. Grit coated her lips and filled her hands when she clawed out to clutch something, anything that felt secure and solid. Overhead a storm-crazed sky roared and flashed. Pain coursed through her body and her very life's blood felt frozen by the cold. But the horror didn't end there. Looming over her in ghastly silhouette was a great dark creature whose features were enveloped in a mat of hair.

A beast. Some kind of marauding beast come to end what was left of this horrible existence. As it reached to touch her, she opened her mouth to scream and choked.

A gush of vile liquid billowed up her throat. She vomited as the sky above her exploded with a bolt of lightning and roar of thunder.

I'm dying, she thought. *And this is the grim reaper come for me.*

Then the creature spoke.

"There, there, lassie." Its voice, male and gently lilting with a Scottish burr, startled her. He rolled her onto her side. "Let it come. Ye must have swallowed half the Atlantic. Ye must get it out."

Battered beyond the ability to resist, she continued to belch up great quantities of brine. A feral terrain poked at her throbbing body. She heard waves crashing on a nearby shore. The sound stirred a flicker of memory, a tiny ember in the darkness of her mind. It extinguished as she vomited again.

Finally she choked up the last and lay with her teeth chattering, racked by cold, pain, and horror. Her shuddering brought a fresh agony racing over her.

"My ankle!" she cried.

"It's broken, lassie." Again the soft, reassuring voice. "I've put it in a temporary splint. Now, come." He gathered her in his arms and she couldn't protest. She hurt in every pore, her head hammered with nauseating pain. She moaned. If this half-human creature meant to kill her, it would be a kindness. She could only pray he proved merciful and did it quickly.

Another bolt of lightning rent the sky. In its illumination she caught a fleeting impression of long, curling dark hair and a heavy black beard torn back in the wind. So it was a man, a wild man with a strangely soothing voice and competent hands.

As he strode through the storm-savaged night with her in his arms, disjointed questions scrambled around in her brain. Where was she? How had she arrived at this weird place on this unholy night? Who was this man-beast carrying her with such strength and tenderness?

The ship. With the next bolt of lightning, remembrance flooded back. The ship caught in a vicious North Atlantic storm. The ship bucking like a thing possessed in the grip of gigantic waves and roaring winds, its bowsprit one moment pointing heavenward, the next plunging into the caldron of the sea. Water hitting her with crippling force. The brutal night alive with screams and frantic cries for help. Splintering wood. Blinding gusts of salt spray. A sailor lashing her to a lifeboat just before it broke free and plummeted over the side. Great masts snapping, cracking like cannon fire as the ship crashed sideways and waves began to gobble her up.

And then nothing.

The memories sent a shudder coursing through her.

"Lady Kathryn, Lady Kathryn..." she mumbled.

"Hang on, lass. We're almost there." Again, the strong, reassuring voice.

He stopped abruptly and kicked out with one foot. Wood creaked and grated, a shaft of light fell upon them, and he carried her out of the rain and wind into a shelter. She became aware of sudden warmth and the blessed glow of a fire on a stone hearth.

He placed her on a crude, blanket-covered bed. As he moved away toward the fire, her fevered gaze roved about the room and she saw that she was in a primitive log structure, its walls chinked with clay and moss, its floor earthen. A pair of benches on either side of a rough hewn table, a few shelves containing bits of crockery above a crude dresser, and a single ladder-backed chair comprised its furnishings. The beast's den, she thought, as she watched him place fresh logs atop the embers languishing on the hearth.

Well fed, the flames leaped to life and she saw him. Tall, over six feet surely, broad of shoulder and narrow of waist, her rescuer stood ramrod straight with not a single strand of gray in his thick hair and beard. Not an old man, then. Worn breeches, shabby knee-high boots, and a ragged coat suggested poverty. He stooped to swing a pot on a crane from over the flames.

Something wet and warm lashed over her face and another furred creature thrust itself against her. She started, a cry of pain lurching from her lips.

"Pilot, leave the lass alone!" The beast at the hearth swung around to admonish the bear-like dog. "She's been through enough this night without ye washin' her with yer great, wet tongue."

3

With a sigh, the dog turned away and went to lie down near the hearth.

The beast turned back to the pot and dipped a mug into it. Then he strode to the dresser and shook some white powder from one of the jars on its top into the steaming cup. He swirled it about as he returned to her bed. There he pulled the ladder-backed chair close, and sat down.

"Drink this." He raised her shoulders gently until she was in a half-sitting position and brought the cup to her lips.

"What is it?" She drew back, turning her head away.

"Something to ease your aches and pains and help you sleep. Donnae worry, lass. I won't be harmin' ye."

A silver key hanging on a chain about his neck glinted in the shadowy firelight and she wondered what secrets it guarded. But only for a moment. His soft, lilting speech gave reassurance and she allowed him to bring the cup to her lips. The bitter, strong potion madc hcr cough.

"A little at a time, lassie."

A feeling of warmth and well-being began to wash over her. Her pain receded.

"Air ye feelin' better, lass?" he asked.

"Yes." She drew a deep breath as he eased her back onto a pillow. "Thank you." Wide green eyes looked up at him, sincere with gratitude.

"'Twas nothin' more than anyone would do." He stood, the cup clasped in his hands. "Now I must be gettin' on the village and organizin' a search for other survivors. I'll chust be leavin' Pilot ta care for ye. Since he rescued ye from the surf, he'll reckon you're his to guard and protect. But first, tell me, lass. What was the name of yer ship?"

Her eyes widened and she sucked in her breath.

"What is it? Can ye no remember?"

"Yes, I remember." The words came out slowly, measured. "But if I tell you, you must promise not to tell anyone I'm a survivor. You must not tell anyone you rescued me or that I'm in your home."

"What? But why in heaven's name, lassie, would you not want anyone ta know you survived? Have ye not family in the Old Country that will be desperate for news of ye? How can ye even consider grievin' them in such a way?" He stared at her, appalled.

"Because there are people..and events I prefer to leave behind in England." She looked up at him, her expression blank. "Because I wish to start a new life here."

"But surely, lass..."

"Do you want to know the name of the vessel?"

"Aye, aye. Very well, I'll agree to yer terms...temporarily. Once ye've fully recovered, we'll discuss this matter again. Agreed?"

She hesitated.

"Trust me, lass. That's the best deal ye'll get from me." Blue eyes hardened with determination, he looked down at her.

"Very well. The ship was the Avon Queen bound for Jamaica. A violent mid-Atlantic storm blew her far off course and the captain decided to break our journey in New Brunswick to make repairs and replenish supplies swept overboard."

"Aye, that's better. I'll be off then. I'll try ta get back by dawn and ye must try ta get some sleep."

"Yes." Already her eyelids were drooping. The potion he'd administered was working its silent magic.

****

He saddled the black stallion he'd named the Lad, led him out of the barn, and swung onto his back. The storm was drifting away, a scrap of a moon peering cautiously out through the curtain of clouds. A stiff breeze ruffled his hair and made him shiver in the wet clothing he hadn't paused to change. Far off across his cleared fields, lightning occasionally brightened the sky but its thunder lagged far behind. Able to count to ten between flash and rumble, he felt confident danger from the storm had passed.

He turned the horse out onto the trail that led past his farm and touched his heels lightly to its sides. The animal broke into an easy canter and he patted its arched neck.

"Good lad! Not too fast, mind. We've a deal to do before daylight and I don't want you winded early on."

As he rode toward the small village of Pine several miles from his farm, he wondered about the woman he'd rescued. Her beauty both attracted and repelled him. Beauty such as hers was all too often skin deep. And yet there was something about her beyond mere physical appearance. An aura of mystery. A lady running away from something; something she was not yet ready to divulge to him.

He understood the desire to leave the past behind in the Old Country. Dear God, how he understood. But surely this girl, this young woman as beautiful and ethereal as a mermaid couldn't have anything in her past as dark and despicable as he did.

"Go on, Lad." He urged the horse to an all-out run. He couldn't hope to decipher her motives, not until he had more time to talk to her, to win her confidence. Meanwhile, there could be other victims of the wreck in need of his help.

****

"Hello, Reverend MacKenzie!" Hamish drew rein in front of the manse at the far end of the little village of clapboard houses and log cabins. "Hello, there's been a ship wreck. Ye'll be needin' ta ring the church bell and draw a crowd."

6

"Hamish, is that you?" The clergyman opened an upstairs window and stuck out his nightcap-swathed head. "What's that you say? A shipwreck?"

"Aye, Reverend." Hamish held his prancing horse in check. "We'll be needin' men ta search the beaches for survivors."

"I'll be right down." He slammed shut the window and within minutes he joined Hamish.

"My, my, where might this wreckage have occurred?" he asked buttoning on his collar. "Do you know the name of the vessel?"

"Near my farm." Hamish swung to the ground and fell into step with the bustling little man. "I believe the ship was the Avon Queen."

"I'm not familiar with the name but that's neither here nor there." They reached the church and the clergyman was rushing up the steps. "There are souls in need of help. Come in, come in, Hamish. You can help ring the bell."

When he hesitated, Reverend MacKenzie turned back to look in surprise at the man whose face was half-hidden in shadows cast by a shy moon.

"What's wrong?" he asked. "I thought you came here to get help and now you balk at ringing the bell."

"I'm not sure such as meself should be enterin' the House of the Lord." He put a hand on his horse's neck and avoided the minister's impatient stare.

"The Good Lord will not be sitting in judgment when there's souls to be saved. Now come on, come on." The reverend waved him forward. "At any rate, I can hardly imagine Him faulting you, a man who has done so much for this community."

"Verrae well." Hamish tied the Lad to the church railing and bounded up the steps behind the minister. "If ye say so, Reverend. But it'll be only this once."

"And who would have discovered the wreck?"

The minister untied the bell rope and handed it to his companion. "There was a vicious storm earlier this evening. I can't imagine you were out walking or riding the bay shore during it."

"Imagine or not, Vicar." Hamish gave the rope a mighty tug and the bell clanged loud and clear. "I was on me way home from seein' someone who was ailin'. Since the nature of his illness was a bit embarassin' I've promised not to talk about it." He pulled the rope again and the bell chimed again.

"Ah, of course. Doctor-patient confidentiality. As a clergyman I quite understand. You may not admit to being a physician, Hamish MacDonald, but you're the best we have at the present in this valley and a most excellent one at that for all your professed lack of formal schooling."

"Thank ye, Reverend, but ye'd best be gettin' outside to greet the folks that will be comin' soon as they hear the bell. They'll be wantin' ta know the nature of the emergency."

Hamish gave the rope another pull and the bell rang out yet again.

"Of course, of course." The little man went bustling off, satisfied with Hamish's explanation.

The man tolling the bell gave a massive sigh as he watched him go. He was grateful the minister had so readily accepted his story. He knew he'd never believe the truth...that some nebulous something had drawn him to the shore. A nebulous something some people would have called fate or even predestination.

****

Hamish, Reverend MacKenzie, and most of the men of the village combed the beaches near where he'd found the woman who called herself Lady Kathryn but found only rubble and wreckage. At one point, however, Hamish did discover a large trunk with the name "Lady Kathryn Sheffield" in gold

8

lettering on its top. Furtively he dragged it back into the trees, determined to come for it later and alone. For now, at least, he was willing to keep her survival and presence a secret.

****

Hamish sat hunched beside the bed, his hands clasped between his knees, staring at her closed eyes, their long, dark lashes spread out on her pale cheeks. Lady Kathryn she'd murmured as he'd carried. Was that her name, the same name he'd discovered on the trunk he'd found on the beach? No, surely not. Fate couldn't be so cruel as to send another such woman his way.

He drew a breath that expanded his chest and hunched his shoulders, then looked down at his calloused hands. Once upon a time he'd been a man with a future. Now he lived in a wilderness cabin that was little more than a hovel and shoveled manure. And all because of a woman, a lady who'd been no lady at heart, a woman more succubus than human.

He emitted a half-groan, half growl. He may as well sound like the beast into which she'd turned him when she'd cast her spell. A spell that would hold him in its power for the rest of his life.

The woman in the bed moved and moaned and he returned his attention to her. *Let her not be a Lady. All that I have left is my body's breath and these hands. I will not let her take those from me.*

In an effort to shove the possibility from his mind, he turned his thoughts to her physical condition. He was glad she'd lapsed into unconsciousness after drinking the potion. Her oblivious state had given him time to set her ankle without causing her more distress. Now her lower leg lay encased in a clay cast supported by thin sticks of wood he'd fashioned with an ax from pieces in his woodpile.

But before beginning, he'd stripped her unconscious body of its drenched, torn clothing. It should have been a natural, impersonal act for him but it wasn't. As he'd set about his work of cleansing and treating her wounds, he'd found himself fighting not to think of her as a woman...a beautiful, shapely woman whose smooth skin and ripe, round breasts tempted him sorely.

He'd been relieved when his task was finished and he could ease her into one of the nightshifts from his trunk. It smelled musty and was heavily creased.

His mouth quirked up at one corner as he gazed down at the high-collared white garment and tried to remember the last time he'd worn it...or anything remotely gentlemanly or civilized. He'd taken to sleeping either in his clothes or, if the temperature dictated, naked.

He wished he'd never found her, that someone else had discovered her battered body and taken her to safety. Why had he felt that sudden, irresistible urge to walk down to the bay shore at the height of a driving storm? It was April 1st, All Fool's Day. Was his finding her some kind of bizarre joke of nature, the essence of which he could not yet grasp?

He stared at the tangle of golden hair laced with bits of seaweed spread out over his pillow. Perhaps she was some sort of mythical creature from the deep thrown upon his shores, her silent siren cries drawing him to her side in the midst of the tempest?

He shook himself. *Reason, man, reason. She's but a woman from a shipwreck. Didn't you see the bits and pieces strewn along the shore. She's only a woman; a woman I will deliver into the care of the village vicar just as soon as she is well enough to travel.*

A shiver shook his body. In his desire to minister to her and search for other victims, he'd neglected himself. He arose and went to stand before the fire. He rubbed cold hands together, then glanced back at her. She continued to sleep.

Hastily he shed his wet clothing until he stood naked in the warmth of the flames. For a few moments he stayed as he was, letting the fire chase the chill from his body. He would allow himself to bask a few more moments before he dressed in dry clothing.

****

She opened her eyes. At first she saw only a blurred image of something silhouetted in a fiery glow. A creature with the upright body of a well-sculptured man but with the hirsute head of a beast. A satyr. Dear God, where was she and what had happened? Horror wafted over her and she shrank back against the wall.

Struggling to find reason in the weird scenario, she forced herself to draw deep breaths. The exercise worked. She became able to focus and pull memory and reason from amid the tangle in her mind. The creature must be the being that had rescued her from the beach. She remembered how he'd brought her here, to his lair, this dark, dingy hovel with the flames on a crude stone hearth casting weird, writhing shadows along the walls, how he'd given her a potion that had almost instantly plunged her into a deep, strange sleep.

As she became more aware, she realized that beneath the blankets and quilts she wore a nightshirt...a man's nightshirt, much too large, buttoned up under her chin. As she clutched the bedcovers to her throat she saw her dress and other clothing hanging over a ladder-backed chair beside the bed.

The creature had undressed her. The thought brought instant panic. She had to leave, get away from this great, hairy monster. Mustering all her strength she tried to rise. And cried out in agony.

He whirled, snatching up his damp shirt from beside the hearth, and swung it over his nakedness.

For a moment they stared at each other. Then he hastily tied the sleeves behind his back and, using the garment as a breechclout, advanced toward her.

"Ye must lay still, lassie."

"Keep away from me, you great brute!" She clutched the bedding to her throat and jerked back against the log wall behind her. "If you dare to touch me…!"

"Lass, I've no the intentions of harmin' ye." He paused beside her, his voice as soft and soothing as she remembered. "Ye've got a broken ankle and a lot of bumps and bruises. Ye'll need time ta heal. Thrashin' about will only make ye hurt more and slow yer recovery."

She looked up and felt her terror receding. Nothing in those intense blue eyes hinted of evil thoughts or desires. She'd trust him…at least for the present. With a groan, she lay back in the crude bed. "Where am I? Who are you?"

"Ye're in my cabin in His Majesty's colony of New Brunswick, it is April first of the year of our Lord 1820, and ye may call me Hamish…Hamish MacDonald. I'm a farmer. I believe ye were the victim of a shipwreck. I found ye on the beach not far from here…Lady Kathryn."

"Lady Kathryn?" Her eyes widened.

"Aye. That's the name ye kept repeatin' as I carried ye back here. Yer name, is it not?"

"And if it is, what would you do? Hold me for ransom?" She adjusted herself against the pillow.

"Hardly, lass. I'm no the highwayman. When ye're well enough, I will take ye ta the village and place ye in the care of the local vicar and his guid wife." His voice grew softer. "Were ye indeed the victim of a shipwreck?"

"Yes. Our ship went down in a terrible storm." She was beginning to remember and shuddered. Memory returned steadily and with it other thoughts, other plans. "You found no other survivors?"

"Nay, lass. I'm sorry." His voice, gentle with concern, comforted her. "Were ye travellin' with someone?"

"With my lady's maid, Rose Jones."

"Sad to say, I'm afeart we must accept the bitter fact that yer the only survivor."

"Only me?"

"Aye, it appeared ta be so." He backed away from her. "Now if ye'll excuse me, I'll chust be dressin' meself. Perhaps ye might choose to close yer eyes or face the wall."

****

"Ye said ye were travellin' with your lady's maid, lass." She opened her eyes to see him once more standing beside the bed, this time fully clothed in breeches, a white shirt hanging loose outside them, and worn, black boots.

"You may address me as Lady Kathryn. And if you dare to harm me..." Her strength and spirit were returning. She had no intention of letting this great beast harm her, at least not without a fight.

"Donnae fret yerself, lassie." He laid a large, gentle hand on her shoulder but hastily removed it when she flinched away. "That should be the least of yer worries. Ye have a broken ankle. I've placed it in a cast. Now drink this. It's only a cup of broth but it will help to build up your strength."

He slid an arm beneath her shoulders. She saw he once again held a mug and was bringing it to her mouth.

"No!" She rolled her head away with a shock of pain and squeezed her eyes shut. She didn't want to

13

drift into vulnerable unconsciousness again.

"It's no the poison." For the first time she heard a note of annoyance in his voice. "Ye must keep up yer strength if ye plan to recover."

She eased open her eyes, turned back to him and looked up into penetrating sapphire ones. A nebulous something told her she could trust this strange creature with the gentle voice and ministering hands. She allowed him to bring the cup to her lips.

Chicken broth. After her first tentative sip, hunger overcame her reluctance. Grasping the mug in both hands she drank greedily.

"Good." He laid her back onto the bed and took the empty cup from her hands. "Now try to get some rest. I must see ta me animals. Then I'll make up a place ta sleep on the floor. Rest easy, lass. I'll not allow any creatures with harmful intent ta get anywhere near yer bed."

With a sigh, she pulled the blankets snug and drifted off into sleep.

****

When she awoke, sunlight was streaming in through a window. She stared about at the moss-chinked walls, smoke blackened stone hearth, and earthen floor and felt her heart plummet. The beast's lair was as primitive as himself.

The creature was nowhere in sight. Escape! The thought charged into her mind. She had to get away before he returned.

She stirred and yelped in pain. Every inch of her body ached and her right foot and ankle felt as if it was encased in lead. Gasping, she fell back on the bed. Gritting her teeth, she tried again and managed to pull herself to a sitting position.

Stifling a moan, she eased the heavy lump that was her foot to the floor, then sat on the edge of the plank bed panting as she gathered her strength.

Her gaze roamed about the single roomed dwelling, recognizing the few pieces of furniture she'd previously noticed and something more. In a far, dark cover sat a large trunk, a pile of bedding folded neatly on its top. She wondered if it contained the secrets of the strange man who'd saved her life.

Her desire to escape overtook her curiosity. The door on the far side of the cabin looked a long way off but even more daunting was the big, black dog lying comfortably across its width. It raised its massive head, looked over at her and muttered

Trapped! She sank back against her pillow and tried to force her tangled thoughts into a semblance of order. She knew she couldn't walk without a support. Her gaze fell on the ladder-backed chair. The beast had used it to sit beside her last night and had left it in position, her clothing draped over its back. If she managed to grasp it, she could push it ahead of her to the hearth. The smell drifting across the room told her some sort of stew was being kept warm in the pot suspended over the embers.

If she could get to the fireplace and upset its contents onto the floor the animal blocking her escape would rush to gobble the spilled food. While it was gorging itself, she could use the chair to escape. Once outside, she'd push something against the panel to keep the brute inside and flee. How and to where she had no idea. She would consider those details once she was free.

Watching the black brute, she eased her hand toward the chair back. The animal stared, but didn't move. Barely daring to breathe, she continued to stretch toward the piece of furniture. As her hand clutched it, she paused, her heart hammering. The dog didn't move.

Encouraged she grasped the chair's top rail. Suppressing a groan, she hoisted herself upright. Dizziness, weakness, and pain made her senses swirl. Willing herself not to give in, she clung to the chair that held her clothes. Once the giddiness subsided she realized this fact would aid her escape. Once out of the cabin, she'd have her own dry if tattered garments to wear.

Fighting to close her mind to pain, she began to ease the chair across the earthen floor. Again the animal muttered but didn't move. Sweating, fighting the nausea threatening to overwhelm her, and keeping the creature in sight, she inched her way toward the hearth.

Finally she arrived. Clutching the chair with one white-knuckled hand she stretched to swing the pot from above the fire. Wet with pain-induced sweat, she struggled the container out over the floor. The delicious smell of chicken wafted from the pot and she realized she was ravenous. How long had it been since she'd eaten? A day…two days ago on the ship? It seemed a lifetime.

She stifled the urge to gorge into the concoction. She'd worry about food later…when she was free. It took every ounce of strength she could muster but she tipped the pot and sent meat, vegetables, and juice spewing over the floor.

This time the animal leaped to its feet but instead of rushing forward to gobble the steaming mess, it moved aside to allow the door behind it to open.

The beast stepped into the cabin, a great dark silhouette that filled the door way and blotted out most of the sunlight. In one hand he carried a musket. A dead rabbit swung from the other.

"What have ye done!" Gone was the soft, lilting Highland brogue as he stared at the spilled meal. "Dear God, woman, do ye not know how hard come-by a decent meal is in this country? I had ta sacrifice one of me layin' hens to make that stew! The contents of that pot would have fed us for two days!"

He threw back his head and let out a great, guttural roar.

"I was just trying to get some and it tipped. Anyway, it's only a bit of meat and potatoes." She clutched the chair back and faced him with all the defiance she could muster. "Surely you're not so hard pressed that you cannot supply more."

For a moment he stood staring at her. Her heart hammered so violently she thought he'd hear it.

He leaned his musket beside the door and drew a deep breath that swelled the broad chest beneath the simple white shirt he wore.

"Ah, well, not ta waste it entirely." He gathered up the chunks of chicken and threw them back into the pot. "I'll chust be salvaging what I can to make more stew." He turned to the dog by his side, its tail wagging slowly. "Now ya may go ta it, laddie." The gentle Scottish tone had returned as he gave the dog leave to eat the remainder of the spilled dinner.

The animal trotted forward, its tail wagging, and began to gobble up the scattered vegetables.

"Surely you don't expect me to eat food that has fallen on a dirt floor!" she cried. "Surely..."

"Surely I do. The boilin' will cleanse it and as I've chust told ye, food is hard come by in this country and especially at this time of year when winter supplies are at their lowest and our gardens have yet to yield."

A great of wave of weakness washed over her. She tried clutching the chair but her hands had lost their strength. She was crumbling toward the floor when he caught her in his arms.

"Ye shouldnae be up, lassie," he muttered as he carried her back to the bed and laid her gently in it. "Ye're injured and ye haven't eaten in more than a full day, I'll wager. But have nae fear. I will care for ye."

"Who *are* you?" she asked, staring up into blue

eyes that seemed to pierce into her soul.

"I told ye, I am Hamish MacDonald, a farmer." He looked down at her. "And I will call ye Kate."

"Kate?" The name surprised her.

"Last night ye told me ye were the Lady Kathryn. Yer voice tells me yer air an English aristocrat, a breed I'll no honor with a title. So Kate ye'll be as long as ye share me roof."

"And how long might that be?"

She resisted the urge to defend her right to be addressed as a lady.

"Until ye're well enough ta travel. Now," he stood up. "Would ya be needin' ta use the privy?" He startled her by reading her mind. "I'll chust be helpin' ye out ta it."

Before she could protest he'd gathered her up in his arms.

"No, really, I'm...quite all right," she protested, embarrassment raging.

"Havers. Ye've not been able ta get up since I brought ye here." He silenced her protest as he kicked open the door and carried her outside.

She saw a muddy dooryard punctuated with patches of melting snow, a log barn backed by forest, and beside it, a long expanse of fenced fields beginning to appear from beneath winter's blanket of white.

"This isn't necessary..." she tried to protest again as he went behind the cabin and pulled open the door of the small outhouse.

"Of course it is." He deposited her inside the little hut and she fell back onto the plank seat. "But since I won't always be at hand whenever nature calls, I'll find ye a bucket ta keep beneath yer bed." He stepped back outside and shut the door. "Call me when yer ready ta go back inta the house."

She knew people didn't really die of embarrassment but she felt she'd come as near to it as she'd ever care to get.

****

When they were back inside the cabin, he urged her to take another cup of broth from the bit of liquid left in the pot she'd spilled.

"You threw the meat from the floor back into that kettle." She drew back from the mug, her face twisting into a grimace.

"Aye, and it's been cleaned by the boilin' as I've told ye. Now drink up. Ye need food and rest, lassie. They'll help ye heal."

****

"What will you do when I'm well enough to travel?" She finished the last of the broth and handed the cup back to him.

"I'll take ye ta the village and leave ye in the care of the vicar and his wife. They'll inform yer kin back in England that ye're alive and well."

"I've already told you. I have no wish for anyone other than yourself to know I survived the wreck of the Avon Queen. I do not wish to be returned to England and that is exactly what will happen if you take me to the village and tell my story."

"But why, lassie? Why would ye not wish to inform yer family that ye're alive? They'll be sick with worry when they learn your ship failed to reach its destination."

"You have no need to know a reason. Just let me stay here until I'm well enough to travel and tell no one how I came to be in your home."

"Ye're talkin' nonsense." He stood up. "But I won't question ye any more at the moment. Ye rest while I see what I can manage fer a meal. At least I'll not have ta feed me dog."

She thought his mouth quirked into a grin beneath the beard as he turned to the dog stretched out contentedly on the floor. She wasn't sure.

But she was certain she wouldn't allow him to

take her to the local vicar. That could only mark the beginning of her return to England and that she wouldn't allow. She would never return to that manor house and the brute who would be waiting.

She'd find some way to convince this strange creature to allow her to stay with him until she could make her own way. In spite of his bestial appearance, she sensed that Hamish MacDonald meant her no harm and was many times more a gentleman than the creature who'd professed to be one yet had attacked her without mercy less than a week before she set out on her ill-fated voyage.

With these thoughts in mind, she drifted off to sleep.

****

He looked down into her sleeping face and wondered what he was to do with her. He hadn't imagined she'd want to stay until she could leave on her own. But where did she plan to go afterwards? A woman alone without either protection or provisions in the wilds of northern New Brunswick would have little chance of survival.

He drew a deep breath as he stood gazing down. Even with her face scraped and bruised, she was a beautiful woman. A tangle of golden curls framed a heart-shaped face with a cream-like complexion. When he'd carried her, she'd felt as soft and light as a rose petal. He rubbed his hands on the seat of his breeches and tried to distract himself from such thoughts. He'd been living alone and feral far too long to be unaffected by such female beauty but he must not let it get the best of him.

What did she think of him? He ran his fingers through the thatch of shoulder-length black curls and stroked his ragged beard. Definitely not a lady's idea of how a romantic, rescuing hero should look.

He drew a deep breath. Just as well. This way she couldn't possibly take an interest in him...as a man. In fact, she'd appeared downright terrified when she'd glimpsed him naked.

"Come along, Pilot," he said, turning to the dog waiting by the door. "It's high time we cleaned the barn. Nothing like shoveling manure to take a man's thoughts away from..." He paused and looked back at her. "Other things."

****

When she returned to wakefulness, sunlight was slanting through the window at such an angle she guessed it was late afternoon or early evening. Turning her head she saw the beast hunkered down by the hearth, putting potatoes and carrots into a pot. When he'd finished he swung it over the fire and got to his feet, rubbing his hands together.

"Shortly we'll be partakin' of the finest rabbit stew west of the Highlands, Pilot," he said to the big dog sitting beside him. "That is, if we can prevent that wee lassie yonder from givin' it ta ye."

"I'm hungry." She spoke and he turned to face her. "I'll not be spilling anything edible."

"I'm right pleasured to hear it." He crossed the room to stand beside her bed. Tall, broad of shoulder and narrow of hip, he was, bodily at least, a fine figure of a man. A man who was, hour by hour, quieting her fears by his respectful behavior. But what of his face? Was it so hideous he had to hide it behind a massive growth of hair and beard? Had he been horribly scarred by disease or accident?

"I must thank you, sir, for saving my life," she said, lowering her gaze demurely. "My injuries and shock, at first, rendered me rude, I fear."

She tried to sit up and he was immediately beside her, one strong arm raising her gently, the other pushing the pillow and a folded blanket behind head and shoulders.

"It's no' me ye should be thankin', lass. It was Pilot as spied ye in the surf and pulled ye ta shore."

21

He indicated the dog. "I chust helped him once he'd dragged ye inta the shallows."

"Pilot." She smiled as she stretched out a hand toward the animal. "You truly were my pilot. Thank you."

The dog's tail wagged and he lumbered forward to cast a large pink tongue over her outstretched hand.

"I had a dog at home," she said wistfully, stroking the animal. "His name was Prince. He was a small dog. He loved to sit on my lap."

"I'm afeard ye'll no be wantin' Pilot on yer lap, lassie. He's nigh on one hundred pounds if he's an ounce." The remarkable blue eyes twinkled and she felt an urge to smile in return. "He's what's known in this country as a Newfoundland Dog, one of the finest, bravest beasts ye'll ever encounter."

"And did you bring him from the Highlands?" She took the opportunity to question him.

"The Hi'lands? Why do ya ask, lass? And, no, I didnae."

"Your accent. On our estate in Scotland we had a ghillie...he was a Highlander and spoke somewhat as yourself. Somewhat, but not exactly."

"Ah, an estate in Scotland, is it? For the huntin' and fishin', no doubt." His tone turned bitter, the sapphire eyes hardening like the gems their color reflected. "A great house that lies empty and useless ten months of the year while crofters round about are burned out of their cottages to make way for sheep! Well, lassie, let me tell ye, I have no love for such 'visitors'!"

He turned and strode out of the cabin, slamming the plank door behind him.

****

When he returned he carried a covered bucket. He plunked it down beside her bed.

"Yer ladyship's indoor privy," he said. "I'll no be

carryin' ye outdoors again."

"Very good." She struggled higher on her pillows and tried to look aloof.

"Well, why donnae ye say it?" he snapped glaring.

"Say what?"

"That will be all, me good man?"

"Why on earth should I say that?"

"Isn't it how ye English dismiss yer servants?"

"Possibly. But it wasn't what I was about to say."

"And chust what that might have been?"

'That I'm hungry and I'd be obliged if you'd fetch me a bowl of that fine-smelling rabbit stew." She struggled to keep her expression haughty but her eyes twinkled.

He paused. Then he burst out laughing, a deep hearty laugh.

"Ye've got the courage of a British lion, I'll give ye that," he chuckled finally. "A mere day from death's door and already ye've spirit ta spare." He turned toward the hearth. "Come along, Pilot, me lad. Her ladyship has spoken. Stew it is."

He went to the shelves above the dresser and began to place bowls, mugs, and utensils on the table.

"If ye're well enough ta order me about, ye're well enough ta come ta table," he said. "As soon as the vegetables are cooked, I'll be helping ye ta it."

****

"That was very good," she commented as she shoved aside the bowl.

"Ye've a healthy appetite, I'll grant," he said, rising to gather up the dishes. "I can see I'll have ta hone me huntin' skills if I'm ta keep us in victuals. And I thought it was only a pregnant woman who was ta be eatin' as if fer two."

"Really, sir! How indelicate!" She adjusted the

shabby jacket that he'd put about her shoulders. "And speaking of indelicate, I assume you undressed me and put me into...this."

She gestured at the nightshirt.

"Aye. Ye were soaked ta the skin. Donnae fret yerself, lass. I behaved as a perfect gentleman." He placed the dishes on the dresser and turned back, his expression suddenly sardonic. "Even if I am only a barbaric Hi'lander." He bent to the hearth and took up a spouted pot. "Tea?"

"I never said you were a barbarian. You're surmising, sir."

He paused, the teapot in his hand. "Ye're right, lassie. Ye've no said anything against Hi'landers. It's no fair of me ta tar all English with the same broom."

"Thank you." She sat up regally. "Now may I please have some tea?"

****

"Where will you sleep?" she asked as she finished the tea amid the deepening shadows of evening.

"On the floor near the door wrapped in those." He pointed to the blankets piled on the trunk. "I could go ta the barn but the nights are still uncomfortable cool. I will leave ye ta yer ablutions now and return when ye are safely ensconced in yon bed."

"I would be grateful for a pan of clean water and a cloth that I might wash," she said as he got up. "And a brush for my hair."

"Och, a certain sign of recovery in a woman." He carried their cups to the dresser. "Vanity."

"Cleanliness is next to godliness." Annoyance colored her tone.

"Ta be sure, lass. I'll chust hie meself out ta the well and fetch the first of yer demands."

"Requests," she corrected but the door slammed

on the word.

****

When he returned he carried a bucket. He placed a basin from the shelves on the table and splashed water into it. She flinched back as ice-cold droplets hit her hands and arms.

He dropped the bucket near the door, then went to the trunk and pulled the key from beneath his shirt.

He fitted it into the lock, turned it, and raised the lid. From her vantage point she couldn't see its contents. Shortly he drew out some toweling linen, a brush, and a hand mirror.

"There." He placed them on the table. "Cloth to wash and dry yerself, a brush ta tidy yer locks, and a mirror that ye may preen ta yer heart's content."

"I do not wish to preen." She gave her shoulders a defiant toss. "I only wish to make myself presentable...something you might consider doing."

"Argh!" The guttural sound belched from his mouth as he turned to lower the trunk's lid and relock it. Muttering he strode out of the cabin.

****

"I'm sorry."

"Whit?" He paused in making up his bed. He'd returned to find her in bed, face clean and the tangles brushed from her hair.

"I'm sorry for what I said...about making yourself presentable. You and Pilot saved my life and I'm most grateful. Under those circumstances, my rudeness is unforgivable." She lowered her gaze to her clasped hand.

He drew a deep breath. Washed and tidy, she was even more alluring. His hand itched to touch those golden curls, to feel the petal softness of her lovely face. And so much more...

"Apology accepted." He returned his attention to making up his bed. "It's no good, us bickerin'. We'll be livin' together for a time. We must not deliberately make each other's lives unpleasant."

He pulled off his boots and lay down in the makeshift bed he'd composed. "Sweet dreams, Kate."

"Kate? No, no, no! I've told you, I'm Lady Kathryn."

"Lass, this is America where all men...and women...are equal. I will call ye Kate. Now go ta sleep. Good night, Pilot," he said as the big dog stretched out beside him. "And good night ta ye as well...Kate."

****

She awoke the following morning to the sounds of his building up the fire under the pot hanging on a hook over the flames on the hearth.

"Good morning," she said softly.

She moved gingerly and realized that aside from the cast and a bit of soreness she felt quite well. She eased higher on the pillow and breathed a sigh when the movement caused only mild discomfort.

"Let me help ye, lass. Yer probably feelin' a good deal better taday but ye mustn't overdo. Ye have ta give yer body time ta mend."

"Very well." She gave up and allowed him help her to a sitting position. "You're the doctor." She smiled.

His hands paused in their work. "A strange description ta apply ta such as meself. I'm only a Hi'lander with little more ta recommend me than a strong back."

"Perhaps." She slanted him a sideways glance. "But you are a strange Highlander, Hamish MacDonald."

"Whit do ye mean?" He straightened up and stared at her with those piercing blue eyes.

"I mean I've known Highlanders and something about your accent doesn't ring true."

"And whit part of Scotland did ye visit?

26

Glasgow, Edinburgh? I'll wager ye never went so far north as the Hi'lands themselves."

"Well, no, I didn't, but still…"

"It's nay good tryin' to put Hi'landers in the same basket with Lowland Scots," he said turning to go back to hearth. "We're an entirely different breed and we speak an entirely different tongue. Now, I'll fetch yer porridge and tea. In a couple of days we'll be blessed with fresh bread. A neighbor woman makes it fer me once a week and delivers it in return fer a bit of fresh game."

****

After he'd left to do his chores, she struggled to the side of the bed, used the bucket he'd provided as a chamber pot, and then forced herself upright with the aid of the chair. Her ragged dress and other clothing had dried and, damaged as they were, she longed to put them on. The nightshirt made her feel vulnerable and invalid.

She pushed the chair to the window and looked out. She could see him through the open barn door, cutting at a stick of wood with a handsaw.

She pulled the nightshirt over her head and dropped it onto the floor. Stifling moans and groans, she struggled into undergarments. With a final effort that took the last of her strength, she pulled on the ragged gown and fastened the buttons on its bodice.

"There!" She sank down onto the chair and drew a deep breath. Now if only she had something to help her walk aside from that awkward chair…

As if in answer, he opened the door, letting in a flood of sunlight and carrying a pair of crude crutches.

"Ah, so ye've decided ta be up and about. That's chust fine if yer careful. Here." He held out the supports. "I made these fer a lad who broke his leg a while back. When he was mended, he returned them

27

ta me. I've cut them down ta fit ye."

She hobbled to her feet to insert first one, then the other under her armpits.

"Perfect!" she beamed. "I was just wishing for such devices."

"Were ye now," he smiled back. "I must be a wizard then, ta read yer mind."

"Perhaps you are, Hamish MacDonald, perhaps you are," she said softly.

"Aye, well, as soon as we're fed I'd best be getting' back ta work. A farm doesnae run itself. I'll be back at midday ta get ye a meal. Meanwhile, I'll place the chair on the verandah. Ye can sit in the sun and mend."

He made them a breakfast of porridge and strong tea before harnessing his team of Clydesdales and heading off across the field beyond the barn.

She wrapped a quilt about her and, grasping the crutches, hobbled out onto the verandah. It was warm in the sun but patches of snow lingered about the farm buildings. Puddles from the spring melt had turned much of the dooryard into a sea of mud and she realized the practicality of the cabin's earthen floor in such a season.

She drew a deep breath. The fresh, clean country air brought back pleasant memories. Otherwise, this country was different from anything she'd ever seen. A hushed wilderness of trees surrounded the little farm. She wondered how far away their nearest neighbor lived.

Deciduous trees hadn't yet begun to open new leaves but already grass in the fields beyond the barn were greening in spite of lingering patches of snow. She heard the rush of a stream through the trees somewhere nearby and assumed melting snow accounted for its exuberance.

She wondered what the farm would look like in summer. Would it perhaps be as lush and exotic as her original destination was reputed to be? She'd never know. She would never complete that journey to Jamaica.

She adjusted her improvised shawl and settled more comfortably into her chair. This crude little farm gave a feeling of contentment she couldn't quite understand. Perhaps it was because it represented the closest thing to freedom she'd experienced in several years.

Her life was her own now but what might she make of it? She stretched languidly. She'd worry about it later. At the moment the peace and the warm spring sunshine soothed and relaxed her to the core. Hamish MacDonald had said he'd let nothing harm her and she believed him.

A little smile tipping her lips, she closed her eyes and dozed in the warmth of the faux spring day.

****

She awoke with a start. Her breath caught with fear.

Three men wearing breechclouts, leggings, robes, and boots of animal skins stood at the foot of the steps. Their hair, long, jet black, and lank, hung about their shoulders, their brown faces grim. One man carried a musket, the other two long spears.

Behind them stood a woman wrapped in a dress of animal skin, tied at the waist with a girdle. She gazed up at Kate with eyes as dark as ebony. She held a basket.

Kate scrambled to her feet, fumbled for her crutches, and fell. As one of the men bolted up the steps toward her, she screamed.

Chapter Two

"Dear God, what now!"

Hamish burst from the barn. "Ah, damn!" He paused as he saw the native lifting Kate, screaming and thrashing, to her feet. "Kate, stop that caterwaulin' at once!" he yelled as he bounded across the yard and up the steps. "These are my friends...Peter, Paul, Michael, and Marie." He pinned her flaying arms to her sides and grinned. "Lass, I do believe ye're frightenin' them."

"I didn't hear them coming." She stared, eyes wide, breast heaving. "I was asleep and when I woke up...they were there!"

"They are a quiet lot." He grinned at the man standing stone-faced beside them on the verandah and spoke in a language she couldn't understand. The man's lips quirked slightly and he nodded.

"What did you say?" she hissed leaning against him.

"I told him you were new to this country and not yet accustomed to its ways or its people."

"And what language were you speaking?"

"Maliseet. My friends are Maliseet, the tribe indigenous ta this area."

The man who'd strode up the steps had backed off a couple of paces and stood perusing her, an inscrutable expression on his dark face. The others remained at the foot of the step, watching the trio.

"Peter, this is Kate." Hamish introduced her to the man beside them.

He grunted in response.

"Michael, Paul, Mary, I'd like ye ta meet Kate." He drew a reluctant Kate forward and smiled down at the trio. "She's come ta live with me till she mends."

"It is time you took a woman, Healer." A slow grin started on Paul's dark face. He spoke to his companions in his own tongue and slowly smiles spread across their countenances.

"I am not..." Kate began but Hamish silenced her with a glance.

"Aye,that it is. Come inside, friends. I'll make tea. Me woman, as ye can see, is not yet able ta serve me."

He handed Kate the crutches, and let her precede the group inside. He helped her to a seat, then turned to the hearth to heat water for tea.

"Sit, friends," he invited the quartet, indicating the benches. "I'll soon have refreshment ready fer ye."

The woman waited until Hamish was busy at the hearth, then approached Kate and held out the basket.

"For me?" Kate looked down at the container and saw it held green plants and a pair of some sort of hide footwear.

The woman smiled, nodded, and thrust the basket onto her lap.

"Fiddleheads." Hamish joined Kate and looked down into the basket. His tone reflected pleasure. "Kate," he turned to her. "Marie has brought us fiddleheads, the first greens of spring. I will cook them fer our supper. They are a verrae special treat."

He smiled at the native woman and spoke a few Maliseet words.

Beaming, Marie reached into the basket and pulled out the foot gear. One was much larger than the other and she pointed to Kate's cast.

31

"Ah, yes." Hamish grinned. "Marie saw that ye have one foot presently much larger than the other and has made ye moccasins ta fit."

"Saw?" Kate glanced up at Hamish.

"They've been aware of yer arrival from yer first day."

"But I...we never saw anyone."

"That is their way. Ye will only see them when they're ready ta reveal themselves. But they are my guid and true friends. Ye must always make them welcome in our home. Marie speaks very little English but Paul has been educated at one of our schools and knows our language well."

"As you are coming to know ours, Hamish." Paul grinned as he rested his musket against the wall and went to take a seat at the table.

"But niver as well as you speak mine." Hamish brought the tea pot from the hearth and made a remark in Maliseet that set his the three male visitors laughing.

"Very good, Hamish," Paul chuckled. "I'm sure the tea is as well brewed as if your woman did it."

"Hamish, please thank Marie for the moccasins...is that what they are called? Say her kindness is most appreciated." In an effort to show appreciation, Kate fondled the footwear in her arms and smiled at the woman.

When Hamish finished speaking, Marie smiled shyly and nodded. She turned and went to squat on the floor near the door.

"Hamish, please tell Marie to join us at the table." Kate was appalled as he poured tea into a mug and took it to the woman.

He returned to the table, leaned over and whispered in her ear. "It's not their way. We must respect it."

"It's not fair..."she began but he silenced her with a look.

32

She sipped her tea in silence as the four men laughed and talked in both languages. She had much to learn not only about this strange man and his farm but also about the people of the region. Perhaps she and Marie might become friends. She would like to have a female friend.

When she'd finished the tea, she slid off her tattered slipper and carefully slid first her good foot and then the one encased in clay into the moccasins. They fit perfectly. She smiled her delight at the woman by the door. Marie nodded her approval, her lips slowly curling upward.

"I wish I had something to give her in return," she whispered to Hamish when he came to stand beside her.

"She's not looking for a reward," he said. "Yer delight in the gift is enough."

"Nevertheless, someday I shall find a means to repay her kindness," she insisted.

****

After they'd gone, Kate looked up at Hamish as he removed the tea mugs from the table.

"They seem like nice people," she ventured.

"If it hadn't been for them, I would have frozen or starved my first winter in this country," he said simply.

"They called you 'Healer'," she continued. "Why?"

"I've a bit of the knowledge of healing," he said bending to add more wood to the fire. "I've helped them when I can. But I will never be able ta repay all they've done fer me. Therefore, lass, I'd be most grateful if ye'd treat them with respect and welcome when they come ta visit."

"Of course." She gazed down at the moccasins. The natives had done much more than bring her gifts. They'd planted an idea in her head; an idea that might just prevent Hamish MacDonald from taking her to the village and on her way back to England.

****

Spring proved illusive she discovered the next day, when a blizzard howled across the farm. Wrapped in a quilt, she huddled in the chair by the fire blazing on the hearth. In preparation Hamish had filled the wood box beside it the previous evening. The pale, ominous clouds that had drifted over the sky late in the day were a warning.

"A blustery one, lass." He came stamping snow from his boots. Pilot, his snout and whiskers frosted, ambled in behind him and shook.

"Our ghillie would have called such a spring snowstorm a lambing blizzard. This is as strange and unpredictable a country as Scotland, is it not?"

"Aye, as unpredictable as a beautiful woman." He pulled off his jacket and went to add another log to the fire.

"And you've had many experiences with beautiful woman?" She was intrigued by his remark.

"Enough." He straightened and checked the porridge pot bubbling on over the fire. "Now ta breakfast. I trust you can stomach oatmeal again?"

****

After the meal and household chores were completed, Hamish hunkered down by the hearth, carving at a bit of wood while she retired to her bed and fell into a peaceful doze in the snug, warm cabin. The wind and snow buffeting its walls reminded her of the great storm on the night the ship had gone down. Strangely the memory offered no terror. In this rugged little cabin she felt safe and secure.

****

"Do you have anything that I might read?" she asked after their noon meal.

"Bored, are ye?" He turned after replenishing

34

the fire.

"I enjoy reading." She drew herself stiff and erect. "We had an extensive library at the manor house."

"Ah. Well, let me see if I can oblige your ladyship."

He drew the key from beneath his shirt and went to the trunk. He opened it and for a few moments stood staring inside. Finally he thrust his hand into its depths and pulled out first one leather-covered volume and then a second. "I have only two that might be of interest. The first is *The History of Tom Jones, A Foundling*, a tale I fear too lusty for a lady's enjoyment. The second is *Robinson Crusoe*. As a castaway yerself, ye might enjoy it."

He placed both books on the table.

"Enjoy what you will of them." He snatched up his jacket from its peg by the door. "Hungry bellies don't stop with storms. I must see to me stock."

He opened the door letting in a gust of wind and snow. Then ducking his head, he went out.

Kate stared down at the two thick volumes on the table. So the beast could and did read. She glanced first at one, then the other. Shortly she was engrossed in *The History of Tom Jones, A Foundling*.

****

"Ah ha!" He stepped abruptly into the cabin. "So the English lady isn't above readin' the tale of a young lad's amorous adventures."

"I was curious." Startled, she slammed the book shut and threw it onto the table.

"So I see." The grin on his face irked and she snatched up the second book, opened it and feigned deep and instant interest.

"I believe ye may find that a bit dull after what ye've just been enjoyin'." He turned to add more wood to the fire and she had to resist the urge to fling the book at his broad shoulders. He made her feel like a voyeur.

"And I suppose you haven't read it? Or do you even know how?" The moment the words were out of her mouth she regretted them.

"Oh, aye, I can read, lassie, never fear." He turned back and she was relieved he appeared more amused than offended. "I am no the total barbarian."

"I'm sorry." She dropped her chin to her chest. "That was thoughtless and unkind."

"Aye, it was. I should have thought an English lady would have better manners."

He sat down on the bench at the table, took up the book she'd thrown aside, and after casting her a roguish glance settled down to read, his forehead knitted into a frown of faux concentration.

****

Hamish MacDonald couldn't sleep and it wasn't the hard, earthen floor or the wind whining around the cabin that kept him from his rest. His choice of reading material had rendered him wakeful and he cursed the desire to annoy the woman that had prompted his taking up that blasted book. Filled with sexual exploits, *A History of Tom Jones, A Foundling* had been one of the worst books he could have chosen given his present circumstances.

He rolled onto his back and stared up at the raw beams overhead. He dared not look across the room to where Kate, beautiful, desirable Kate, lay sleeping peacefully in his bed. *Robinson Crusoe* apparently had proven a more relaxing tale.

Damnation! He clinched his jaws until they felt like cracking. Why did this damn blizzard have to arrive and trap them together in the cabin for hours on end? Why couldn't he view her simply as a patient? Why couldn't he just forget about women, all women and continue his hermit's life? Hadn't he learned anything from past experience?

She'd taunted him, seduced him until his life

had been left in a shambles, worthy only of a hangman's rope. Now, sleeping peacefully in his bed was another English lady, one for whom he lusted although he'd known her but a few days.

He turned to face the flames languishing on the hearth and wished his desire for Lady Kathryn would burn out as well. There was only answer. He had to get rid of her as soon as possible.

****

"Kate, come and see this."

She opened her eyes to be momentarily blinded by a glare of sunlight bursting through the window.

"Get up!" Standing over her he reached down to take her arm.

She gasped and shrank away from him, eyes widening. In an instant it all flooded back. The man looming over her, demanding...

"Lass, I've slept on the floor in the same room with ye these several nights and haven't made a single move to molest ye." The words smacked of exasperation. "Surely ye must trust me by now. Donnae let foolish fears let ye miss out on something wonderful. "

It was all right. It wasn't him. It was Hamish. He wouldn't harm her.

She held out her hand.

"Very well," she muttered. "But this had better be worth waking me from a restful sleep and dragging me out into the cold."

"Aye, it will be." He helped adjust the crutches and slung a blanket about her shivering shoulders. "But it'll be lastin' only a wee while."

At first when he pulled open the cabin door the brilliance hurt her eyes and made her turn away, rubbing them. But as they became accustomed to the glare, she gasped. The dooryard sparkled with thousands of sun diamonds in the fresh blanket of show. Trees beyond the clearing were frosted in

37

ivory beneath a sky so blue it put sapphires to shame.

"It's beautiful," she breathed.

"Aye, that is it." He leaned against the doorjamb, a slight smile quirking up the corners of his mouth. "I wanted ye ta see the wonder of it before it dissolves into a sea of mud and slush. It'll be the last snowfall until next winter. This country is as beautiful as it is surprising in its changing seasons. The colors of the trees in autumn can fair take yer breath away."

"Are you trying to convince me it's a good place to live?" She squinted in the sunlight.

"Nay, just show ye the wonder of it. I've been here five years and sunlight on a fresh snowfall still astonishes me." He turned back into the cabin. "I'd best be gettin' us something ta eat. Man...or woman...cannae live on beauty alone."

He headed back inside and she heard him shuffling pots about on the hearth. She gazed at the sparkling beauty and drew a deep breath of the crisp, clear air.

"Mr. MacDonald?" she called after him. "Where does the road lead that runs past this farm?"

"If ye turn to the right, ye'll end up at the bay shore and if ye turn left, ye'll be on the way to the village of Pine. Why? Aire ye thinkin' of takin' to the road? If so, I'd advise against it. This is a rough country. A woman alone, niver mind one with her ankle in a cast, would be welcome pray to any number of savage beasts and villains."

She ignored his dire warning but tucked away the directional information for future use.

Later that morning she discovered that with the melt came bird song and the joyous rush of the stream that ran through the trees nearby in full happiness of its spring freshet. Following the sound, she left her chair on the verandah and hobbled gingerly across the yard, around puddles and into the edge of the mossy forest.

As she paused at the water's edge, a deer appeared out of the trees on the opposite side, a small spotted baby by her side. Kate felt her breath suck inward at their natural beauty. For a moment all three stood staring at each other.

A musket blast ruptured the moment. The pair wheeled and leaped gracefully back into the bush.

"Kate, where are ye?" Hamish's voice hailed her.

"Over here," she called.

"So here's where ye go ta." He joined her, a dead partridge swinging from one hand, his musket in the other. "Ye mustn't stray too far until yer a good deal better. This is a rough, unforgiving country."

"I just saw the most beautiful deer and her fawn. I was enjoying their company until you decided to kill that poor little bird."

"In this country, one cannae waste the opportunity ta get food, especially in spring when any type of fresh meat is scarce. This--" he held the bird up before her. "Will make a fine stew."

"I expect it will," she sighed. "It appears to be of the grouse variety and they do make an excellent fricot."

"Och, so you know a tad aboot cookin' wild game, do ye now. A rare bit of knowledge fer a lady."

"We had a hunting lodge," she said bringing herself primly back to her lady stance. "As I've already told you."

"Aye, that ye did." He turned back in the direction of the barn. "If ye enjoy woodland creatures, ye'll find much ta delight and amuse yerself around the farm. Chust don't wander far. I've no the time ta go searching fer ye if ye get lost or injured. And I plan to deliver ye in good condition ta the vicar in Pine first thing tamorrow mornin'."

"No!" She scrambled after him as fast as the

crutches would allow. "No, he'll send me back to England, he'll…"

"Lass." He swung on her. "It isn't right, you and me sharin' a cabin. We are no the married couple. And while my native friends might accept that arrangement, white society willnae. I donnae wish ta ruin yer reputation and I will do chust that the minute any of me white neighbors discover us. These first few days I could say ye couldn't be moved but now ye're runnin' about the place, frisky as a rabbit. Ye must go, lass."

He hefted his musket over his shoulder and strode back toward the cabin.

Her mind racing, Kate stared after him. She had a plan. A bold and daring plan. All she needed was for one of his neighbors to pay him a visit to put it into motion.

****

"Thank you!" Kate cast her eyes heavenward an hour later as she heard a wagon rattling at high speed into the dooryard. Grasping crutches, she hobbled to the door in time to see its driver pull his galloping team to a mud-spattering halt in front of the barn.

"Hamish, will you come, man! We've a great need of you!" the shabbily dressed man at the reins yelled.

Hamish straightened from checking a shoe on one of his massive Clydesdales.

"What is it, Andrew?" He came around the animal's haunches.

"It's Neil, Hamish! He's been gored by our bull and he's bleedin' something fierce!"

The man paused for breath as he caught a glimpse of Kate on her crutches in the cabin doorway.

"You didn't tell me…" he began but she was quick with the explanation suggested during the

Maliseets' visit.

"I'm Kate, Hamish's wife." She bobbed an awkward curtsy. "We've just recently married."

She cast a besotted smile over at her newly declared husband. His mouth gaped open. One hand on the rump of one of the Clydes, Hamish MacDonald stood frozen in the warm spring sunlight.

A triumphant imp of mischief drew a coquettish smile to her lips. There. She'd done it and there was no way out...for either of them.

"Mrs. MacDonald." The man touched the brim of his battered hat, his face mirroring his surprise. "Hamish has been keeping secrets, it appears."

"Aye, he's a close one, is my Hamish." She slanted him a shy smile through lowered eyelashes.

"Hamish, will you come, man?"

"Whit?...oh, of course, Andrew." Hamish drew himself up. "I'll just be getting' me things from the house. Turn me team out into the pasture, will ye, and fetch the Lad. I'll be needin' him ta get me back home. Chust bridle him. There's no time for a saddle. I'll borrow one of yours to get home."

He headed toward the cabin with long, pounding strides. The glance he threw in her direction as he passed her might have curdled milk. She didn't care.

Now he'll be forced to allow me to stay with him for as long as I chose. The thought sent a smug, comfortable feeling coursing through her veins.

****

Andrew Currie strode out of the barn leading a big black horse, the mount Hamish had referred to as the Lad. The farmer led the stallion to the rear of the wagon.

"My husband is a fine healer," she said softly as Andrew knotted the animal's reins to the backboard.

"Aye, Missus, he is that. Some folks say it's a warlock he is but that's pure foolishness. He's been

41

gifted, that's all; gifted with the powers of healing and put among us to help in our times of need. It appears yourself has required his skills of late." He looked pointedly at her crutches.

"Yes. A foolish wagon accident. Hamish was driving too fast. He was eager to get back to the cabin after our wedding." She paused as she struggled to attain the image of a bashful bride.

"Oh, aye." Andrew's expression and words were full of comprehension.

"The wagon hit a bump at a curve in the road. I was thrown clear and this--" she glanced down at her encased foot, "--was the result."

"Well, I must say, Mrs. MacDonald, if you had to suffer an accident, you couldn't have had a better person at the ready to help you."

"How long ago did it happen, Andrew?" Hamish burst out of the cabin and ran toward the waiting wagon, a small black bag in hand.

"Nigh on a half hour. I came straight here as soon we'd carried him into the house. Do you think you can help him, Hamish?"

"I'll have ta see him first. I can't make any promises." He leaped onto the wagon's high seat and Andrew Currie scrambled to join him.

"Kate, if I'm not back by nightfall, open the barn door so that Pilot might herd the cow and her calf inside. Niver mind Calvin and Clyde. They'll be all right in the pasture until I return. And I will be havin' a wee word with ye when I get back so mind ye wait up." His eyes narrowed threateningly as he looked down at her.

"Of course, my dearest." She smiled up at him. "I could not sleep without you by my side."

"Aye, well, perhaps ye shan't have ta concern yerself about it verrae long."

He turned back to the man seated beside him. "Now, Andrew, urge up this team. Let us see if yer

Percherons are all they're reputed ta be."

"Yah!" Andrew flapped the reins and his team broke into a gallop.

Pilot came and sat beside Kate. She placed her hand on his head.

"Goodness!" She smiled down at him and tried to overcome the shakiness. "I didn't think telling such a tale would take so much out of me. Did you see the look your master gave me! We shall have to do some serious plotting and planning while he's gone. Otherwise..." She paused as she recalled his parting remarks. "But as he's said himself, he's made no inappropriate advances to me thus far although he's had ample opportunity. I cannot see him becoming a rogue now. Come, Pilot, let us explore his farm. I shall have to begin acting as a good wife and learning more about this place will be a beginning."

The animal wagged his tail slowly and looked up with gentle, brown eyes.

"You're as much an enigma as your master." She smiled at the dog. "You certainly don't have the look of a jailer but that's exactly what you are." She heaved a sigh and gazed about the farm buildings. "Well, that being the case, you can help me explore without any dereliction of duty."

Pilot wagged his tail in his slow, lazy fashion and started around behind the house.

"Oh, so I'm to follow?" She caught up her dress, gripped her crutches more securely beneath her arms and set off behind the dog.

At the back of the house she discovered a large outdoor oven, a freshly plowed kitchen garden, and a small orchard, its bare branches just beginning to show evidence of unfurled leaves.

Pilot barked and trotted to a small, windowless building nearby, its entrance blocked by a thick door. Staggering, hampered by her crutches, she finally managed to drag it open.

A gush of cold air rushed out and she paused, peering into its dark interior. As her eyes became accustomed to the gloom she saw great heaps of sawdust. Empty meat hooks hung from the rafters and several barrels stood in its centre. Half-buried were several large jugs that looked as if they could contain milk.

"An ice house!" she breathed in delight. She hobbled inside.

Brushing away some of the sawdust, she revealed a great block of ice. Delighted, she gazed about at the largesse the little log structure had to offer.

Ten minutes later she was filling a basket she'd fetched from the cabin. She took butter and cheese out of the wooden casks and pulled a jar of milk from beneath the sawdust where it lay nestled against a great block of ice.

Just before she left, she placed the basket on the floor and took down the partridge he'd left hanging on a hook near the door. Then, with her basket looped over one arm and the bird in hand, she nudged the door shut and headed for another on the side of a small rise above the house.

"Unless I'm much mistaken, Pilot, that's your master's root cellar," she told the dog padding at her heels.

She had to struggle to pull open the barrier. With a sigh, she set to work. Finally she peered into the dark recesses of a well stocked root cellar. Returning to the outside, she picked up the basket and returned to top it off with potatoes and carrots. Tonight she'd make him a fine meal. She hoped that would be sufficient to satisfy his physical needs on this, his wedding night.

****

At dusk she went out to the barn and opened the rear door. The cow and her calf immediately came

44

shambling across the field and walked past her into their stall. She heaved a sigh of relief. Then she gasped. Heading toward her at a full gallop were the Clydesdales. She flattened herself against the wall and fervently prayed they'd manage to pass her without running her down.

The first gelding, the one she had heard Hamish call Clyde, slowed to a trot at the door and went quietly into his stall. The second, the one named Calvin, slowed to a walk and stopped in front of her. He turned in her direction and snorted. Then he moved closer, lowered his head, and nuzzled her.

"You're just a big baby looking for affection," she chuckled in relief as she straightened his forelock. "I do believe you and I are destined to be good friends."

In answer, Calvin rubbed his nose into her hand and snuffled.

****

As Hamish rode home through the moonlight, he was filled with roiling emotions. First, he felt pleased that he'd been able to save the life of the young farmer. Second and most powerfully, he felt frustration bubbling in his soul like a witch's caldron at the situation Kate had forced upon him. He could see no way out of it that would leave both of them appearing blameless. He could still hear her light, happy voice declaring herself his wife, see her casting him demure glances, and Andrew Currie lapping it all up as gospel truth. Damnation, the woman must be out to drive him as mad as her predecessor.

He put his heels to the stallion and vented his frustration with a savage yell. The Lad vaulted forward through the shadows as man and horse bolted down the trail toward his farm and the quandary awaiting him there.

****

Twenty minutes later as he led the Lad into the

barn, he stopped and stared. In the moonlight flooding into the barn through a window, he saw hay missing from the pile near the door and his water buckets and hay fork a little to the left of their usual position.

Surely she hadn't attempted to feed and water his stock. But when he peered into the stalls, he saw contented animals including the Clydesdales settled for the night. Next he checked on his hens. The remains of their supper of grain littered the floor of the coop, the birds were settled on their roosts.

She couldn't have. But she must have. She had.

****

"How is Neil?" She got up as he entered.

"Goin' ta survive, I believe. Nasty wound. I hope the calf in my barn doesn't inherit any of her father's bad temper." He spoke automatically because from the moment he'd opened the door, all medical thoughts had vanished.

She'd wound her hair into some new style and she'd cleaned the ragged dress. In the glow of lighted candles and the shadows cast by the fire on the hearth, she appeared more beautiful than ever. No, more than beautiful; bewitching.

The word set warning bells clanging in his head. *Don't get involved, you fool. Don't let this one strip you of what little you have left.*

"I'm sure she won't." The golden haired vision was speaking, bringing him back to the moment. "She followed her mother into the barn like a perfect lady."

"And you would know all about that. Perfect ladies, that is." He felt himself bristling, his nerves raw. *Damn her, damn her.* And damn his traitorous body. He hadn't asked her to come here, didn't want her in his house. Was this some kind of insane test to see if he'd learned a lesson, to see if he could resist temptation?

"Of course." Her tone turned stiff and cold.

"I'm right sorry for that remark." He immediately felt no better than the brute he resembled. He placed his black bag on the floor and drew a bench across the floor to join her before the fire. "Ye did a lot of work out there in the barn and I'm beholden ta ye, lassie, I truly am. It couldn't have been easy."

"It appears you had a more difficult time than I did." She glanced at his blood and sweat stained shirt.

"I'm no a thing worthy of company at the moment." He arose. "I'll chust go and wash up."

"You'll find clean water in the basin on the washstand on the verandah and a fresh shirt on the peg above it," she said to his retreating back. "When you return, I'll have supper ready."

He paused. "Thank ye, lass."

He opened the door and went back out into the spring night feeling for the first time in a long time as if he'd come home.

****

"Now, lassie, you and I have to talk..." He struggled to sound authoritative as he stepped back into the cabin, washed and wearing a clean shirt.

The scent of stew warming on the hearth pervaded the softly lighted room. The table neatly set for two had a bouquet of wild violets in a dish and a pair of burning candles at its center.

"I've heated up our supper," she said softly. She spread her hands as best she could with the crutches tucked under her armpits. "I used the partridge you shot this morning to make us a fricot."

"Ye plucked and gutted the bird yerself?" *A rare lady indeed.*

"Aye." She aped his Highland word as she slanted him a mockingly demure glance. "Wouldn't any farmer's wife?"

47

"Verra guid. But it cannae undo the mischief ye set in motion earlier this day. Unless…" He planted his feet firmly apart and hooked his thumbs into his wide belt. "Ye're ready to make yer words a fact by comin' ta me bed." *Give her a damn good scare, make her sorry she'd been so brazen before his neighbor.*

"Don't be foolish!" She shrugged aside his crude suggestion. "I merely told Andrew I was your wife to explain my presence. Your failure to deliver me promptly into proper hands has made all other explanations unacceptable."

"I failed ta deliver ye into proper hands because ye were injured and needed ta rest before being transported!" he bellowed.

"And I do thank you, Mr. MacDonald." She bent forward and calmly thrust a ladle into the bubbling pot. "Now if you've finished your beastly posturing, come and sit at the table. Our supper is ready."

****

She awoke to the sound of horses stamping and blowing in the yard. Sunbeams filled with dancing dust motes slanted across the cabin and she realized it was early morning.

She struggled to her feet, pulled a quilt about her shoulders, and grasping her crutches, made her way to the door. She opened it to see Hamish harnessing the Clydesdales to a wagon.

"Where are you going?" she asked.

Fear shot through her. Had he decided to risk her threats and take her to the vicar?

"It's none of ye're concern," he said curtly climbing up onto the wagon's high seat. "I'll be back afore dark. In the meantime, Pilot will be yer guardian."

He flicked the lines over the horses' backs and they headed out of the yard at a brisk trot. "And mind ye have a meal ready when I return, *wife*."

****

She was tidying the cabin after her breakfast of porridge and tea when she heard a wagon approaching. Hamish. He must have forgotten something and turned back. She hobbled to the door to see an unfamiliar conveyance driving into the yard, a woman in a straw sunbonnet at the reins.

"Whoa!" she admonished, bringing the team to a halt at the verandah steps. A heavy set woman with a plain, weathered face, the visitor beamed a wide, welcoming smile as she looked down at Kate.

"Good morning to you, Mrs. MacDonald," she called out as she tied the horses' reins to the brake and began to lower herself awkwardly to the ground. Her skirts caught in the wagon wheel and Kate was treated to a view of long bloomers and sensible boots.

"Blast!" she muttered as she pushed her dress back into position. "These accursed garments must have been designed by men. No woman would invent such cumbersome rags!"

She turned to Kate and let another broad smile erase her look of annoyance. "Excuse my ill manners, Mrs. MacDonald. I must introduce myself. I'm Jessie Currie, Andrew's wife. I make bread for the Healer. This week I've added a couple of pies and a batch of scones. It's the least I could do seeing as how he saved Neil's life. I don't know how Andrew and I would manage to run the farm without his brother."

She reached into the back of the wagon and withdrew a large basket covered with a snowy white cloth.

"Thank you Mrs. Currie," Kate smiled. "Won't you come in? I've tea still warm on the hearth and I'd enjoy sharing a cup with a neighbor."

"That's right kind of you, Mrs. MacDonald." The woman gathered up a handful of skirts and headed up the steps. "I'd also enjoy hearing all about this sudden marriage of yours...that is, if you've a mind."

"Of course." Kate turned and followed the woman inside. "I'm sure many of our neighbors are curious."

Her eyes sparkled as she led Jessie Currie inside. What a tale she planned to tell!

****

It was early evening when Hamish drove the team into the yard and reined them to a halt.

"Kate!" He jumped down from the wagon's high seat. "Come and see what I've found on the shore."

She hobbled out onto the verandah to find him pulling a large, familiar-looking trunk from the back of the wagon. Her hand flew to her mouth.

"It's labeled Lady Kathryn Sheffield." He hefted it up beside her. "I'm presumin' it belongs ta ye."

"Of course it does! How many titled ladies named Kathryn Sheffield do you suppose would be aboard a single ship?" Nervousness caused her to snap. "I'm sorry." She modified her tone. "I'm astonished you recovered it. I'd no idea you'd gone off searching for my belongings. Please. Bring it inside at once."

He dragged it into the cabin and she followed him. Then he turned to her.

"The key?"

"I barely escaped with my life. What would make you think I have the key? In fact, I never had it. My lady's maid was in charge of it. I wasn't in the habit of wearing it about my neck."

"Aye. Well..." He ignored her inference to the one he wore and continued, "Do ye want me ta force it for ye?"

She hesitated.

"Well? Are you no anxious ta hafe yer belongings again?"

"Yes...of course."

He went to the dresser and took out a thick knife. He returned to the chest, inserted it under the

50

lock, and heaved against it. It gave with a sharp snap. He lifted the lid to reveal a tangle of water soaked garments and toilet items. She moved to his side to survey the contents.

"They donnae look too bad," he said. "If ye wash out the salt, they should be decent enough ta wear."

"Perhaps." She lifted the skirt of a green satin gown gingerly between her fingers. "However, they're hardly suitable for a farmer's wife."

"Ye're no a farmer's wife!" he howled. "I never married ye!"

"And would it be all that horrible a fate if you had?" She slanted him a sideways glance and fluttered long lashes.

"Aye, it would but donnae go askin' why."

"Very well." She shrugged. "By the by," she continued turning away with a swirl of her ragged skirt. "I had a visitor today. Jessie Currie, Andrew's wife, brought fresh baking and stayed for a bit of conversation."

"Oh, aye?" He looked over at her, his eyes narrowing.

"I told her we'd met in Scotland, on my father's estate where you were a ghillie." She felt her heartbeat upping as she began the tale she'd told the woman. "I told her we fell in love but, of course, could never marry...a servant and a lady. So you came to America to build a life for us. It took you a number of years...?" Her gaze posed the question.

"Five," he breathed, shaking his head slowly.

"Well, five then it is," she continued brightly. "Five years to get your farm in a condition where you saw fit to send for me. I, of course, had to run away. Therefore, it's important no one in the community betray me. Otherwise, my father will send someone to fetch me and you and we will never, ever see each other again."

"A damned fairy tale, woman!" he muttered, a

scowl as dark as a thunder cloud covering his countenance. "Do ye seriously think anyone will believe such a yarn?"

"Yes!" She swirled back to face him, her eyes glinting emerald sparks. "Because most people, unlike you, are romantic. Most people believe in love and happily ever after."

"Then most people air fools!" he bellowed. "Ye've forced me into supportin' lies. Now I will have ta commit yer yarns ta memory so not ta be branded as a rake or a roué who keeps young women in me house without benefit of clergy."

"Rake or roué? Really, Mr. MacDonald, I'm sure no one would liken you to either of those sophisticated, if disreputable individuals."

The moment the words were out of her mouth she regretted them.

"On that score, ye're correct, Lady Kate. This vulgar lad will chust be off the barn where I trust I'll be more appropriate company."

"I'm sorry. I didn't mean..."

"Ye don't have ta apologize." He turned away. "I'll see ye in the mornin'."

"Wait. Have you had anything to eat? I've kept bread and cheese on the sideboard and I can steep tea. You must be hungry."

He paused. "Aye, I could do with some food."

"Then sit at the table." She smiled up at him. "And you don't have to leave for the night. I mean," she hastened on. "You could sleep in here...on the floor...as you've done previously. I'm sure it can't be comfortable out in the barn with the animals moving about all night."

"That it isn't, lass. But it's the mosquitoes that fair drive me ta distraction. Mosquitoes and blackflies. Their buzzin' and bitin' fair drives me mad."

"Then, by all means, stay inside." She went to

the hearth and swung a pot over the fire. "The water will be hot by the time you've seen to the animals. I'll have food on the table by then."

"Thank ye. I am weary and food and hot tea will be welcome." He started toward the door.

"Mrs. Currie told me Pilot has been coming to their farm quite regularly to visit their Newfoundland dog named Black Beauty," she called after him. "Were you aware? Perhaps we should be keeping him at home."

"I hardly think that would be fair...or possible." He turned back to her, a slow grin kinking up the corners of his mouth. "Ye see, lass, Black Beauty is in whelp with Pilot's pups."

After he'd gone, she returned to the trunk, removed the soggy gown and held it gingerly up to her shoulders. It sagged in front of her, six inches too long and nearly the same measurement in girth. With a sigh she laid it over the chair and began to rummage through the rest of the trunk's contents. Where was that sewing kit?

As her hands searched through the layers of fine lady's apparel, she suddenly remembered the jewels. Struggling to her feet she looked out the window to make certain Hamish wasn't close by, then began to unpack.

When it was empty, she carefully slid her fingers into a small, barely visible niche in one corner and lifted. As the section of false bottom raised, she caught her breath. There they lay in all their splendor. The jewels. Her ticket to freedom.

Chapter Three

The following afternoon Hamish drove back into the dooryard as the sun was slanting down behind the trees. She'd heard the horses and wagon approaching and had come out onto the verandah. As he reined the Clydes to a halt, she saw a collection of packages and sacks in the back.

"You've been shopping?" She gazed at his load.

"Aye." He swung down. "If ye're determined to pose as me wife and if ye want me ta support the fiction, I expect ye ta at least cook fer me so I've brought ye the means."

He went to the rear of the wagon and lowered the tailgate. "Flour." He hefted the first bag to the verandah. "Sugar." He hefted the second and placed it beside the first. "Oatmeal." He threw a third to join the other two. "I trust ye can make decent porridge?"

"Of course." She drew herself up proudly. "And even if I didn't, living with a Highlander, I'd have to learn, wouldn't I?"

"Aye, that ye would. And I've brought ye even more surprises. Our supper." He reached behind the wagon's seat and pulled out a large basket.

Intrigued, she hobbled to his side and removed its covering. She'd expected to find a freshly killed rabbit or partridge. Instead her eyes rounded as she saw cheese, ham, bread, a pie, and a bottle of wine.

"How…where?"

"Village ladies. News of our nuptials has spread like wildfire. This is their gift ta the bride."

"But we don't deserve..." she began.

"I quite agree. Still it was ye who declared yerself me bride. Now ye must live with the consequences...publicly at least."

He reached up and pulled down a cloth bag.

"I believe ye'll find clothin' inside," he said. "Apparently Andrew found me bride a trifle shabby and the ladies set about to right the situation. Now I must see ta the team."

****

When he'd finished stabling his team, he returned to the cabin to find Kate wearing a plain blue cotton gown that he assumed had come from the bundle of clothing. She'd tied her hair back with a bit of matching ribbon. Beyond her, the table was set for supper and lighted by a pair of candles.

"Good evenin', lass," he said. "Yer lookin' bonny...as does the cabin and meal."

"Thank you, sir." She bobbed him an awkward curtsy, then quickly drew herself up proudly. "I've fed Pilot. He appeared hungry."

"He's right good at feignin' hunger," he chuckled. He laid a hand on the dog's head as the animal came to greet his master. "Ye'll have ta get used ta his posturin' or he'll have ye makin' him as fat as a pig."

"According to you, he saved my life, therefore I can hardly neglect him. Now come." She seated herself daintily on the single chair and spread her skirts carefully about her. "Our meal awaits. Will you pour the wine, sir?"

A sardonic smile twisted his lips. It had been a long time since he'd been asked to pour the wine. Or perform any civilized duty at a meal. He drew himself up, favored her with a courtly bow, and advanced to the table to do as she'd requested.

In the centre of the table he saw a pot of freshly boiled potatoes, a bowl of oatmeal, and a saucer of butter. When they sat down to eat, she offered him the vegetables. She took one herself and proceeded to roll it first into the oatmeal and then in the butter. When he failed to follow her example, she looked over at him questioningly.

"Well?" she asked.

"Well, whit?" He met her gaze squarely.

"I boiled those potatoes especially and set out oatmeal and butter. I thought you'd enjoy them. It's a great favorite in the Highlands."

"Oh, aye." He reached for the bowl of oatmeal and proceeded to roll his potato in it. As he dipped it into the soft butter, he looked over her.

"It's been so long since I had any of the food of the Hi'lands, I clean forgot," he said.

"Have you now?" She glanced over at him but he avoided her gaze and kept his attention focused on his food.

****

"A fine meal, lass." He leaned away from the table and caught himself just in time to keep himself from toppling backward. "Damnation, I forgot I was sitting on this confounded bench." Annoyed he righted himself.

Glancing across the table he saw her eyes twinkling. He hesitated, then slowly let a grin curl up the corners of his mouth. "Perhaps I should be purchasin' a second chair."

"Perhaps you should, Mr. MacDonald," she replied her lips twitching, her emphasis on the first syllable of his surname in the Scottish manner in which he pronounced it.

Blue eyes met green, humor sparkling between them. It slowly melted away until only the gaze of a man and a woman remained. Meeting, questioning, wondering...

"Aye, well." He aroused him with an effort. "I must see to the stock and close up the barn."

"Yes." She got to her feet. "And I have dishes to

wash."

Again both paused, sapphires looking deep into emeralds. Hamish fancied the air between them suddenly crackled with some sort of static charge as he felt again the unwelcome reaction of his body to this enchantress.

Damn! Sorcery, magic. He wanted nothing to do with any of it. He swung and strode out the door, slamming it with unnecessary force.

For a few moments Kate stood staring after him, her confidence in her power to control their relationship eroded. What she'd seen in those piercing blue eyes had been lust; pure, unvarnished lust. What would she do if he insisted on becoming her lover? She looked at the bread knife on the dresser, the musket standing by the door and knew she could defend herself with either of them. But she knew those weren't the weapons she would need.

In spite of his long hair and beard, Hamish MacDonald had become attractive to her; mysterious, earthy, virile, and with a strong, muscular body that caught and held her attention. And blue eyes that appeared to pierce her very soul. Perhaps he was some sort of mystical creature who held more than the powers of healing within his grasp. If he did make amorous advances she'd have to steel herself mentally more than physically to repulse him.

One thing she did know for certain. He was not like *him*. No, most definitely Hamish MacDonald was not like *him*.

****

He cleaned the stalls, put fresh food and water into each, brought the three horses, the cow and her calf inside for the night, and locked the hens in their coup. He paused to scratch the Lad's forelock as the stallion stuck his head out of his box stall.

"She's a beautiful, charming woman," he told the

horse. "And an intriguing mystery to boot. Not an easy combination for a man to resist." He drew a deep breath as the big animal nuzzled him, searching for his bedtime treat.

"You've not been listening to a word I said," he chuckled drawing a carrot from his pocket. The sensation of the horse's velvety snout on his hand sent his thoughts racing back to the woman inside the cabin. He wondered if her cheeks would feel as soft as they looked. He wondered if she'd resist if he tried to take her face in his hands, if he tried to raise it up so that their lips might meet.

He shook himself. The animal, startled, threw back his head.

"Sorry, my boy." He rubbed the stallion's forehead. "I had to shake off the thoughts I was having before they went any further. Sleep well, my handsome prince. I pray your rest is not disturbed by visions of a pretty young mare."

He turned and headed for the door. Halfway there he stopped abruptly, pulled the front of his work-stained shirt out from his body and sniffed it.

"Damnation! I reek of barn and animals and sweat. I've been living alone so long I haven't noticed how repulsive I've become." Disgusted, he strode out into the night.

****

He paused on the bay shore and looked out over the calm, black waters. A scrap of a new moon was rising, lending its slender reflection to its surface. Benign and peaceful at the moment, the bay appeared incapable of the death and destruction that had cast Kate upon this shore.

Kate. Why had he chosen to name her such? Had it really been because he refused to acknowledge her as a titled lady or did it reach deeper than that, right down to his penchant for nicknaming people he cared for. Like Margaret, his

Maggie.

Crazy thoughts, he reprimanded as he stripped off his clothes. Lady Margaret and Lady Kathryn. Maggie and Kate. Dangerous thoughts.

Naked he waded into the cold, spring waters of the bay and flinched as they covered his thighs and groin area. The sensation scrambled his thoughts as he dove forward and stretched out with long, powerful strokes away from the shore. To hell with women, all women, he thought as he swam into the shaft of moonlight streaming along his path. A woman had exiled him here, turned him into a creature who appeared more beast than man. He wouldn't allow another female to destroy this new life he'd made for himself.

****

He returned to the cabin to find the dishes washed and replaced on the shelves above the dresser, the hard-pressed earthen floor swept, and the fire banked against the chill of the spring night.

Kate, wearing his nightshirt, apparently asleep, lay in the bed, her crutches leaning against the wall nearby.

Pilot, on the floor beside her, raised his head at his master's entrance, flogged his tail a few times, then, with a sigh lowered it again to sleep.

For a few moments Hamish stood staring at her, at the soft hue of her complexion, at the beauty of her heart-shaped face, and tangled golden curls. *She was like a mythical princess, cast by fate on this wild, remote shore. Damnation!*

He brought his thoughts up short as he felt his body begin to lust and strode to the chest in the corner to gather his bedding from its top. Maybe he should sleep in the barn.

The fire burning low on the hearth felt good. He hesitated. Surely he hadn't become such a brute that he couldn't sleep in the same room with a woman without losing control.

He snatched up the quilts and blankets and headed for a place near the door. Soon he was stretched out, warmly wrapped in bedding, his head resting on a rolled-up jacket. Exhausted from a full day and a long swim, he fell asleep almost immediately only to dream of the woman lying there in the flickering firelight.

But when he knelt beside her bed, he discovered she had glossy black hair. When she turned to him, brown eyes sparkling with desire looked up at him from a breath-takingly beautiful oval face. She smiled that dark, seductive smile he remembered all too well as her name slipped through his lips. "Maggie."

His heart hammering he bent to kiss her. Her soft, full lips parted in the old, familiar way, arousing him in every inch of his body. The cabin dissolved and they were once again in the manor house. The bedcovers were silk and the room illuminated by dozens of candles, their play of light and shadow dancing seductively.

"Maggie, ah, Maggie," he breathed as he moved to join her on the bed.

He awoke with a start. A dry stick had snapped in the fire. His chest was heaving, he was sweating. *Sweet Jesus, would that woman never leave his soul in peace? Couldn't she be content with having destroyed his life? Wasn't once enough! Why did she have to come back to haunt his dreams?*

"Mr. MacDonald, are you all right?"

Kate's voice startled him. She'd raised on one elbow and was staring at him, concern crinkling her forehead. "You were moaning."

"I'm verrae well, thank ye. Chust a bad dream." He turned on his side, his back to her.

Don't look. The last thing you need after such a dream is another beautiful woman close to you, lying in your bed, in your nightshirt.

He closed his eyes and tried to blot out the image.

****

She slid back down under her covers, wondering. His hair and beard had appeared damp...as if he'd bathed. Had he decided to become more civilized? Had she inspired him?

No, of course not. She turned her back. He wanted only to be rid of her. If she hadn't tricked him into this pretense of a marriage, he'd have cast her into the vicar's care as quickly as his horses could trot. And, anyway, why should she care? As soon as her ankle healed, she'd be off to seek her fortunes elsewhere.

****

When she awoke one morning a week later, she heard him urging his team into motion and then the creak and rattle of the wagon as he drove out of the yard. So he'd left, gone off somewhere again. She yawned and stretched. Good. No need to rush with her morning ablutions. Looking forward to time alone, she struggled to her feet and saw he'd left porridge, bread, and tea ready.

After she'd dressed, eaten, and tidied the cabin, she looked about and wondered what to do. She considered altering some of the clothing in the trunk Hamish had rescued from the shore but decided against the idea. It would be a waste of time, most of it being inappropriate for farm work. Even the material used in the gowns was ill-suited for alternation into anything she could use.

Sunlight was streaming in the windows. Abandoning any idea of sewing, she opened the door on a beautiful spring day. She'd inspect the garden. She knew he'd been working at it. She was also eager to see how the orchard was progressing.

Grasping her crutches, she hobbled around to

61

the back of the cabin. There she paused, breath catching in her throat, overwhelmed by the beauty of the small orchard in full bloom. Blossoms of pink and white had turned the previously barren apple and plum trees into clouds of soft, sweet-scented beauty.

Next she looked at the garden laid out in straight, neat rows. Already a few tender green sprouts were forcing their way through the rich-looking earth. Hamish MacDonald was a man of foresight who planned and planted to sustain himself.

But what of her? She hobbled over to an apple tree and touched a blossom-laden branch. Who would provide for her once she was well?

She let the branch snap back into place and returned to the cabin. One by one she pulled the elegant garments from the trunk and began to shake out their tangles. If she couldn't stay on the farm perhaps she'd have need of them and the secret that lay beneath that false bottom.

****

When he returned that evening he found his clothes line crowded with female attire swaying gently in the breeze. Very little looked fitting for a farmer's wife. He led the team, tired and dirty like himself from plowing, into the barn. But the lacy undergarments and nightshifts had brought back memories he knew were best subdued under the present conditions.

When he'd finished his barn chores, he went up to the house to find a basin of clean water, a piece of soap, and a drying cloth on the bench near the door with a clean shirt hung on a peg above it. A grin twitched beneath the beard as he pulled his work-soiled garment over his head. Even if this was her way of telling him he needed washing, it was a treat to find the hint so complete and convenient.

As he scrubbed, he felt a sudden urge to shave and cut his hair, to look human again. But no. That would never do, no matter how much he longed to be rid of the tangle. He exhaled in disappointment as he rubbed soap into an armpit.

****

She peeked through the crack in the doorway. She felt a sudden desire to see if the man matched the magnificent creature she'd thought she's seen standing naked before the fire on her first night in the cabin. A smug smile tipped as she watched him strip off the shirt and begin to wash vigorously.

Yes, she was quite certain he and the creature of her tangled vision were one and the same. His body was hard and lean and bore the structure of a Greek god she'd seen in books in the manor library. She wondered if the physical labor farming required was responsible or if he'd simply been blessed with a hard, muscle-rippled form. Either way he was a pleasure to look upon.

She remembered seeing Callum the head groom thus washing and how fascinated she'd been by his powerful physique. But then she'd been merely a curious child of fifteen. Now she was a mature woman of twenty and she understood the feelings aroused within her all too well.

She also knew nothing could ever come of such sensations. She could never truly marry this man any more than she could return to England. And she was not about to sleep with him unwed. She had enough with which to concern herself without adding an illegitimate child to her problems. Reluctantly she turned back to her chores.

****

Kate put the last of the vegetables into the pot and swung it over the fire. Although last summer's produce was still firm from their storage in the root cellar, she was eager for the fresh offerings of the present year. In another week, the radishes and lettuce would be fit to eat and she'd be able to provide more variety in their meals.

Their meals. Already she was in the habit of thinking of her and Hamish as a couple. A very strange couple. A lady and a beast.

Pilot barked and she came out of her musings. The dog stood at the door.

Grasping her crutches she hobbled to let him out. As she opened the door she saw that the sunshine had vanished. Now, as evening approached, ominous black clouds had darkened the sky and a gusting wind was raising dust devils in the dry yard.

Glancing toward the slope of the far hayfield where Hamish had finished loading his wagon and was heading for home, she saw a bolt of lightning crack open the sky above him.

Clyde, the more fractious of the team, half reared and in the ensuing boom of thunder, began to prance and kick. The loaded wagon tipped precariously as the terrified horses shuffled wildly, then broke and bolted down the hillside toward the barn at a dead gallop.

Hamish, sawing on the reins and yelling, would surely be killed if the team tried to find refuge in the barn.

Oh, God, no! Clutching crutches and skirts, she scrambled out of the cabin and down the steps.

Chapter Four

Hobbling as fast as one good leg could take her, Kate scrambled down the steps and across the yard.

"Calvin, whoa! Stop!"

The big horse pricked his ears and swerved just as she slammed the barn doors before the frenzied team. She barely had time to dodge aside and avoid being trampled before the team skidded to a dust-raising halt, great white feathered hooves churning up the earth. Snorting, pawing and shivering as another bolt of lightning lighted up the sky, they shook their massive heads, rattling bits and harness.

"Sweet Jesus!" Hamish leaped from the seat, caught the frantic horses by their bridles, and turned to look at Kate. "Ye could have been killed, woman! Whoa, Clyde! Easy, Calvin, lad!"

"Never mind that now." She struggled to her feet. "Just get those frightened creatures unhitched and inside before they're further maddened by the storm."

"Aye. And ye get yerself up ta the cabin. There's goin' ta be a cloud burst any minute."

****

After Hamish struggled the team into the barn, unhitched them from the wagon, and led them into their stalls, he paused, breathing hard. *Kate was quite a woman.* He wiped sweat from his forehead with the back of his forearm. He could have been badly injured or even killed.

And yet there she'd come, at a hobbling run, across the dooryard, dragging her cast to put herself between him and quite possible death. He'd never known a woman with that kind of courage. He couldn't imagine Maggie racing out of the manor to throw herself in front of a crazed team of Clydesdales.

He drew a deep breath and shuddered, partly from shock, partly from memories that, even after years, still had the power to stir him to the depths of his soul. *Would he never be free of her?* Or of comparing every woman he met with Lady Margaret Blackwell.

****

He dodged into the cabin as the storm volleyed across the sky and great bursts of thunder shook the log house.

"A bad one," he said wiping water from his face.

"Get out of those wet clothes." She handed him a quilt. "I've tea and a hot meal ready for you."

She turned her back and busied herself at the hearth until his deep, sensuous chuckle made her pause.

"You find something amusing?" she asked.

"Aye, more like amazin' and that something would be ye, Kate. Ye may once have been a useless aristocrat but not any more. Nay, not any more. Ye've the courage of a lion and the nurturing soul of a mother, lass."

She turned slowly as he stood by the bed swathed in the quilt.

"It's a lady's duty to show courage in adversity," she said, a flock of butterflies beginning to flutter in her chest.

"Oh, aye." The two words reeked of skepticism. He sat down on the bed and the quilt parted over his legs.

Trying to suppress the thought that the beast had very nice, manly limbs she turned to tend their supper.

"But how would a lady such as ye come ta know what ta do in such an emergency?" he asked. "I'm sure most would have nary an idea of what a runaway horse would do or where it would head. They're accustomed ta leavin' such knowledge and concerns ta their grooms and footmen."

"My father was an avid horseman," she stirred the pot on the hearth. "He often took me with him to the stables. I overheard talk of what to do about runaways."

"And anythin' else? A stable can be a right bawdy place with language often no' fittin' a lady's ears."

"No one would dare speak improperly with my father by my side." She swung to face him, spoon in hand. And gasped.

He'd dropped the quilt and was pulling on a pair of dry undertrousers. But not quickly enough for her to avoid seeing much more than she'd expected. She swung back to the meal on the hearth, blushing as she heard his deep-throated chuckle.

"A hundred thousand pardons," he chuckled. "I'd no idea ye were about to swing round. But, then, as ye have expressed a desire ta remain under me roof, perhaps ye will have ta get accustomed ta me in various stages of undress. As I perhaps will have to become accustomed ta ye."

"There should be no need for any such accommodations," she snapped stirring the pot so violently some of the contents splashed over the edge. "Even in this tiny cabin, it is not difficult to maintain our privacy. And our dignity."

"Oh, aye, our dignity." She heard him pulling on boots and a moment later he came to stand beside her fully clothed. "We must, above all, maintain our dignity."

Lightning flashed and in the ensuing roll of thunder she looked up. The electricity of the storm seemed to flush through her veins in mad desire for the earthy, mysterious man.

Later she could only assume he'd fallen prey to similar magic. In that moment, he turned and before she could move to stop him, he was kissing her, kissing her as she'd never been kissed before. Lightning flashed, thunder broke over the cabin like cannon fire as her consciousness reeled. Her body suddenly weightless and floating, was engulfed in a magnificent, all-consuming sensation she'd never imagined.

His tongue thrust between her lips and ran gently over the tip of hers. His hands slipped to the small of her back and thrust her against his risen desire. She floated, she whirled. And when he finally stopped, she staggered, every ounce of strength drawn from her body.

"Aye, well." He looked suddenly embarrassed and shy as he backed away, rubbing his hands on the seat of his trousers. "Sorry. It mustta been that brush with death and the storm and yerself lookin' so lovely. It willnae happen again, I promise." He turned toward the table. "Now let us get ta that supper. It smells downright allurin'."

Kate could only nod. Fumbling, she served the meal. He didn't press her to speak. Instead he ate and drank silently as the storm raged. Then, as it began to recede, he made up his bed by the door as if nothing had happened, as if he'd never forever changed her world with that mesmerizing kiss.

Where had a creature she'd termed a beast learned to kiss in that seductive, mind-whirling manner? She wondered as he left for a final check on the stock. Was he indeed some kind of warlock who could easily lead her astray? Well, he wouldn't succeed. She'd lived through a shipwreck. Surviving an onslaught of sexual desire should be easy.

She cleared the table, set the dishes to soak in

the pan of water, and hastily prepared for bed. By the time he returned, she was beneath the covers, her back to the door, feigning sleep.

****

He was gone with the team when she awoke the next morning. She rose, washed, dressed, and made herself a pot of tea. Then she took a mug and hobbled out onto the verandah to sit on a bench against its back wall. It was a beautiful day. She drew a deep breath and savored its clearness. She could be happy here.

Thoughts of the previous evening suddenly filled her mind and she hugged her arms about her body at the remembrance. He'd made her feel more truly alive in those moments in the storm than she could ever had imagined. The sensuality of his kiss, the intimacy of his embrace, his body's obvious attraction...

She felt herself blushing. Surely ladies didn't dwell on a man's bodily reaction. Yet, it was exciting and, in a way, comforting to know how he felt about her, even if only in a physical sense. If he was attracted to her, if he felt a pull of desire that he nevertheless appeared capable of controlling, that meant he would not be completely anxious to be rid of her.

And given time to heal and make plans, she'd be much more equipped to make her escape when the right time arrived.

Reassured by her reasoning, she went back into the cabin.

****

Hamish arrived as she was preparing the noon meal.

"Come out here, Kate!" he called.

As she opened the door, he jumped down from the wagon's high seat and strode around to the back of it. Lowering the tailgate, he waved an arm. "Come

69

and see what I've bought."

Intrigued, she made her way across the yard.

"Look." He indicated a new ladder backed chair. "A second chair so that we might both sit comfortably at meals."

"Very thoughtful."

"And I've bought one of these." He pulled out a carved piece of metal. "A reflector. George Loggie, the proprietor at the general mercantile, tells me it's a wonder for baking on a hearth when the weather's too bad to cook outdoors."

"Yes, it is. I'll bake you some scones directly. Thank you."

"But wait, there's more." Grinning he jumped into the wagon and drew out an object swathed in cloth. "Here, fer ye. Fer savin' me skin yesterday."

He handed it down, then joined her on the ground to watch as she gazed at the package. "What...?" she glanced up at him suspiciously. He was still grinning.

"Open it and see."

She unrolled the wrapping. Trimmed with hand painted roses and completed with a daintily handled cover, a china chamber pot came into view.

"Now ye can give me back me bucket. I've few enough ta spare." Impish jesting sparkled in those expressive blue eyes and she chuckled, then laughed.

"My, if this is what I receive for stopping your team, whatever elegant gift would you get me for a really important occasion?" She finally managed to control herself enough to speak.

"Ah, lass, allow me that special occasion and ye'll find out."

She couldn't mistake the sexual innuendo in his words or the sudden change from teasing to passion in his eyes.

"That won't be necessary." She handed him the chamber pot, adjusted her crutches, and hobbled with all the dignity she could muster toward the cabin. "These gifts are all I could possibly want."

****

Kate removed the pan of scones from the reflector oven and smiled down at them. Golden and light as feathers, they looked perfect, exactly the right treat to present to Hamish after his thoughtful shopping.

She placed them on the table, then headed out to the barn to invite him up to the cabin for scones and tea. Such a ritual might have the effect of civilizing and formalizing their way of life after those tumultuous moments during the storm. Lord knew she wanted to do all she could to prevent its repeat and the possibility that *she* might not be able to bring it to a halt before they were completely carried away on a wave of physical desire.

As she crossed the verandah and hobbled down the steps, she heard a fine tenor voice issuing from the barn. He'd gone out there earlier to mend harness. The strains of *Flow Gently Sweet Afton* lilted out into the fine afternoon as naturally as the most soothing of summer breezes. She paused to listen, a delighted smile tipping her lips.

****

"My Mary's asleep by thy murmuring stream,
Flow gently, Sweet Afton,"
Disturb not her dreams."

He stopped abruptly when she joined him in the last line.

"A lovely tune, is it not, Mr. MacDonald?" She tilted her head and smiled.

"Aye, Mr. Rabbie Burns had the gift, that's fer certain." He returned his attention to the old cavalry saddle in his hands focusing on it and not the way the sunlight was turning her hair to gold or how easily her voice had blended with his.

"You're planning to use it again?" She gestured at the scarred leather. "It's a bit the worse for its years, isn't it?"

"No, I'm not plannin' ta use it. I just thought that fixed up and polished it might bring in a few bob."

"Are we hard up for money?" She looked at him, concern furrowing her forehead. "Because if we are, I can take in washing and mending..."

"We're no the paupers!" he snapped. "I'm chust lookin' ta buy a bit of new farmin' equipment. This old saddle, not bein' of any use, can be sold to facilitate such a purchase."

"Oh." She stepped back, hands clasped behind her back. "You're a fine singer," she continued. "You should use your gift more often."

"Aye, well, I've not had a great deal to sing about these past few years." He drew the sweat-stained girth through his hands and examined it closely.

"But now you do?" He caught the teasing curiosity in her words.

"Aye, sometimes now I do." He squinted up at her in the shaft of sunlight streaming in through the open barn door. "I've a couple of people I've been called upon ta help who are makin' excellent progress. That's enough ta spur any man into song, do ye not think?"

"Oh, aye." The two words wobbled light, as if she were dancing around him, gently taunting him.

"Now look ye here, lass." He dropped the bit of harness and stood up to tower over her. "Donnae go thinkin' yer presence has anythin' ta do with me singin'. I sang before ye got here and I'll..." He stopped himself short.

"And you'll sing again after I'm gone." The brightness drained from her face and she turned back toward the house. "I only came down to invite you for tea and scones but perhaps you're far too busy."

She hobbled back toward the house and he sat down heavily on the bucket, cursing himself.

****

"I've come fer a taste of those scones, if ye've still a mind ta feed me."

She turned from placing tea leaves in the pot to see him standing in the cabin doorway. He looked so contrite she had to suppress a smile.

"Of course I've still a mind to feed you. Sit down." She indicated the table where she placed a plate of scones and a pat of butter. "Tea will be ready directly."

"These are lookin' verrae fine." He sat down and reached for a scone. He bit into it, chewed for a moment, then continued, "And they taste chust as good. Ye're ta be complimented, lassie."

"Thank you, kind sir." She poured hot water into the tea pot, swished it about, then carried it to the table. "We'll let this steep a moment."

"Ye're a puzzle, lass," he said holding his half-eaten scone in one hand. "Ye profess to be a lady, ye have the speech and manners of one, and yet ye can act like an experienced farm wife when the need arises."

"Ah, yes, now there you have the answer to your puzzle." She took two cups from the dresser and placed them on the table. "When the need arises. A true lady is always ready for any occasion even if it is a bit out of her usual field of endeavor. I am one who made certain I would be ready for most common necessities by watching the tenants and servants at work. Tea?" She picked up the pot and held it over his cup.

Stymied, he could only nod.

****

That evening they sat on the verandah and

73

listened to the frogs and crickets as a full moon rose over the woodlands beyond the pasture. The warm spring night breeze set the pines behind the cabin soughing softly, and in the forest back of the ice house the brook giggled contentedly.

Hamish felt a sense of satisfaction he hadn't felt for years. He'd been lonely for female company, for the sight, scent, and sound of a woman. And now he had Kate. Kate who couldn't have been further from what he'd thought he wanted in a woman and yet who he now was beginning to believe might be exactly what he needed. But, of course, that wasn't possible. Would never be possible.

"Mr. MacDonald?" She brought him out of his reverie.

"Hmmm?" He leaned back and drew a deep breath of the sensuous night air. He'd sleep in the barn for certain tonight. He was getting those all to familiar longings that he had to deny around the woman sharing the evening with him.

"Will you always be a farmer, do you think?"

"Probably. I like the land, I like the life. Why?"

"Just wondering. Sometimes I get the feeling you don't belong here. Sometimes..."

"Well, I do. Now stop yer wonderin' and just enjoy this perfect night."

"I think I'll be going inside." She arose haughtily and turned toward the door.

"Now donnae go gettin' yerself all in a knot just because I donnae feel like givin' yer speculations any credence." He turned to her without getting up. "Woman, ye air gettin' as irksome as if ye truly were me wife."

She shot him an annoyed look that even the darkness of the evening did not hide before she hobbled inside the cabin and gave the door a hard push shut.

"Argh!" He leaned back in his chair and slapped

his hands down hard on its arms. The blasted woman was wondering away too much. Why couldn't she just accept him for what he was, what he would always be, and leave his past buried deep, where it belonged?

Chafing with annoyance, he arose and headed for the barn.

"Come along, Pilot," he called to the dog loitering by the cabin door. "Her ladyship will be havin' none of us this night. Anyway, it's a lovely night. Sleepin' in the barn will be a treat."

He spoke loud enough for Kate to overhear.

****

At the sound of a wagon approaching on the road, Kate turned from hanging clothes on the line. She knew it couldn't be Hamish. He'd said he and the team were working in a field beyond the trees in the opposite direction. As she watched two strangers, a young man and woman in a truck wagon appeared. The man was urging the horses to a gallop while his companion clung to her distended belly, her face distorted with fear and pain.

"Are you Mrs. MacDonald?" The young man dragged the team to a halt beside her. Dust rose to film her wash.

"Yes."

"Is Hamish about? Lizzy's gone into labor...too early. We need him right bad."

Lizzy moaned and clutched herself.

"He's in the back field." Kate hobbled forward and reached up a hand. "Come, Lizzy. I'll make you comfortable in the cabin while your husband fetches mine."

She helped the woman down, recognizing that she was hardly more than a child. Perhaps they married young in this country, she thought, as she urged the girl towards the cabin.

Lizzy's husband flapped the reins and left at a

gallop.

"Come inside, Lizzy," she said. "We have a bed where you can make yourself comfortable until my husband arrives."

Together they went up the steps into the house. Once inside the girl doubled over, moaning.

"Just a little further," Kate urged. "Look. Over there. A nice, soft bed for you and your babe. Hamish will be here any minute."

But will he be able to help, she wondered, as she assisted the groaning young woman into her bed. He might be fine for patching up wounds and mending broken bones, but a premature baby was an entirely different matter.

"Mrs. MacDonald, your man will be able to help me, won't he?" Lizzy looked up, her face wet with sweat, her eyes round with fear and desperation. "I couldn't bear it if we lost this wee one. Leam and I want it so very much."

"Mr. MacDonald has healing hands," Kate said soothingly, adjusting a light blanket over her. "He's mended my ankle and Neil Currie's wound. Birthing a wee babe should be a simple task for a man of such skills."

Reassured the girl settled back with a sigh.

"Rest," Kate smoothed the tangled hair back from Lizzy's brow. "You will need your strength to bring this wonderful new life into the world."

****

By the time Hamish arrived at the cabin, Kate had settled Lizzie in her bed, had water on the boil, and was preparing dressings. He took it all in with a single glance, then turned to the young husband close on his heels.

"Go care for your team and mine, Leam. Then stay in the barn until I call you. There's nothing you can do here."

"Leam!" Lizzy's voice rose in a scream of agony

as she arched on the bed.

Kate, kneeling beside her, took her hand. "It will be all right, now, Mrs. Fraser. Hamish is here," she said softly.

"Go!" Hamish stopped the father-to-be as he attempted to go to his wife.

"But she needs me." His face glistened with sweat.

"Nay, right now she needs me and--" He looked at Kate bathing the young woman's sweating face and making soothing sounds. "--me guid wife."

He went to the basin of water Kate had prepared and began to wash his hands and arms. The young father, after a last glance at his writhing wife, left the cabin.

"Kate, I'll be needin' ye ta assist." Hamish dried his hands and turned.

"Of course." She spoke confidently.

"Guid. Hold Lizzy's hands while I see just how far along she is."

****

When he arose from examining the expectant mother, he turned to Kate and she knew all was not well.

"Kate, a word with ye on the verandah," he breathed into her ear. Aloud he said, "Lizzy, Kate and I will chust be steppin' out for a wee moment. Try to rest. We'll be right back."

He took Kate by the arm and drew her quickly outside. Once the door was closed behind them, he paused.

"Lizzy's baby is breech," he said.

"Oh, no!" Kate's hand flew to her mouth. "I've heard of such occurrences. Don't they often end in damage to the child at the very least? At worst..."

"We won't visit that possibility chust now." He drew a deep breath, then continued, "I believe I can successfully turn the child but I will need your help.

You must comfort that girl and keep her as quiet as possible during the process. I cannae chance her causing me hands ta slip and make a mistake. Do ye think ye can do it, lass?"

"Yes, of course." Kate spoke with a great deal more confidence than she was feeling.

"Well, then, let us get ta it. The wee lassie is in a deal of pain and we mustn't allow her strength ta be completely sapped."

He cupped his hand beneath her elbow and guided her back into the cabin.

Chapter Five

During the next few hours Kate sweated and sometimes despaired but didn't cease to marvel at the skill with which Hamish worked, painstakingly repositioning the baby within Lizzy's womb that it might be borne as nature intended.

Lizzy gripped her hands, writhed and screamed until Kate felt the young wife would tear her throat asunder.

Finally, Lizzy seemed to give up. She lay spent, her breathing labored, her complexion a glistening waxy hue. She released Kate's hands and let them fall from hers.

"Hamish!" His name was a gasp from Kate's lips.

"Get cold water and bathe her face and throat. I'm almost done. The child should be free directly. Keep talkin' ta her, Kate. Keep reassurin' her that she and the bairn will be chust fine."

Five minutes later, Lizzy opened her eyes so wide Kate feared they'd pop out of their sockets. Then she screamed.

"Good lass, good lass, chust a little more. That's it." Hamish's voice was full of confidence and encouragement.

Lizzy screamed again, then fell back limp upon the pillows.

"Ah, yes." Hamish's face brightened as he gathered the new life in his hands and held it up. "Lizzy, ye have a fine, wee laddie. One of the finest I've ever seen."

"Mrs. MacDonald, does he speak true? Can you see? Do we have a healthy little boy?"

Kate looked and then smiled back at Lizzy.

"That you have, Lizzy. Now I must go and wash him while Hamish tends to you. I'll be bringing your son to you shortly."

****

As the wails rent the air Kate set about the task of making the small boy presentable. In the bed Lizzy lay spent but happy.

"And he's well and whole, Healer?" she asked for the third time.

"A right robust fellow, wouldn't ye agree, Kate?" Hamish rolled down his sleeves.

"He's beautiful." She smiled down at the child, fresh from his first bathing. "You may give him to his mother now, Mr. MacDonald." She gathered her crutches and struggled to her feet as he picked up the blanket-wrapped bundle.

"Oh my." The new mother gazed down at her firstborn. "He's got his father's eyes...and chin...and nose."

"And his mother's hair and lips and forehead." Kate stood smiling down at the pair. "Congratulations, Mrs. Fraser."

"And it's thanks in no small measure to you and your good man." Lizzy beamed at the couple standing beside the bed. "I should have died of pain and fear if you hadn't helped me. When your turn comes, Mrs. MacDonald, rest assured I will be there for you."

Kate cast a swift glance at Hamish but he merely smiled kindly down at his patient.

"That's verrae guid of ye, Mrs. Fraser," he said softly. "Mrs. Macdonald will take comfort in yer offer, won't ye, me darlin'?"

He turned but Kate had focused her gaze on the new mother and appeared oblivious to his words.

****

Later that same afternoon Kate sat on the verandah while the exhausted young family slept inside the cabin.

Hamish had saddled the Lad and set off down the road a half hour earlier. He'd not explained where he was going and Kate hadn't felt the need to inquire.

Everything was under control. If he needed a few moments respite, he was certainly entitled after the stress of the past few hours.

She heard hoof beats pounding up the road toward the farm. Hamish and the Lad burst into view at a dead gallop. Man and horse were as one.

As they entered the yard, Hamish slowed the stallion to a sedate canter, turned about, then headed for the pasture gate at the other end of the yard.

Kate felt her breath catch in her throat as horse and rider cleared the five foot barrier with such grace and ease they seemed to be flying.

They galloped about half-way across the field before Hamish turned the horse and headed back toward the gate once again. Again they cleared it with such grace it appeared man and horse had invisible wings.

He drew to a halt before the verandah and grinned from the back of the prancing, blowing horse.

"He's quite a lad," he said, patting the horse's arched neck. "He dearly loves ta jump but I rarely have the inclination ta allow him such pleasure. However, taday is a verrae special day so I'm indulgin' him."

"And yourself, Mr. MacDonald," she couldn't help adding as she recognized his flushed exhilaration.

"Aye, well, I must admit I do enjoy a good

81

canter." He backed the horse away from the steps and turned him toward the lane. "And successfully birthin' a fine young lad like the one in the cabin gives me an excuse ta celebrate. I'll chust be coolin' the boy off and then I'll be up ta join ye."

"On the verandah," she called softly. "The family is asleep inside."

She watched as he trotted the horse down the lane, then walked him back. She'd never suspected he could ride as he had just demonstrated. Watching him had been pure pleasure.

But then she'd never known he had a fine tenor voice. He'd called her a puzzle, but she was nowhere near the enigma he was proving to be.

****

"Are ye sure ye'll be comfortable out here?" Hamish watched as Kate adjusted quilts and blankets in a bed of hay in barn that evening. "Givin' the cabin over ta the young couple and their babe for the night was a verrae kind gesture, but ye're not yet healed yerself."

"I will be perfectly fine, thank you, Mr. MacDonald." She finished her bed making and sat down upon it to face him. "Besides," she looked up at the roof as the Lad blew and moved in his stall nearby. "I love the sound of rain and contented animals."

"Aye, well, ye'll have lots of both this night." He dropped on one knee and began to arrange his own bed a few feet from hers. "I donnae think this downpour will let up any time soon. As for contented animals..." He gestured to Pilot stretched out across the end of Kate's improvised bed and snoring. "Pilot seems ready to oblige."

He grinned and she smiled back.

"Hamish, how did you know what was wrong with Lizzie?" she asked. "How did you know about breech births?"

"I've dealt with a few in me time," he said turning away. "It's one of the first things ta check when a young woman who is about ta become a mother for the first time begins ta give birth ta her babe early. When a child goes full term, it has time ta turn in the womb and be ready ta be delivered the proper way, headfirst. However, if the wee un decides ta come afore its proper time, then oftimes it hasn't had that chance."

"You know a great deal about medicine for a man who professes to be nothing more than a farmer with healing hands." She looked at him, eyes narrowing.

"Not so surprisin'." He adjusted his blankets and settled beneath them with a sigh. "A farmer often has ta tend birthin' and sick animals."

"But not all farmers have your gift of healing," she persisted.

"Perhaps I've chust been blessed." He reached toward the lantern. "Ready?"

"No. I have more questions."

"Then they'll have to wait." He blew out the candles inside the glass and turned on his side. "Good night, me darlin'."

"Humph!" She gave a disgusted grunt as she settled noisily.

"Ye did a fine job today, Mrs. MacDonald," he said softly in the darkness. The words of praise came easier when he didn't have to face her. "If I didn't know ye were a lady born and bred, I'd suspect ye'd assisted in a birth before this day."

"Hardly." The word was a scoff in the darkness. "But a lady is taught not to shirk a duty when it's required of her. And..." Her haughty tone moderated abruptly, then stopped.

"And?" he pressed.

"I once had a cat that gave birth to her kittens in my bed."

"Ah." He repressed the chuckle rising in his throat.

"Are you laughing at me?" Indignation peppered her words.

"Nay, nay, lass. It's chust good ta know ye've had the experience."

"Good night, Mr. MacDonald." Her tone hadn't grown any less irritated.

"Good night, Mrs. MacDonald. May angels guide ya ta yer rest."

****

Apparently no angels were available to help him to his rest. Long after her regular breathing told him she slept, he lay awake revisiting the events of his life since Kate's arrival.

Too many inconsistencies made it impossible for him to accept her for who she claimed to be. But whoever that might be, she'd proven to be a fascinating woman who demanded his most concentrated efforts to resist. Another week and he could remove her cast.

Then what?

She'd said she'd leave. But to go where and how?

He wasn't about to give her one of his horses. And how could she leave now that she had his neighbors believing she was his wife? Damnation!

Finally exhaustion overwhelmed and he slept only to dream of Kate limping off down the trail, a portmanteau in her hand while he stood watching, unable to make a move to stop her. When he tried to call out, to ask her not to leave, he had no voice beyond a froggish croak.

****

She awoke to discover Pilot snuggled tightly against her.

"Pilot, move!" she hissed. "You're too warm."

The big dog sighed and reluctantly crawled off a few inches. As he did, she realized the rain had ceased and moonlight was streaming in a window. Its beam fell on the face of the man asleep a few feet away. He was lying on his back, his hands clasped on his chest. She had a horrifying flash that he was dead. The image sent her heart racing with fear.

What would she do without him? She knew she'd soon be well and physically able to make good her expressed intention to leave, to walk away from this wilderness farm that she'd begun to think of as home.

He had healing hands and a caring heart. He'd tended her most carefully without making a single inappropriate demand upon her person. In short, the feral beast had behaved with more decency and honor than many so-called gentlemen she'd known.

She turned and tried to blot the problem from her mind. Still it was just before the dawn when she finally drifted into a fitful sleep.

****

"Hamish! Come and join us, man! Your good wife has made us a fine breakfast...porridge and bread and tea. Sit yourself down. You must be hungry."

Leam was sitting at the breakfast table when Hamish stepped into the cabin. Lizzy was propped up in bed with a cup of tea, the baby snuggled close.

"I was feedin' the stock," he replied closing the door behind him.

"I forgot!" Leam bolted to his feet. "My horses!"

"Sit, man. I fed and watered them. Now I'll chust take a minute with me patient before I settle down ta this fine repast. How are ye today, lass?" he asked, smiling down at the pair in the bed.

"Very well and happy, thanks to you, Hamish," she beamed up at him. "We've decided to name our son James. That's English for Hamish, is it not?"

"It is indeed." Hamish ran a hand down his beard. "I'm honored."

85

"Mr. MacDonald, your breakfast awaits." Kate drew his attention and he went to the table. Kate placed a pot of tea beside the bread and butter, then went to fetch a bowl of porridge from the pot bubbling over the fire.

"Do you think I can take Lizzy and James back to our farm this morning, Hamish?" Leam asked as Kate poured tea. "There's a ship loading fish and lumber destined for the Caribbean at the wharf in Pine and I've a stack of timber I'd like to get sold aboard her before she sails on the twentieth a mere week from today. Lizzy and me could use the money from that sale, especially now."

"I don't see why not." Hamish reached for a thick slice of bread and began to spread it with butter. "That is, if ye drive a mite slower than ye did yesterday."

"Oh, aye, of course. My team can move like turtles if I ask them."

"I've no doubt. Kate, sit yourself down and eat, woman. I'll be needin' you ta help me make Lizzy and James comfortable in the wagon and you cannae work on an empty belly."

****

"Well." Kate watched Leam drive his team carefully down the road an hour later, his wife and babe ensconced in blankets in the back. "That was an unexpected event. Are you often called on to birth babes, Mr. MacDonald? I thought you were simply skilled at stopping up wounds and mending broken bones." She gave him a suspicious glance. "If your speech and manner of living didn't brand you as a feral farmer, I'd be inclined to suspect you were a trained doctor."

"Oh, aye?" He looked down, frowning. "And where do ya think such as meself would be gettin' the money ta afford such an education?"

"I have no idea. I first suspected you might have

gained experience on a battlefield when you mended my ankle and patched the goring your neighbor received from his bull. But I cannot attribute your skill at birthing babies to such a past."

"Wars and battles donnae stop babies from bein' born," he said. "Some women follow husbands and lovers who are soldiers. Babies are the natural result of such attachments."

"So you're telling you were a stretcher bearer or medical assistant in the army?"

"I'm no tellin' ye anythin'." He turned and headed for the barn. "And yer time would be a lot better spent cleanin' the cabin and seein' what's for our dinner than wonderin' about me."

****

Kate sank down on a chair with a deep sigh. She'd finished setting a batch of bread and now she was weary. It was the first time she'd attempted such a feat. Although she'd never admit it to Hamish, doing housework on crutches while dragging a clay cast about was both irritating and exhausting. She'd promised to work by his side as a good farmer's wife should and she wasn't about to give him cause to doubt her, no matter how her back and arms ached.

"Well, now, lassie." The man himself stepped into the sunny kitchen and put his hands on his hips. "Whit have ye been about?"

He glanced at the mound of dough she'd left rising in a bowl on the dresser and stopped short. "Ye've been settin' bread?"

"You needn't look so surprised, Mr. MacDonald." She slanted him an exasperated glance. "Jessie Currie instructed me during her visit. It's a relatively simple task."

"Oh, aye, for a farmer's wife, I've no doubt, but for a lady..."

"Ladies have brains and capable hands as well."

She arose and hobbled to the hearth. "Now would you care for a cup of tea? I have some still warm."

"Nay, nay, lassie. That's no the reason I've come in chust now. Unless I'm greatly mistaken, it's time for that great lump ta come off yer ankle. Let's give it a look." He knelt before her and took the cast in his hands.

"Do you really think so?" She could barely believe her good fortune. "It would be wonderful to be free of it."

"Aye, I'm sure it will be." He went to the trunk in the corner, drew out the key hanging on the chair about his neck, and opened its lid. "I'll chust be gettin' something ta ease it off."

****

Ten minutes later he helped her to her feet. The cast lay in a shattered mass on the floor around them.

"Slow and careful," he said softly as she gingerly eased weight onto her newly bare ankle.

"Ah!" She caught her breath and stumbled back against him as small shards of pain shot from it.

"Slow and easy," he said again and this time she managed to stand on it. Slowly he took his arm from about her waist and she was standing free of the cast for the first time in weeks.

"It's a miracle!" she breathed.

"Try a couple of steps." He stayed in position to catch her. "Chust a couple, mind. There's no need ta do it all at once. Nor is it wise."

She did as he advised, feeling the ache of an ankle not yet accustomed to being on its own. But it was only for the first steps. She could walk free and easily again. She whirled to face him, nearly lost her balance, and tumbled into his arms.

"Thank you, Hamish," she breathed, looking up into his face. "Thank you so much."

"Och, lassie." He set her gently away from him.

"Anyone would have done as much."

"But not with such skill. Hamish MacDonald, you definitely are the Hermit Healer. You're probably the most valuable man in this entire community. It gives me pride to be your wife."

"Ye're no me wife!" he howled. "Damnation, how many times must I remind ye? And in a few days I'll be takin' ye to the village and handin' ye into the care of the Reverend MacKenzie and his guid lady."

Exasperated he turned and strode back to the barn.

Humming a little tune, Kate walked at first cautiously, then with confidence and only a slight flinch to the dresser to check on her bread.

We'll see about that, Hamish MacDonald, her stubborn mind declared.

****

Kate waited until Hamish had ridden to a neighboring farm two days later before she put her plan into action. As closely as she could reckon from the time frame Leam had given, it was the nineteenth of May. Early the next morning, probably at dawn, that ship loaded with lumber and fish destined for the Caribbean would be leaving the wharf in Pine. She intended to be aboard.

She'd ride to Pine, hide in the woods nearby overnight, and in the morning, convince the captain to take her along in return for the smallest portion of trunk's jewelry she could convince him to accept. She couldn't afford to be overly generous. She was setting out on a new life, alone and with only her wits as protection. Carefully she wrapped food stuffs and a few articles of clothing in a blanket and tied it securely.

Then she lifted out the false bottom of the trunk Hamish had rescued from the beach. She selected a diamond and ruby necklace.

"This should pay for my keep and anything I'll

be taking away with me," she said placing it open on the table. The most precious and easily concealed from the remainder she thrust down her bodice. The remainder she thrust into her improvised packsack. "No point in putting all my eggs in one basket," she murmured.

She went to the sideboard and picked up the Tom Jones novel Hamish had left there and which she'd secretly been reading. Opening it to a remembered page, she laid it on the table, went to hearth and selected a slender, half-burned stick from the smoldering fire. She waved it about to cool, then returned to the table. Carefully she used the blackened tip to underline two words. "In Payment." She placed the necklace beneath them. In the absence of paper and ink, this was her only way she could think of to leave him a message.

"Goodbye, Pilot." She turned to the dog that stood watching her. "We're friends, aren't we, so you won't try to stop me." She bent and gave him a hug. "I'll miss you but your master leaves me no choice. I won't let him take me the village."

She headed toward the door but halted as Pilot trotted to stand between it and her.

"Now, Pilot, we both know I have to go." She cocked her head to one side and spoke firmly. "I owe you my life. Please let me get on with it."

Squaring her shoulders, she marched past the dog and out onto the verandah. She dropped her sack of provisions, closed the door behind her and tied it with the bit of rope that served to secure it.

Inside, as if suddenly aware of his mistake, Pilot began to bark and jump against the door.

"Good bye," she called struggling down the steps with her provisions. "And thank you."

In the barn, she pulled out the old cavalry saddle Hamish had been mending when she'd gone to fetch him to enjoy her scones. Dusting it with her hand, she carried it into Calvin's stall. Pleased to discover Hamish had mended the girth, she took the milking stool from beside the cow's stall, placed it beside the Clydesdale, and stepped up on it to throw the saddle over his broad back.

"Good boy," she cooed as she led him to the pasture fence a few minutes later and urged him against it.

Scrambling into the scarred saddle, she checked her bag of provisions tied to it, then nudged the big gelding into motion. He snorted and pranced, unaccustomed to the contraption on his back, then as she reassured him with soft words and gentle hands, he trotted out of the farmyard, his gait as smooth as a rocking chair.

****

"Kate!" Hamish swung down from his mount, looped the reins over the verandah, and strode up the steps. "Kate."

An impatient "woof" replied from inside the cabin.

At the door he paused and frowned at the rope latch secured with an awkward knot.

"Pilot?" he called as he untied it and pushed his way inside.

The big dog greeted him with drooping head and feebly wagging tail.

"What? Why was the door secured? And," he glanced around the interior of the cabin. "Where's Kate?"

Then he saw the open jewel case on the table.

"What's been going on here?" He stared at the gleaming ornaments. "Pilot?"

In answer the dog barked and loped out the door. Hamish followed him to the barn and inside. Pilot stopped at Calvin's empty stall and barked again.

"Sweet Jesus, she's stolen my horse and run

away! Pilot, quickly!" He turned and was running toward his stallion. "Pick up her trail! We must find the daft woman before something happens to her."

****

Kate walked Calvin down the shore. The day was hot and humid with a heavy grey cloud cover. Her clothing clung to her sweat-drenched body like a second skin. Mosquitoes and blackflies swarmed around the pair. Calvin frequently shook his head and wriggled his skin in an effort to free himself of the pests.

"I'll find you shelter as soon as we get to the village," she promised, swatting at the buzzing, biting hoard. "Surely there must be some abandoned cabin where we can both spend the night out of the reach of these terrible pests. If I were of a superstitious nature, I'd be tempted to think the elements were conspiring against my escape by sending these nuisances and cloying temperature upon us."

Gazing out to sea she found memories of the horrendous night of the ship wreck reentering her mind and struggled to push them away. She had another sea voyage ahead of her. She couldn't let fear deter her embarking. The West Indies wasn't her choice of destinations but it was her only one at present. Perhaps the ship would dock at some port along the American coast and she would be able to slip off and find a new home. No matter what its first port of call, Kate intended to get to shore in some new community where her past could truly be left behind.

Suddenly Calvin stopped, raised his head, and whinnied. He half turned back in the direction they'd come and she saw Hamish and the Lad racing after them at a full gallop.

"Go, go, go!" She slapped her legs against the startled gelding, sending him forward in a leap and then a shambling gallop. "Go, go, go!" Her urgings became cries of desperation as the thunder of hooves behind her grew closer.

Suddenly a powerful arm swept about her waist, lifting her from the saddle and pulling her onto the pursuing animal. She fought and kicked but he was too strong. Shortly, as he reined his mount to a stop, she was deposited on the beach with a thump.

"Whit do ye think ye're doin'?" He leaped to the ground to confront her, his face glistening, his shirt soaked and plastered to his sweating body. His expression mirrored anger and exasperation. "Stealin' me horse and runnin' off without even a 'by yer leave' after all I've done fer ye!"

"I didn't steal your horse!" She faced him, green eyes snapping emerald fire. "I left a necklace in payment! Surely my care and one horse can't be worth more!"

"It's no the amount!" he yelled back. "It's the idea that I cannae trust ye. I thought we'd come ta an understandin'."

"An understanding you were about to violate!" she shouted. "You'd said you'd keep the circumstances of my arrival a secret if I told you the name of the ship on which I'd been sailing! Then the minute you remove that miserable cast from my ankle, you make plans to turn me over the local vicar no doubt with a full account of how I came into your life and the fact that I am not truly your wife!"

"Did I say any such thing? No, I did not! I simply said I'd take ya ta the vicar. I planned ta make up some story as ta why ye were leavin' me!"

"Oh, aren't you the clever one! I cannot wait to hear your tale!"

"Well, ye won't be hearin' it now." He caught her about the waist and was about to fling her up onto the Lad when she suddenly grabbed him about the neck and pulled his face down to cover his mouth

Gail MacMillan

with hers.

For a moment, he did nothing but when she started to draw away, he caught her back to him and kissed her, kissed her until her body turned molten and malleable, until she whirled off the ground and floated into a time and place where there was only this mysterious man and his mind-boggling sensuality. All the magic she'd experienced when he'd kissed her on the day he'd nearly been killed by his runaway team flooded back. When he finally released her, she staggered away from him, staring in mute astonishment.

"There." He put his hands on his hips and let a sardonic smile kink his lips. "Is that what ye've been wantin'? Was that what ye were lookin' fer?"

"Of course not, you great oaf!" She scrubbed the back of her hand across her lips and managed the outraged response. "I thought...I thought that was the payment you were seeking in addition to my jewels."

"Lass, your most precious jewels don't lie in a velvet chest." The wicked suggestiveness of his words enraged even as they inflamed.

Trying to give the former full power, she swung away from him but he caught her about the waist and flung her up onto his horse. The stallion shied and she caught at his mane.

"Now enough of pleasurin' ourselves." His good-natured grin rankled. He'd been playing with her, tormenting her, nothing more. "We've both chores to do and it's gettin' late. I have a stop to make along the way as well."

Ten minutes later they rode into the dooryard of the Curries' well-kept farm. Andrew Currie came out of the barn to greet them.

"A pleasure to see you, Hamish," the farmer said catching the Lad's bridle. "Do you and Mrs. MacDonald have time to climb down and visit? I know the wife would glad to have the company."

"Sorry, Andrew, not at the moment. Right now I'm wonderin' if ye're still interested in that old saddle Calvin is sportin'? I've a mind ta get rid of it."

"For certain." Andrew looked up and Kate saw questions in his expression. "But I could have come over for it. No need to ride over here with it displayed on your animal."

"We were headed out for a bit of a ride so it's no hardship." Hamish swung down, leaving Kate in the saddle to breathe a sigh of relief. After that wild kiss that had left her lips and body tingling, the movement of the man's hips against hers during the ride had been almost more than she could bear and maintain an outlook of haughty annoyance.

"How much are you asking for it, Hamish?" Andrew asked as the healer began to loosen the girth from about Calvin's broad rib cage.

"A couple of yer layin' hens would make it square." Hamish pulled it free and handed it to the farmer. "I had ta banish one of mine ta the pot and I've few enough as it is."

"Not enough. Six hens and a rooster. Otherwise I'll not do business with you, Hamish MacDonald."

"Verrae well. Thank ye. I'll come over with the wagon in a day or so ta collect them. Good day ta ye, Andrew."

He swung back into the saddle with Kate, touched his forelock, and urged the Lad into a trot.

"So I'll be trapped at your farm until such time as you see fit to get rid of me," Kate said, bitterness coloring her tone once they were well on the road.

"I wouldn't put it exactly like that but since ye've charmed me animals into being useless in keepin' ye safe, I have ta take action." He shifted against her buttocks. She felt a hot thrill flash through her and had to stifle the gasp that almost escaped her lips.

95

"Hold tight," he muttered into her ear, his lips against her hair and something in her solar plexis moved...pleasurably.

Holding the Lad's reins in one hand, Calvin's in the other, he nudged the stallion into a brisker trot that didn't help Kate's situation.

When they arrived at the farm, he rode through the yard and out into the trees beyond.

"Where are you going?" she asked, suddenly alarmed. "Surely not the village, to the vicar?"

"No, although that's probably what I should do." He drew rein beside a deep pool in the brook where she'd come upon the deer and her fawn. "I'm sweat soaked and filthy. I need a bath and this pond is the only source available." He swung to the ground, reached up and pulled her down to join him. "Do ye care ta join me?"

"Don't be daft!" She put her hands in her hips and faced him angrily. "Have I not just tried to run away from you? Do my actions inspire you to think I'd care to romp naked into a forest pool with you?"

"Verrae well, then. Perhaps ye'll oblige me by handin' over the rest of those jewels ye have stowed about yer packsack and on yer person. I'll not have ye tryin' to trade it for anymore of me livestock in future efforts ta run away."

"And just what make you think there's more?" She backed defiantly away from him.

"Because, me darlin', while you do have a lovely shape, I've perused it frequently enough to realize it's grown considerably at its topmost since this mornin'. Furthermore, no lady ever traveled with a single diamond necklace. There has to be more, much more. Now will you hand over the booty or must I search fer it meself?"

He stepped forward, hands reaching for her.

"Damn you, Hamish MacDonald!" She stumbled away from him. "Very well. Turn your back and you shall have all of it!"

"A moment." He gathered up the reins of both horses. "Chust a safety precaution, ye understand. I'm not in the mood ta go chasin' after ye again this hot day."

"You may turn around now." She turned back to him, holding a glittering collection in her hands. And gasped.

He'd opened her improvised packsack. The remainder of the jewels lay spread out on it.

"How dare you!" she cried. "Here, take it all!" She flung the necklaces and bracelets in his face. "For a man who fervently declares time and time again, he wants nothing more than to be rid of me, you're taking away my only means of leaving!"

"Leavin' as ye've proposed is too dangerous." He looked her squarely in the face, diamonds, emeralds and rubies about his feet. "While I may not relish bein' forced ta pose as yer husband, I'm not about ta let ye endanger yerself by runnin' off with no idea of what ye're ta do. When ye're fit and have solid, definite plans, I'll be only too glad ta assist ye with them. Until then, I'd advise ya not ta try stealin' any more of me stock."

He pulled off his shirt and boots, then began to open his trousers. "Now will ya be joinin' me or not? A cool swim will make ye feel a whole lot better, guaranteed."

"I hope you drown!" Grabbing up her scattered garments, she turned and stomped off in the direction of the farmhouse, hot and dusty and wishing she were the one cooling her passions in that deep pool.

****

As Hamish swam leisurely about in the cold, clear water, he felt his tension easing. From the first moment he'd discovered her missing until he had her safely back on the farm, he'd been a roiling mass of raw emotion.

He had to get rid of her and soon. She was etching herself all too indelibly into his mind and body. He'd even found himself riding back to his farm with the thought that he was returning to Kate foremost. If she were anyone but an English lady, if she were simply a farmer's daughter, anyone other than a member of aristocracy, he might be willing to take a chance on truly putting his past behind him and setting out to make her his true and legal wife. But she was who she was and nothing would change those circumstances.

And soon he'd have to rid himself of her, let her get on with her life.

He dove deep into the black depths of the pool, then broke the surface to shake water from his long hair and beard like a dog. A dog. A beast. And he'd never be able to be anything else.

****

"I'm thinkin' it might be time we went ta the village." Hamish arose from the breakfast table the next morning. "I'll harness the team while ye clean up in here."

"No!" She jumped to her feet, bumping the table and making the dishes rattle and totter. "I've told you I will not be shipped back to England!"

"Now did I say anything about shippin' ye anywhere?" He put his hands on his hips and faced her squarely. "No, I didnae. I simply thought ye might fancy a change of scene now that yer foot is free of that great bit of clay. But if ye're goin' ta go accusin' me of tryin' ta shanghai ye…"

"No…no, no, no!" She rounded the table, yelped, and clutched her hip as pain shot up.

He caught her gently by the shoulders and helped her onto the chair.

"Aye, now see whit ye've done," he reprimanded. "Ye may be free of the cast but ye've still got a deal of healin' ta do. Perhaps ye'd best stay here…"

"No, Hamish, please!" She caught at his work-calloused hand. "I want to go! Please! I do so need an outing!" She gazed up, her eyes pleading.

He straightened. "Well, if ye're sure ye will behave yerself…"

"Yes, yes, yes!" She tightened her grip and he was amazed at the strength in it.

"Verrae well. I'll go harness Calvin and Clyde. But mind, ye keep yer word, lass, or there'll be no more outings for ye for a verrae, verrae long time."

****

It was a beautiful day for a wagon ride, Kate decided an hour later as, perched on the high seat beside Hamish, she was headed for the village called Pine.

Trees sported the delicate green fuzz that, in another week or two, would become full-fledged leaves. Along both sides of the rutted wagon path, grass was turning green and small, shy wildflowers were beginning to peek out. The air was clear and warm, the sky a vast blue vault above towering pines soughing softly in a gentle breeze. From time to time rabbits scampered across their path and the bush was filled with birdsong.

Kate drew a deep breath and began to sing:

"Oh, ye'll take the high road
And I'll take the low road
And I'll be in Scotland afore ye
For me and my true love will never meet again
On the bonnie, bonnie banks of Loch Lomond…"

Hamish joined in and they sang together until Kate's voice cracked over an especially high note and they broke off, laughing.

"It's really such a sad song," she commented when their mirth ended. "Legend has it was written by a Scottish rebel awaiting execution in England who'd parted from his true love on the banks of Loch Lomond. Others say while it was indeed written by a rebel awaiting hanging, he wrote it to a friend who'd escaped the noose. He claims he'll be taking the underworld road to Scotland while his friend will be traveling overland and the rebel will, being a spirit by then, get there first."

"Ye seem to have a rare knowledge of Scottish music," he commented.

"That shouldn't surprise you," she said. "I've told you my family had a hunting lodge in the Highlands."

"Aye, aye, that ye did." He flicked the reins and brought the team back to a trot. "I chust didnae think such tunes would hold any attraction fer an English lady." He glanced over at her; a quick, quizzical glance. "I'd a thought the meanderings of the likes of yer Lord Byron would be more ta yer taste."

"You know the works of Bryon?" It was her turn to turn a questioning gaze on him.

"Aye, well, I've heard the name bandied about. I wasn't born a hermit, ye know."

"I didn't suppose you had been." She kept a penetrating gaze pinned on him. "And what, may I ask, were you born? What were you before you decided to secret yourself away?"

"That's of no concern ta ye," he said turning his attention to the horses.

"Oh, but it is...husband." Knowing how the term irked him, she spurred him with it.

"I am not yer husband, woman!" he howled. "Ye proclaimed yerself my wife and blackmailed me inta keeping up the fantasy."

"Don't tell me you haven't benefited from it!" she snapped back. "I'll wager it's the first time in months, perhaps years, that your shirts and drawers have been regularly washed and mended, your table properly laid, and your meals decently prepared."

"Aye." His tone moderated. "But ye've given me no medals for livin' with a beautiful woman and still managin' ta keep myself ta myself. Other men might not have been so gallant especially when that woman has taken it upon herself ta publicly declare him her husband."

"But you're not. Therefore I cannot understand your bewailing the denial of a condition which you yourself admit you have no right to."

"Argh!" He flicked the reins and sent his lagging team into a brisk trot.

For the next few minutes they drove in silence. Then she ventured a question that had been haunting her.

"Do you sometimes wish I truly was your wife?"

He pulled the team to an abrupt halt and turned to look at her, blue eyes seeming to pierce through to her very soul.

"You said I was beautiful," she faltered.

"Whit? Air ye proposin' ta me, lassie?"

"No, of course not. I just wondered..." She looked away from him, focusing on the horses' twitching ears.

"Aye, well, wonderin'." He turned back and clucked to the team.

As they started off at a brisk walk, he stared ahead at the road for a few moments. Then he spoke.

"I have wondered whit it would be like," he said, his voice barely audible above the creak of the wagon and the plod of the horses' hooves. "More than wondered, if ye must know the truth. I've been a man alone these five years. I willnae disgust yer sensibilities by explainin' male needs and desires but I will not deny that I have them."

He paused and drew a deep breath.

"That bein' said..." He glanced back, his tone

strengthening. "I'll answer yer question. Yes, there have been times, for carnal reasons, I've wished ye were me true wife, that ye could fulfil me needs without destroyin' yer future and reputation. Times like now when I long ta halt this team, take ye down from this wagon, and carry ye into that stand of trees yonder ta a place by a brook where the banks are soft and green with fresh, sun-warmed moss. There I'd lay ye down and stretch out beside ye ta run me fingers through yer mermaid's hair and down your slender, white throat, ta unfasten those little buttons on yer bodice...one by one by one."

His gaze traveled downward, his words slowing over the last few, becoming as sensuous as if he were actually plucking them open. His tone had grown deep and throaty. The horses as if sensing his inattention had come to a plodding stop.

She felt her breath suck backward and she nearly choked. Her heart hammered, her hands clutched the board seat to become white knuckled. She felt hot and cold, flustered and flabbergasted. Good Lord! The man was undressing her with words!

But he hadn't finished.

"Then," he continued, eyes hot with passion. "I'd slide it from yer shoulders, yer beautiful pale shoulders until it fell to your waist and follow its descent with kisses, tasting yer soft warm flesh until..."

He paused. Her breath was coming in gasps and she felt blood rushing to her face.

Chapter Six

"Enough." He swung away, slapped the reins, and yelled to the horses, sending them forward at a gallop.

She clutched the seat and welcomed the speed even though it threatened to throw her clear off her perch. The air rushing past dried the sweat from her overheated body and cooled at least a bit of the passion he'd aroused. Most importantly, it kept his attention elsewhere.

****

Pine, she discovered, was a lively, crude little settlement, its several wharves along the river piled high with timber products. Interspersed between the wharves were four ocean intended vessels in various stages of construction. Behind these forest-based industries was a village consisting of one rutted main street with plank and log houses and shops lining its length.

Hamish reined to a halt before the one nearest the edge of the community. A sign above its wide doors announced it to be a livery stable.

"We'll leave the horses here until we're ready ta return ta the farm," he said.

He wound the reins around the brake, jumped to the ground, and held up hands to lift her down. As they fitted snugly about her waist the memory of his passionate words flooded back and she felt a hot rush.

"Mrs. MacDonald, I do believe ye're blushin'," he said softly leaning close to her ear, blue eyes twinkling wickedly as he placed her on the ground. "Does that mean ye werenae unaffected by my words back in the glen?"

She was spared a reply as a big, burly man with a crop of red curls and a like-colored bushy beard emerged from the stable.

"It's yourself, Hamish," he greeted, grinning broadly. "And this must be the new missus I've been hearing about. My, my, she is a pretty colleen. You've chosen well, my lad."

"Patty, I'd like ye ta meet me wife Kate. Kate, this is Patty O'Brien, owner of this establishment and the best blacksmith in the province."

"Kate, is it now?" The man extended a big, work-scarred hand and enclosed the small one she offered in return. "Sure, and it's a pleasure to meet you. It's high time Hamish took himself a wife. 'Tain't natural a man his age living alone even if he's some kind of warlock healer." He winked and grinned at Hamish as he finished speaking.

"Enough, Patty. Ye'll have the lass terrified. I'm beastly enough without the likes of ye addin' fuel ta the tales of the ignorant."

"Sorry, my friend." Laughing, Patty slapped him on the back. "I wouldn't want to be throwin' cold water on newlyweds." He turned and led the team away, chuckling.

"Ye might check Calvin's right front hoof," Hamish called after him. "I'm thinkin' he's got the loose shoe." He turned to Kate. "Come along, *wife*. I've a feelin' that's only the beginnin' of many such comments we'll be forced to endure taday. The good thing is that after this first outing we'll be accepted...at least pretty much."

"We had to face the village sometime." She heaved a great sigh as she struggled to keep up with his long, determined strides. "Let's get on with it."

Their next stop was at a shop not far from the

livery stable. Pieces of wood and shavings littered its front and once they went into the building, Kate saw the interior was much the same. But amid the clutter sat chairs, tables, and cabinets of amazing craftsmanship. A small, stooped man, glasses sliding down his nose, hobbled forward to greet them.

"Hamish MacDonald, this is a pleasure." A wide smile brightened his wizened face.

"It's good ta see ye as well, Arthur." Hamish shook hands with him, a grin curling up the corners of his mouth. "I've brought me wife ta choose some furniture. Me house is sadly lackin' in such commodities, I've come ta realize."

"Of course, of course. A pleasure to meet you, Mrs. MacDonald. What may I show you?"

"A pair of rockers for the verandah," Hamish surprised her with his request. "The weather's getting' fine and I cannae abide pullin' furniture in and out of the house."

"I've just the pair for you. Come, look."

He led them to a collection of chairs near the back of his shop and pointed out a handsomely carved set.

"They're lovely." Kate ran her hands over the smooth, rich wood.

"We'll take them. And that chest of drawers yonder." He indicated a small dresser. "Mrs. MacDonald had had naught but an old trunk in which to keep her finery." Hamish dug into his vest pocket and pulled out a pouch. "What will I be owin' ye, Arthur?"

"I'll not take coin from you, Hamish MacDonald." The old man drew himself up indignantly. "I'm insulted you'd make such a gesture."

"Arthur..." he began to protest but the cabinet maker stopped him short.

"Mrs. MacDonald, I reckon this man of yours

never told you how he saved my life when a tree I was felling hit me last winter. I would have died except for his attentions."

"That's wonderful!" Kate's response reflected her pleasure. "I'm so glad my husband could help."

"As am I, my dear," Arthur chuckled. "So now you understand why I will never take payment from him for any piece of furniture he may desire from my shop. I owe him my life."

"Arthur..." Hamish tried again.

"Hush, my boy. I refuse to sell you a single shaving from this shop. I will, however, put these chairs and the chest out in front for you to collect on your way home. If you're too stubborn to take them, then they'll rot in the street or be stolen by some of the rabble that frequents the tavern."

"Verrae well, ye stubborn Englishman. I declare, I've not only been cursed with a bull-headed wife. Now I find me guid friend and cabinet maker is cut from the same bit of cloth. Thank ye, Arthur." His tone moderated from jesting to sincerity over the last three words. "I will pick them up shortly. Come, Kate. We've more shoppin' ta do and I want ta get back ta the farm afore dark."

At the general mercantile store he instructed her to buy cloth for two dresses suitable for the farm and any other "feminine trappins" she required.

The shop keeper, George Loggie, leaned on the counter, his big, strong hands palms down on its plank surface, watching Kate as she moved gracefully about the store, a grin on his wide, good-natured face.

"She's a beautiful woman," he commented softly to Hamish when she wandered to the rear to peruse the shelves of dress goods. "Congratulations. But you surely surprised us. We had no idea you were considering taking a wife."

"Ay, and ye'd be thinkin' no woman would have

the likes of me," he grinned back.

"No, no, Hamish..." George Loggie stumbled. "Look here, lad..."

"No need ta apologize for an honest thought, George," he chuckled. "At any rate, it's of no account. I have Kate and we're happy."

"Good, good, my boy. That's what we've all been hoping for you. You've done so much for us."

"Mr. Loggie." A large-bosomed, middle-aged woman in a rustling black dress and wide bonnet bustled into the store. "I've a list of things we need sent up to the manse this afternoon." She pulled a scrap of paper from her reticule. "Will you please see to it?"

"Of course, Mrs. MacKenzie," the shop keeper took her list, then turned to Hamish. "Hamish, perhaps this would be a good time to introduce Mrs. MacKenzie to your wife."

"Ah, yes." The woman crossed her arms under her heavy breasts. "I've heard about her. The woman you married somewhere else. The woman you didn't see fit to bring to my Alexander to wed." She fixed him with a frowning, accusatory stare.

"I'm right sorry about that, Mrs. MacKenzie." Hamish shuffled his boots. "It's just that we had ta travel back ta me farm alone tagether and it wouldnae hae been proper unless we were wed."

"True, true," the woman relented. "And just where might you have been traveling from? News of your nuptials has spread through the community like wild fire, but not the details."

"Saint John, New Brunswick." Kate had come quietly to join the group.

"My ship docked in Saint John," she continued smiling up at Hamish. "We were married immediately. After waiting years..."

"You knew Hamish in the Old Country?" The minister wife's surprise was mirrored in her words.

107

"Yes, of course. He worked as a ghillie on my grandfather's estate in Scotland." Kate continued to smile as she extended the lie. "That's why we could never marry in Scotland. So Hamish decided to come to this country, set up farming, and send for me when he could."

"So you defied your family and ran away to marry a servant?" Mrs. MacKenzie had fixed a penetrating gaze on the young woman.

"Yes." She gathered Hamish's arm in both of hers and hugged it. "And I'm not one bit sorry. I've loved him since I was fifteen."

"But a lady as a farmer's wife in this country..." George Loggie had stood listening to her tale, his eyes widening with each detail.

"A lady in love." Kate looked shyly up at Hamish from under long lashes. "That explains everything, does it not, Mrs....er...MacKenzie?"

"Indeed." The woman drew a deep breath that expanded her large bosom still further and smiled. "And since your husband has so far failed to do so, let me introduce myself. I am Mrs. Alexandra MacKenzie, wife to the Reverend Alexander MacKenzie. I'd be delighted if you'd come up to the manse for tea. I'm sure Hamish has errands to accomplish that do not require your attention." She looked over at him pointedly.

"Of course, Mrs. MacKenzie." He inclined his head. "I'm sure me wife would enjoy a civilized tea. I'll chust pick her up at the manse in about an hour."

His words were cordial but inside he was in a turmoil. Just exactly what fantastic yarn would Kate spin about their past? God only knew. He'd learned he could never anticipate her.

He freed himself from Kate's grip and headed for the door.

"And, mind, don't go loitering in the tavern," Mrs. MacKenzie called after him. "One must make certain to keep one's husband in check at all times, my dear," she continued turning to Kate. "This is a rough, raw country. Many a good man has turned to drink. Now come along." She took Kate's arm. "I have some lovely scones and blueberry jam."

"There's nothing quite as frightening as a truly good woman, now is there, Hamish?" George Loggie grinned after the pair had gone.

"Ye're right, George. She's one powerful female."

"Is there something I might get for you, Hamish?" the store keeper asked when the man lingered.

"A bottle of ink and a couple quills,George,if ye don't mind." He drew a deep breath. "I've a mind ta be updatin' me will."

****

As Hamish strode up the street he cursed softly under his breath. Bringing Kate to town had been one huge mistake. It had begun on the way to the village with that ridiculous urge to make her feel all the frustrated lust he did, to make her ache and long until she could stand it no longer. He realized now, all his suggestive words had done was inflame his own desires still more.

Then there'd been the encounter with Mrs. MacKenzie; an encounter that had allowed Kate to further spread the story of their fictitious past, one he'd have to remember in perfect detail in order to maintain the lie that was their marriage.

"Damnation!" he muttered, then realized he was in front of the tavern. The place was alive with some sort of feverish excitement.

"What's happened?" He waylaid a young man who came dashing out.

"Robbery in Newcastle!" he exclaimed referring to the shire town five miles further upriver. "The shipping office has been robbed of a chest of gold coins! The clerk was shot dead but not before he hit one of 'em with a musket ball. The constable is inside right now looking for men to join him in chasing down the three bandits. If you'd care to join up, there'll be a bit of pay in it."

"No, thank ye. I've a farm ta run and a wife ta fetch. Good luck ta ye in catchin' those criminals. They'll be dangerous and desperate, so take care."

****

At the manse, Kate arose, teacup and saucer in hand, and went to the parlor window as she heard the rattle of an approaching wagon.

"It's Hamish coming to collect me," she said. "I must be going. Thank you so much for a delightful tea, Mrs. MacKenzie. I only regret I did not have an opportunity to meet your husband."

"Reverend MacKenzie is seldom at home." The woman sighed and placed her cup beside Kate's. "He's the only minister in miles, his parish much too large for a man of his years. But," she sighed again. "It's the life he's chosen and I've chosen him so I mustn't complain. It must be much the same with you, my dear. Hamish is so often called out to treat the sick and injured. There's not a doctor in miles and he does have a healing touch."

"Yes." Kate smiled. She liked Mrs. MacKenzie and it had been good to chat with another female whose interest was a level above babies and farm chores. "But as you've said, we've chosen our mates and are now bound to love, honor and support them."

"I can see you'll make our healer a fine wife," the plump woman accompanied Kate to the door. "Now if you can convince him to become a little more civilized in appearance and perhaps attend church once in a while…"

****

"Did ye enjoy yer tea?" Hamish asked as they drove back toward the farm. Late afternoon sunlight glinted through the trees making a play of light and shadow. It flitted over her hair, turning it to flashes of gold.

"Yes," she replied. "Mrs. MacKenzie is a kind and gracious woman."

"Is that a fact?" Hamish glanced over at her. "I've always thought her a thoroughly bossy woman whose capacity ta do good works knows no bounds and can be terrifyin'."

"You mean because she ordered you to stay out of the tavern."

He caught the teasing in her tone and chuckled.

"Aye. And I'm no alone. I believe she's taken it upon herself ta so instruct every man in her husband's parish, a large area indeed. Get along, Calvin. Clyde, pick up yer great feet. We want ta get home afore moonrise."

He'd left Pilot guarding the farm but the idea of armed bandits in the area made him uneasy.

"Kate, there's something I need ta tell ye," he said, as the team picked up their pace. He knew he had to inform her about the robbery for her own protection.

"Ah, but first there's something I must tell you." She half turned on the seat and put her hands over his holding the reins to slow the horses back to a walk.

"You have told me what you'd do if we were truly wed," she said softly, seductively. "Now I shall tell you what I'd do. No, don't try to stop me," she raised a hand as he made to speak. "It's only fair."

"Verrae well." He halted the team and squinted over at her in the waning sunlight. "Tell me...if ye must."

"If we were truly wed..." She cast her gaze demurely down to her hands which she'd clasped over his. "I'd love you and honor you and support you."

He heaved a sigh. He'd thought she'd been about

to torture him. If this was her way of getting even, it was mild indeed.

"Thank ye," he said. "Now I'll chust be gettin' on with what I have ta…"

"Not just yet." She looked up at him, long lashes lowering seductively over sly green eyes.

"If we were well and truly wed, Hamish Macdonald," she began, her gaze locked on his, her tone becoming soft and sensual. "I'd put my hands on either side of your bearded face and draw you to me until our lips met. And then I'd kiss you and taste you as you've never, ever been kissed and tasted before. And while you were lost in that kiss, I'd slid my hands down your neck and over your chest to open your shirt. When it gaped wide to your belt, I'd slide my hands inside and run them over every inch of your flesh until they reached your belly…your flat, hard belly."

The last was a breathy whisper as she leaned close, her eyes never wavering from his.

"Enough!" The word was a bellow. He cracked the reins over the team's flanks and sent them forward at a gallop that all but unseated her.

Her throaty chuckle scrapped across his soul like a fingernail over a slate board. Damn the woman! She must indeed be some kind of siren or succubus sent to drag his soul further into Hades.

He drew the horses to a dust-raising halt in the yard. The abrupt stop unseated Kate and she would have been flung to the ground had he not caught her about the waist. As the dust settled he held her in one arm and controlled the prancing, snorting team with the other.

"Are you trying to get us both killed?" she cried, struggling free, her eyes snapping green sparks as she glared at him.

"Ye've no understandin' of men and their desires, lass," he glared back. "None whatsoever."

"Oh, but I think I do, Mr. MacDonald, I really think I do." She struggled down over the wheel before he could stop her and dropped with a grunt to the ground.

"Now see what ye've done." He leaped down beside her. "Damaged that ankle again, I'll wager."

"I certainly have not!" She threw back shoulders and faced him defiantly. "I'm perfectly fine. Now, if you'll excuse me, I've supper to prepare. Pilot must be getting hungry."

She turned toward the house but he caught her by the arm.

"Pilot!" he hissed. "He's no come runnin' ta greet us! Something is verrae wrong. I was about ta tell ye that there's been a robbery and murder in the area. Three criminals are on the loose, one of them wounded."

"And you think..." Her voice dropped to a whisper and she cast a gaze about the farm yard.

"Aye, it's a possibility. They may be seekin' medical help. And now with no Pilot about..."

"You don't think they've harmed Pilot?" Her words were suffused with concern.

"I donnae know. But we must be verrae careful."

"What should we do?"

"We climb back onta the wagon and drive out of here. I'll get some of the neighbor men together and return after ye're safe."

"But Pilot..."

"There's nothing we can do fer him under the circumstances." He couldn't tell her he believed the dog dead. "Now slow and easy," he said softly. "Let me help ye back onta the seat and follow my lead.

"Damnation, woman!" he barked. "Where's yer brain! How could ye forget the oatmeal! What's a man ta eat for breakfast, I ask ye! We'll have ta go all the way back ta the village and it's gettin' late. We won't be back afore moonrise!"

113

"It's only your stupid Scottish craving for that mush that will be taking us back to Pine!" she snapped back, catching his plan. "I swear, I'll never understand your Highland passion for such miserable fare."

"Hush yerself, woman. It'll soon be dark and I've a great load of work still ta do before I see our bed."

He started to help her up onto the seat but the cabin door burst open. Two dirty, unshaven men appeared on the verandah. Each held a musket leveled at them.

"Hold it right there, Healer!" One of them ordered, coming down the steps. "We're needing your services. My brother is inside your cabin, a musket ball in his shoulder. You'll take it out before we ride on or your woman won't live to see the sunrise."

Hamish let Kate slip back to the ground to stand beside him.

"I take it ye're the bunch that shot that man in Newcastle," he said facing them squarely.

"Clever, aren't you! That's exactly who we are and as such you know we're men with nothing left to lose by killing again. So get a move on, Healer. We've no time to waste."

"Verrae well," he said. "But I'll haff yer word ye'll leave as soon as I've patch yer companion and ye'll no harm me wife or damage me farm."

"Of course, Healer." The second man cackled. "We give our word as gentlemen."

"Shut up, Morrisy!" The first speaker, apparently the leader, snapped. "Joe's my brother and he needs help. Now get a move on, Healer! There's no time to waste!"

Inside the cabin they found the injured man lying on the bed. His dirty shirt was blood soaked, his weathered face and straggly hair drenched with sweat. Hamish dropped on one knee beside him and carefully lifted his filthy clothing to examine the wound. The man flinched and groaned, his eyes glazed with agony and fever.

"I'll need hot water and the instruments from me trunk," he said getting up and beginning to roll his sleeves. "Kate, build the fire."

As he moved toward the trunk and she toward the hearth, the leader suddenly grabbed her by an arm and held his musket to her side.

"Take care, Healer," he breathed. "Pull a single trick from that box and I swear I'll kill your woman."

"No tricks." Hamish drew the key from beneath his shirt and inserted it into the lock.

"You got any gold in there, Healer?" Morrisy moved to Hamish's side and leered up at him.

"Do I look like a wealthy man?" Hamish swung on him in all his bestial fury and the man, even though armed, took a step backward.

"Don't talk like any bigger fool than you are, Morrisy!" the leader snapped. "If he had gold he wouldn't be living in this hovel with his woman dressed in rags. Just leave him to get on with it!"

Hamish raised the lid and took out a small black satchel.

"Let me wife get on with boilin' that water. He turned back to the pair with it in his hand, his voice as low and threatening as a wolf's growl. "There's no time for nonsense."

"Morrisy, you boil that water," the leader ordered. "You, woman..." He turned on Kate. "Go down to the barn and tend our horses. They'll need food and water if they're to get us to the American border. If you fail to come back, rest assured we'll kill your man the minute he finishes patching Jesse here. Understood?"

"Do as he says, Kate." Hamish relocked the trunk and headed back toward the bed. "These bastards are leavin' us no choice."

****

The shadows were lengthening across the yard as she hurried toward the barn.

"Pilot!" she called softly, hoping against hope that the dog would come out of some hiding place. "Pilot!" She paused just outside the barn door and called again. Still no big black creature bounding toward her. With a sigh she pulled it open and stepped inside. And gasped.

There, stretched out on the hay, lay the Newfoundland.

"Oh, Pilot!" she breathed and moved apprehensively toward the motionless body. "Oh, Pilot." She dropped on her knees and touched his shoulder gingerly.

He flinched.

"Pilot?" she said again, afraid to hope.

The dog stirred and slowly opened his eyes. As he struggled to raise his head, she saw the gaping wound just below his ear. Gently she helped him onto his belly and examined it, all the while stroking him and talking softly.

"What did those terrible men do to you, Pilot?" she whispered. "They must have thought they killed you and threw your body in here that we wouldn't be alarmed when we saw it. Miserable creatures!"

Pilot began to pant and struggle to his feet.

"No, no, you have to rest!" She tried to keep him down but he refused to obey. Instead he shook himself slowly, stretched tentatively as if testing his body and limbs, then he walked unsteadily toward the door.

"No, Pilot." She arose and went to stand between him and the entrance. "You can't help us...not wounded as you are. But maybe..." A thought had come to her. "Pilot, the Currie farm. Can you go to the Currie farm for help? Go to Black Beauty! Go now!"

She stepped aside, holding her breath.

Pilot stepped outside into the approaching dusk. For a moment he paused, sniffing the air and looking toward the cabin.

"No, Pilot. Not the cabin. Go to Black Beauty. Go to the Currie farm!"

The dog looked back at her, wagged his tail twice, then headed off at a shambling trot into the woods behind the barn and a shortcut she hoped to the Currie farm.

"What's keeping you, woman!" Morrisy stepped out onto the verandah and bellowed. "The Healer says he needs you to help him!"

"You had no right to kill our dog!" she cried, hoping she was appearing sufficiently broken hearted and outraged. "He wouldn't have harmed you!"

"The big black bastard bit Jesse," he yelled back. "I took the butt of my musket to him. Now finish tending those horses and get back in here!"

Kate swung about with the best display of outrage she could muster and headed back into the barn to see to the horses. When she'd finished, she heaped a pile of straw together about the size of Pilot and covered it with a horse blanket. When and if they returned to the barn for the horses they might be fooled into thinking the dead dog lay under it.

Inside, she found they had laid the injured man on the table and Hamish had arranged his instruments and clean clothes on one of the benches. His sleeves were rolled above his elbows and his expression was grim as he looked up at Kate's entrance.

"I'll be needin' ye ta help me, wife," he said. "Wash yer hands and roll up yer sleeves. This isn't going ta be easy."

"Yes." She obeyed, then went to stand by his side.

"Ye'll hand me the instruments as I need them," he said. "And wipe the sweat from me forehead."

"Yes," she repeated but felt her stomach roil as she saw Hamish pick up a sharp pointed instrument that looked like some form of pinchers.

"Come closer," he instructed. "Ye'll have ta keep wipin' the blood away from the wound so that I can see what I'm doin'." He picked up a bottle of whiskey opened on the dresser.

She watched as Hamish raised the man's head and proceeded to pour a goodly measure down his throat. The wounded man coughed and sputtered but managed to ingest a fair amount.

"Good." Hamish paused and drew a deep breath. "Well, what air ye waitin' for, woman?" He turned to Kate. "Get inta position. I've got no time ta spare if this villain is ta have a fightin' chance."

She did as he said and tried to steel herself for the ugliness ahead.

****

"That's the best I can do." Hamish stepped back from the unconscious man on the table and dipped his bloody hands into the basin of water Kate had ready for him. "Now it's up ta him and God whether he lives or dies."

"You'd better hope he lives, Healer." The leader hefted his musket and wiped a dirty hand across his mouth. "Otherwise we might be forced to take yer pretty woman along with us to make up a third. What would you say to that!"

"Bastard!" Hamish snarled and when he looked over at the outlaw leader, his eyes above the growth of hair and beard snapped blue fire. "Touch her and I swear I'll drive my scalpel so deep inta this bit of slime, it will pin him ta the table!"

"Just make sure he doesn't die." Hamish's bestial reaction made the armed man falter for a moment. Then he regained himself. "We'll have a couple of bottles of that whiskey you were so quick to drain down my brother's throat. I saw you had a goodly supply in the drawer of that dresser. It'll help pass the time until it's full dark and the horses are rested."

"Ye cannae be thinkin' of puttin' this man on a horse tanight!" Hamish dried his arms on a bit of cloth and began to roll down his shirt sleeves. "He'd not last a furlong!"

"Well, we'll just have to see, won't we? We can't be waiting around here for the constable and his bunch to arrive. We led them a merry chase in the opposite direction, then doubled back through a stream but if they're not entirely fools, they'll realize we'd be seeking help for Joe and your farm would be the best bet. Now, come on! Whiskey, I said! Fetch it for us, woman!"

He shook the musket at Kate.

She looked at Hamish.

"Fetch it, Kate," he said softly and she caught the nuance in his words.

She turned and pulled out a drawer in the dresser. She selected a pair of bottles and extended them toward the bandits. Each of them grabbed one, opened it, and began to gulp the contents.

Kate looked past them at Hamish who nodded slightly in her direction and she understood.

She gave the slightest of nods in return. Her heart was banging against her ribs but she knew it was their only chance.

"And, woman, we want food!" Morrisy ordered sitting down on a bench. "Lots of food."

"I'll have to go out to the ice house to fetch meat and butter," she said.

"Well, then, do it! And mind you be smart about it or this musket butt might just connect with your man's belly or lower," he leered at her over stained, broken teeth. "Wouldn't want that, now would you?

119

Wouldn't be able to pleasure for a long time, maybe never."

"Go, Kate." Hamish applied a wet cloth to his patient's sweating face. "The sooner they're fed, the sooner they can be on their way."

"Yes, of course." She caught up her skirts and headed for the door but the leader, Brandon, caught her by an arm and drew her close.

"You're one pretty woman," he muttered his foul breath making her want to retch. "You could make time pass real good on the way to the border. What say you come along with us?"

"Let her go, man, or I swear I'll rip you limb from limb."

Feral outrage turned the Healer's words into a snarl as he faced the pair, teeth barred, hands clinched into white-knuckled fists at his sides. Like a marauding beast he advanced toward them.

"Hamish, no!" Kate caught at his arm. "Please, no!"

Chapter Seven

"All right, all right." Brandon released her arm and gave her shove toward the door. "There's no need to get yourself upset. We'll be leaving as soon as it's dark. You and your woman will be free to fall into that bed yonder the minute we're out of sight and do as you please. Although what such as her wants with the likes of a brute like you I can't fathom. Or maybe that is what she likes...a great, hulking brute slavering over her!"

For a moment Kate feared Hamish would leap over the table on which the stricken man lay and attack Brandon. She watched as he drew a deep breath, then shuddered and shook himself. The best thing she could do was leave before she became an intolerable bone of contention between the men.

****

When she returned from the ice house with meat, butter, and cheese, she saw that Morrisy and Brandon were already well on the way to being drunk. She placed the food on the table. Casting Hamish a furtive, sideways glance, she went to the dresser to fetch bread and plates.

She placed the food on the table but before she could cut the bread, Morrisy fell upon it, tearing off great chunks and stuffing it into his mouth like a famished animal. Brandon ripped chunks off the joint of ham with his teeth. She moved to stand beside Hamish and watched the pair devouring the food.

"Soon," he breathed into her ear and she

inclined her head slightly.

****

"Get the horses, Healer!" Brandon jolted to his feet. It was pitch black outside. "We'll be leaving. And don't try to escape while you're saddling them or your woman here will live to regret it. Understood?" He was weaving as he held the musket unsteadily aimed at Kate.

"Understood." Hamish grabbed up his jacket and strode out the door.

"Now, woman," the outlaw leader turned to Kate. "Wrap us up a good package of whatever food you have. We'll be needing nourishment and we can't risk going into any villages between here and the American border."

Kate nodded, went to the dresser, and began to gather foodstuffs into a cloth. Out of the corner of her eye she watched the pair gulp more whiskey. The injured man on the table was breathing in great, trembling gasps. He'd surely die on the journey they were proposing, but she could conjure scant sympathy. In Newcastle a good, decent man lay dead.

"Yer horses are ready." Hamish stepped back inside, one hand behind his back.

"Good. Morrisy, hoist Joe to his feet."

The injured man roared in pain as Morrisy did as instructed.

"He'll die if ye persist in this madness!" Hamish barked. "Leave him with us. I'll tend him, I swear."

"Toward what end, Healer? So that he can swing from a hangman's noose?" Jesse Brandon laughed harshly. "Do you think I'd leave my brother, my own flesh and blood to such a fate! Better he dies in the saddle. Bring him along, Morrisy. We've no time to spare."

He flung the nearly empty whiskey bottle into the fire. It smashed with a great burst of flame. He staggered backward.

"Now, Kate!" Hamish lunged at Brandon, a stick he'd held concealed behind his back crashing out to give the man a mighty blow on the side of his head. Kate threw herself at Morrisy who was struggling to keep the injured bandit on his feet. All three crashed to the floor amid a scream from the patient.

"It's over, Kate." Kate heard Hamish's victorious voice as she struggled to extricate herself from the two fallen men. She scrambled to her feet to see him holding the musket. The outlaw Brandon lay unconscious on the floor.

"Bastard!" Morrisy raised himself on one elbow and spat contemptuously. "Your woman's probably killed Joe here."

The injured man was moaning semi-consciously, rolling about.

"I'm certain she's done him no good but at least by her preventin' his leavin', he'll have a chance. Ye two were about ta kill him in a saddle. Now crawl over in that corner and stay there. Kate, run out ta the barn, if ye'd be so good, and fetch a length of rope that we might bind up these good lads until the constable can collect them."

With a nod, she hurried off to do as he'd instructed. She had to do it quickly...before her trembling knees and quaking nerves deserted her.

****

"Pilot?" Hamish asked softly as she was binding the outlaws' hands and ankles a few minutes later. She heard the dread in his voice.

"Quite well except for a bump on the head," she smiled reassuringly up at him. "I sent him off to the Currie farm for help."

"The Currie farm? Ah, lass, that could prove a mistake. They'll think he's chust payin' another family call on Black Beauty."

The sound of horses breaking into the yard at a

full gallop followed close on his words. Seconds later Andrew and Neil Currie burst into the cabin, muskets in hand.

"Good God, Hamish!" Andrew bellowed when he saw the subdued bandits. "How did you manage this, man? When Pilot arrived at the farm, wounded and kicking up a fuss we knew something was terrible wrong."

"Kate and I make a guid team," he grinned. "It takes more than a few highwaymen ta git the better of a pair of MacDonalds, right, me love?

"Right, Mr. MacDonald." She put her hands on her hips, cocked her head to one side, and grinned back at him. The next instant she sat down hard on her chair. Her knees suddenly felt like mush.

****

A half hour later the Curries headed back out of the farm yard, the three bandits bound in the back.

"We'll deliver this bunch to the constable in Newcastle," Andrew had promised Hamish and Kate as they loaded them aboard. "You two look as if you could use some rest. And you've got Pilot and your team to see to, Hamish, lad. You can't go neglecting your animals simply because a bunch of ne'er do wells have been causing you grief."

He indicated the dog laying on the verandah and Hamish's team still standing harnessed to the wagon where the highwaymen had forced them to be left hours earlier.

"Thank ye, Andrew." Hamish slammed the backboard into place and stepped aside. "We are a might tuckered and I still have work ta do."

"Then get to it, lad." Andrew flicked the reins over his team and he and Neil drove off into the night.

Hamish draped a weary arm over Kate's shoulders and drew a deep breath.

"Do you think you can see ta Pilot while I put

the team away?" he asked her gently. "I know you're weary but if you'd be able…"

"Of course." She looked up at him and even in the darkness he could see her smile. "I'll take him inside and clean his wound."

She turned away and started up the steps. "Come along, Pilot."

"Kate?" He stopped her.

"Yes?" She turned back to him.

"Ye did good in there…helpin' me with that man's wound. Most women and a good many men would have fainted dead away."

"I didn't have any choice, did I?" She continued on her way.

"Nevertheless, I'm admirin' ye, Lady Kathryn."

She swung back to see if he was mocking her but he'd moved off into the darkness to begin unhitching the team.

When he came back into the cabin, she was sitting on her chair. She was deathly pale. Pilot lay on a blanket on the floor by her feet, the fur on his head damp from a recent washing. He wagged his tail faintly at his master's entrance, then replaced his snout between his paws, and with sigh, closed his eyes.

"He's exhausted," Kate said softly reaching down to run a hand gently over the dog's shoulders.

"As are ye," he said. "But I'm thinkin' ye'll not be able ta sleep just yet…not without help."

He went to the dresser, removed another bottle of whiskey from a drawer, and took two mugs from the shelves.

"A wee dram, that's what this Healer prescribes," he said, pouring a generous measure into both containers. "And a bit of fresh air. Come. We'll go out onta the verandah for a few minutes before we try ta sleep."

She gathered up a blanket, then followed him

outside. He'd placed the two rocking chairs he'd purchased in the village that day side by side just outside the door. With a sigh, she sank into one, pulled her improvised shawl about her, and accepted the mug he offered.

"It's a warm evening," she said, wrapping her fingers around the container. "I can't think why I'm so cold."

"Shock," he replied, pausing to gaze up at the moon rising above the barn. "It can drain all the warmth from a body. I've felt it meself by times."

He sat down in the second chair, took a deep drink of whiskey, then let out a deep breath. "A bit of an unexpected evenin', was it not, me lady?" he chuckled.

"Aye, that it was, Healer," she replied, her tone matching his enlightened one. "But I do believe we acquitted ourselves verrae well."

He chuckled again.

"Aye, that we did, lassie, that we did. Even if yer performance lacked somewhat in lady-like behaviour, your courage didnae. I could not have asked for a better partner under the circumstances, either by the operatin' table or durin' the fightin'."

"Nor could I." She took a sip from the cup and coughed.

"A little at a time, lass. That's pure Scotch whiskey with a fair ta middlin' kick ta it."

"And you have a goodly store," she said remembering the contents of the drawer.

"Aye, that I do. But if ye're wonderin' if I'm a drunkard, I will relieve yer mind. I keep it for medicinal purposes such as tanight. Sometimes it's all I have ta kill pain when someone comes ta me hurt or wounded."

"But what about the potion you gave me when you brought me to the cabin that first night and the following day?"

"I get that from me native friends," he said. "It's made from the leaves of a plant that has not yet matured and what I gave you was the end of last summer's supply."

"Can you make it yourself?"

"I'm afraid it's one of their secrets. While they're not averse to supplyin' me with the powder, they don't want ta share its exact source with me. And I know better than ta try ta winnow that information from them."

She took another sip and he saw her eyelids were drooping.

"Here." He put his cup down, took hers from her hands, and scooped her up in his arms. "Ye're ready for the bed and no mistake."

She didn't protest as he carried her inside and sat her on the chair by the fire. She watched while he stripped the soiled blankets from the bed and made it up with clean ones, thinking that she should be doing such work but not having the strength. But when he lead her to the freshly made bed and began to unbutton her dress, she lurched away and stopped him, her small hands covering his.

"No."

"Lass, I've no intention of..."

"Hamish, we're both exhausted, I've drunk just enough whiskey to feel lightheaded. I could very easily fall into your arms under these conditions for very wrong reasons." She looked up at him, green eyes weary. "Please. I'm vulnerable just now so, as you profess to be a gentleman, leave me alone before I make a very big mistake."

He swallowed hard. For a moment he could only stay as he was, standing beside her bed, his hands on the top button of her dress, her hands over his. Was ever a man so tempted, he wondered, as he gazed into her eyes and saw a longing he could barely stand mirrored there.

"Verrae well." He let his hands fall to his sides. "I will sleep with Pilot by the door if ye donnae mind. I think he's needin' a little love and attention."

"Of course." She breathed the two words and crumpled onto the bed, her eyes closing.

Gently he raised her feet onto the bed, removed her shoes, and pulled the quilts over her. Feeling weariness rising through his own body, he gathered his blankets and went to join Pilot near the hearth. He longed to groan aloud but knew he couldn't. Across the room, Kate slept. Beautiful, amazing Kate. The woman he was coming to desire above all else in the world.

But he was a beast, the Hermit Healer, not a man a woman such as Lady Kathryn would desire when she was rested and in her right mind.

Body and soul aching, he rolled up in bedding and, fell into an exhausted sleep.

****

When she awoke in full sunlight, he was gone. She sat up slowly, rubbing the sleep from her eyes. He'd done a rudimentary cleaning of the cabin. However, it was a man's cleaning. She pushed back bedcovers and swung her feet to the floor, ready to do it properly.

A pot of tea sat warming on the hearth. She poured herself a cup and then cut a thick slice of bread from the loaf on the table. *A poor breakfast for a man who'd had an arduous night.* She'd make it up to him by preparing a fine meal at midday after she'd scoured the evidence of those filthy bandits from the place. She put her cup on the dresser and rolled up her sleeves.

When she'd finished, she saw Hamish's clothing hanging on pegs above the trunk. They needed a good laundering. With a sigh, she gathered the lot and headed outdoors.

She finished the chore an hour later and stood

back, hands on hips to admire the display of men's apparel fluttering from the clothes line. She'd even scrubbed his under clothing to a snowy whiteness. A bath would be in order now that she was free of the cast.

She looked at the tub. She might fit into it but she longed for the kind of washing where she could stretch out and luxuriate. Suddenly she remembered the stream beyond the house and barn and the lovely little pond where she'd seen the doe and her fawn drinking, the same one Hamish had bathed himself in on the night he'd brought her back from her escape attempt.

Picking up a square of soap, she lifted her skirts and scuttled off into the bush.

****

"Kate!" Hamish came out of the cabin, frowning, and called her name. "Now where did that woman get ta this time, Pilot?" he asked the dog by his side. "I knew I shouldn't have left her alone. I swear, she'll be the death of me yet. Go find her, boy. Go find our Kate."

The dog wagged his tail, then trotted down the steps and sniffed the earth. He circled several times, then headed out of the yard toward the stream. Hamish had to run to keep pace with him.

He stopped when he saw her.

Unaware of his approach she was luxuriating in the small, deep pond, the water barely covering her breasts. She was rinsing her long, golden tresses and humming. Truly, he thought, she was a woman from the sea, a mermaid temptress if ever there was one.

He knew he should call out, inform her of his presence but instead he stood savoring her forbidden loveliness. Damnation but he admired her beauty, her strength, her courage. Last night she'd assisted him as ably as any man with an operation that would have left many ill and fainting and still had the strength to fight by his side like the bravest of soldiers.

He turned away and started back to the cabin. Let her enjoy herself. She'd had few enough pleasures since she'd come to live with him. As he headed for the verandah he noticed the clothes line and its attachments for the first time. A hot blush gushed up his cheeks. Good God! The woman had washed his drawers and set them flapping in the breeze. Had she no respect for a man's dignity?

Lips drawn into a hard line of exasperation and embarrassment, he went up the steps and into the cabin.

****

"Hamish, you're back early." She entered, her hair damp, her cheeks flushed. "I'd planned to make you a large meal for midday repast. You had little breakfast."

"I'm chust fine, thank ye." He sat at the end of the table, two slices of bread and a chunk of cheese on the plate before him.

"I'll make fresh tea." She went quickly to the hearth and knelt to take up the pot languishing there.

"No need." He pushed the chair back with a loud, scrapping sound. "I had a dram with me meal. Now I'll be getting' back ta the fields. There's a lot of work ta be done."

"Then I'll see you have a fine supper." She looked up at him, frowning. "Bread and cheese washed down with whiskey is far from a decent meal...especially after the exertion of the past night. You must built up your strength."

"Me strength is chust fine." He started for the door, then paused and looked back into her confused face. "Lass, I no mean ta be short with ye but chust now I saw ye bathin' in the bush." His tone softened. "And I am a man, no matter what my appearance, with a man's desires, desires that must, in our circumstances, be kept in check. Ye're too fine a lady ta be sullied simply ta fulfil me lust."

He went out, Pilot at his heels.

Kate sank onto the chair and put her hands on her warm face. Did the man not know women had desires as well?

****

Hamish rode back from Callum Maclean's cabin late in the afternoon. His thoughts were occupied with the elderly recluse. The old man lived alone in a ramshackle log structure back in the bush. Hamish had discovered him one day while out hunting and had tried to befriend him. Although suffering from arthritis and several maladies of advancing years, the hermit at first had refused help.

Hamish continued to visit him and finally the old man had accepted medication to ease his discomfort. He had no magic potion to slow time or cure the ills of years of neglect and poor food. Still, it was better than doing nothing.

He wondered what had driven the old Scotsman to bury himself in the forest and become such a cantankerous hermit. Maybe, in his younger days, Callum MacLean had had his own version of Lady Margaret.

Hamish dismounted at the stable door and led the stallion into the shadowy barn, a sardonic smile tipping his lips.

The next instant it faded. Calvin was missing from his box stall.

"Sweet Jesus, not again!"

He tied the Lad and was about to further investigate his loss when he heard the slow clop of hooves walking toward the barn and a woman's voice singing:

"Every lassie has her laddie

Nae they say ha'e I..."

Long strides took him to the barn door in time to see Kate mounted on Calvin reining the gelding to a halt a few feet away. She was riding bareback and astride, her skirts hiked up to reveal shapely legs in white stockings. The horse wore his working bridle, complete with blinders.

She stopped singing when she saw him, tilted her head to one side, slanted a coquettish grin, then finished,

"Yet all the lads they smile at me
When comin' through the rye."

"Where have ye been and just what do ye think yer doin' ridin' about the country like a peasant wench with your skirts hiked up about yer waist? And that's no a song fer a proper lady to be singin' either."

He strode forward and reached up with strong hands. She yelped indignantly as he dropped her abruptly on the ground in front of him.

"I am not your prisoner, sir." She shrugged free and adjusted her dress. "I can go visiting whenever and wherever I choose. Did you really believe selling that old saddle would keep me tied to your farm?"

"Och, and who might ye have been favorin' with yer company this day?"

"I was returning Jessie Currie's visit if you must know." She gave him a haughty, annoyed glance before she shrugged free and swung away from him.

"Oh, aye? And I suppose ye favored young Neil with a fine view of your nether limbs as ye rode into their yard?" Irritation chafed him like sack cloth.

"Neil is still recovering from his injury as you well know. He was doing light work in the kitchen garden behind the barn from where he could neither see me arrive or depart. It's none of your concern. Aren't you the same man who keeps howling about how we're not truly married?"

She swung away from him, and head held high, marched toward the cabin.

"Och!" He took Calvin's bridle and led the Clydesdale into the barn. "A woman'll be the death of me yet, Calvin. You mark my words."

****

"I believe we should go to church on Sunday." She was clearing table after their evening meal.

"And chust what would have inspired that thought?" He sat back on his chair.

"Mrs. MacKenzie invited us and today Jessie Currie made me realize that it's the right and proper thing for a married couple to do."

"Oh, ye do, do ye? And what about me? You thought I was a beast when first we met. What have ye observed since that time that would lead you to believe I might also be the heathen?"

"I never suggested such a thing." She turned to face him. "You're a kind and generous man who cares about the well being of the local people. Therefore, whether you're formally a Christian or not, you exhibit the proper spirit to qualify. Now what is your answer? Will you come to church with me?"

"I'll gladly drive ye to and from the service, lass, but I'll not attend." He got up and headed for the door. "I donnae belong in the House of the Lord."

"How can you say that?" She pursued him. "You care more about your fellow man than anyone I've ever met. You practice the Golden Rule daily, you..."

"Ye still know little about me, lass." He paused with his back to her. "There are things in me past that even the Guid Lord would be hard pressed ta forgive."

"Hamish..."

He brushed aside the hand she tried to put on his arm and strode out to the barn. Inside he paused by the Lad's stall and drew a deep breath.

"I wish I could go with her, my boy." He rubbed the stallion's arched neck. "But I don't believe murderers are welcome in the House of the Lord."

****

Early the next morning rising clouds of dust announced their coming. Kate paused in hanging bedding on the clothes line and watched as the half dozen farm wagons laden with men, women, children, and building materials drove into their yard.

"Whit's all the racket?" Hamish stepped out the barn.

"Our neighbors, I believe." Kate shielded her eyes against the sunlight. "They seem to have come visiting."

"Whoa!" Andrew Currie drew to a halt and jumped to the ground. "'Morning, Mrs. MacDonald, ma'am, Hamish. We've come to make you a wedding gift. It's not fitting you should be sleeping on a bunk in a corner of your kitchen now that you're wed. And we owe you both a heavy debt for ridding this community of the Brandon Bandits. So we've come to build you a proper bedroom."

He turned back to his loaded wagon and helped the woman from its high seat. "Mrs. MacDonald, I believe you've already met Jessie, my wife. You'll not have to worry about providing dinner for this lot. She and the other women have brought enough food for a small army. Come on, lads," he called to the men. "Help your young ones and ladies to the ground and let's get to work. We've a full day ahead of us."

****

Evening found a new room of freshly sawn lumber attached to the back of the cabin. Inside a double bed built against the wall held the luxury of a feather tick and pillows. Opposite stood the chest of drawers Hamish had bought from the cabinet maker in Pine. Near the door was a wash stand complete with basin. There were even curtains on the window. Kate stood at its centre and gazed about in awe-struck delight.

"It's beautiful," she breathed to the women who'd gathered around. They'd led her into the room after they'd put their feminine touches on the men's handiwork.

"You've thought of everything!" she breathed, looking at the container of wildflowers beside a pair of candles on the chest of drawers. They'd even hung a small mirror above it. "I'm quite..." Suddenly tears rolled down her cheeks. "Overcome," she gulped.

"It's small enough payment for all Hamish has done for us in his years among us, never mind your both risking your lives to rid us of those highwaymen." Jessie Currie put a motherly arm about Kate's shoulders. "There's not a family for miles he hasn't helped through sickness or injury. He's a miracle worker is your man, Mrs. MacDonald."

"And so are you." Lizzy, with baby James in her arms, stepped forward. "I'll never forget what a comfort you were when my little lad was born."

"I did very little, I'm afraid. It was all Hamish's work."

"What was all my work?" Hamish appeared in the doorway.

"Delivering little James, my dear." Kate immediately fell into her role as loving spouse.

"The men have been urgin' me ta come and see this new addition," he said and the women fell silent.

He advanced slowly into the room, Pilot by his side, his booted footfalls loud on the plank floor. In the centre, beside Kate, he paused and turned slowly about to take in every detail. Finally he stopped.

135

"A fine place, is it not, Mrs. MacDonald. Indeed, a man would be hard pressed ta find better in this country."

"He certainly would, Mr. MacDonald." She moved forward, circled his arm with both of hers and gave him a little squeeze. "We will be very comfortable here."

The sound of a fiddle tuning filtered into the room and Jessie turned to the others. "Dancing is about to commence! Everybody outdoors! It's been too long since we've had a good Ceilidh."

The women scuttled out, leaving Hamish and Kate alone in the room that smelled of freshly sawn lumber and wild roses.

"Well." Hamish put his hands on his hips and looked down at Kate. "With a bedroom this fine, the neighbors will soon be expectin' the word of a wee bairn on the way. If no such announcement is forthcomin', the men will begin ta wonder about me manhood and the women about yer barrenness. Will ye be able ta face up ta such censure? Or would ye prefer we try this excellent mattress tagether and give their hopes a possibility?"

"I'll risk their censure and pity." She stepped briskly away from him. "And I personally will never doubt your claim to manhood."

She slanted him a coquettish glance, then with a swirl of skirts, headed out of the room to join the music and dancing in the yard.

****

"Another dram, Hamish?" Andrew offered him a flask.

He hesitated.

Then Kate danced past, laughing and glowing in the light of the bonfire, Neil Currie her partner. She seemed to have time for every half-decent young buck in the dooryard that evening.

Except him.

He remembered her taunting words on the drive back from the village and felt hot anger. If she was out to torment him, she was succeeding.

"Aye, thank ye, Andrew, I will." He accepted and took a long pull. Seeing Kate the object of all delight was gnawing a great hole in his self restraint. He remembered her ride to the Currie farm astride Calvin, her skirts pulled indecently high. *Damnation! She'd declared herself his wife. She had no right, no right at all to carry on that way.* Visions of her swimming naked in the pool flashed through his head.

The dance came to an end and suddenly bagpipes wailed from the verandah.

"It's old Robbie with the pipes he brought all the way from the Highlands," Andrew Currie breathed as silence fell over the gathering.

In the hush of the summer's night the notes of the pipes stretched hauntingly out into the firelight. Expressions of sadness and remembrances slid over faces and a woman stifled a sob.

Hamish saw Kate straighten up proudly and stick out her chin. *What manner of English lady was she to be so affected by the pipes?* She became more of a mystery with each passing day.

The tune changed and someone called out, "The sword dance. Come, someone must be willing to try."

Two sticks were crossed on the ground and suddenly Kate was in position between them. *What does she think she's doing?* Astonishment held him in place. *Surely she wasn't about to attempt something she can know nothing about.*

But then she was holding up her dress and her feet were moving nimbly over and about the sticks as if she'd been born to do the intricate steps.

Onlookers, at first silent in surprise, began to clap hands and cheer her on.

She whirled until she suddenly fell sideways

over her newly healed ankle. Hamish, in a single, long stride was there to catch her before she toppled to the ground.

A burst of applause and cheers accompanied her as he helped her to the sidelines.

"Whit did you think ye were doin' out there?" he hissed in her ear.

"A sword dance." She looked up at him in feigned surprise. "I would have thought you, a Highlander, would have recognized it."

"Argh!"

Their neighbors surrounded them to compliment and congratulate her.

"Another dram, Hamish?" Andrew Currie held out the bottle as he started to make his way out of the crowd around Kate.

"Thank ye, Andrew, but I have me own bottle in the cabin. I'll chust be fetchin' it."

He turned and strode into the cabin. He'd never been much of a drinker, but by God, that woman dancing around his yard, lighting lust in the eyes of every young buck in the gathering, was driving him to it.

****

The fiddlers slowed the pace to a waltz. As Neil made a move to claim her once again, Hamish stepped forward and took her arm.

"Ye'll be excusin' me, Neil, if I claim me wife for this final dance," he said in a way that left no room for argument.

"Of course, Hamish. Thank you, Mrs. MacDonald. It's been a pleasure." The younger man bowed to Kate and backed away.

"Mrs. MacDonald?" He opened his arms in invitation and grinned.

"Of course." She inclined her head and drifted into his embrace as the slow, sensuous strains of the last dance engulfed them.

He drew a deep breath as she eased against his arms, as he caught the light female scent. He shouldn't have gone drinking alone in the cabin. Again he saw her, a beautiful naked mermaid in that pool, her hair streaming out over the water in the dappled sunlight filtering through the trees. The whisky was forming a soft, swirling cloud in his mind. And in the cloud a hazy kind of rationalization was taking hold.

He shouldn't have to torture himself. She was his wife in the eyes of the community, had shared a house with him for weeks. Furthermore she'd incited him with those shameless words on that wagon ride from the village. No woman could speak to a man in such a manner if she didn't harbor a carnal interest in him. He wanted her, he needed her, she wanted him, she needed him, and to hell with the rest of it.

She looked up and her eyes told him all he needed to know.

Tonight would be the night.

****

They stood together, Hamish's arm about her waist, thanking their neighbors as the families climbed aboard their wagons. Then they waved farewell as the group rumbled out of the yard and off into the darkness.

"Well, Mrs. MacDonald." Hamish turned slowly to face her in the shadows of the dying fire.

"Well, Mr. MacDonald?" She glanced up at him, then lowered her gaze.

A deep chuckled rumbled in his throat as he caught her up in his arms and carried her into the cabin and through to the new bed chamber at the back. His mouth covered hers and he paused in the doorway to savor a deep, exploratory kiss.

When she moaned softly, he continued inside.

"Kate," he breathed as he let her feet slide to the floor beside the bed. "Oh, my beautiful Kate. I need you like air, like water, like life itself."

"Show me how much, Hamish MacDonald." She freed herself and in the flickering candlelight, unbuttoned her dress and let it float to the floor.

As it puddled about her feet, he put out his hands to cup her breasts.

Her breath caught in her throat and didn't release until his mouth covered her left nipple to suck gently through the soft cotton of her chemise.

"Hamish!" His name was a soft cry.

"Say it, Kate." He raised his head to look into her eyes. "Say you want me...in our bed."

"I...want...you." The words were a staggered gasp of passion.

With a triumphant laugh, he slid the last of her garments from her body and scooped her up into the bed.

Chapter Eight

Kate awoke the next morning to find him gone from the bed, only the tangled covers and her own nakedness bearing evidence of what had transpired during the night.

"Hamish?" She struggled from the bed and pulled the chemise over her head. Barefoot and bewildered she went into the kitchen.

He arose from stoking the fire and turned to her, fully dressed down to his boots. She felt a sudden flush spreading through her body as she recalled his nakedness in the night, his ardent kisses and caresses. He'd made her feel supremely alive, supremely feminine, the most beautiful and desirable woman on earth.

But now he was looking at her as if she were a stranger.

A chill slid over her.

"Hamish?"

"Lass, I'm that sorry."

Her heart plummeted as he spoke.

"I'm so verrae, verrae sorry. I had no right ta do what I did last night. It was the case of too much whiskey fer a man who's lived sober and celibate too long and yerself too beautiful fer even a beast like me ta resist. If I could undo these past hours at any cost, believe me, I would."

"Oh, you would, would you!" She swirled toward the kitchen bed. In an instant she'd grabbed the china chamber pot from beneath it, swung on him, and drew back her arm.

"Kate, no!" He put up his hands to shield his face. "Not the chamber pot! It cost a wee fortune!"

He ducked outside as the pot crashed against the door.

"Kate, for God's sake!" His voice came from the verandah. "I'm sayin' I'm that sorry."

His answer was another crash of crockery.

"Keep talking, Mr. MacDonald! Every word will cost you a dish!" Another vessel hit the door.

"Argh! I'm goin' ta the barn. I'm sure the beasts will be happy ta see me this morn."

Kate let her hand fall to her side. Her bosom was heaving, the desire to kill the creature headed for the stable hot in her blood. With a final outraged cry she flung the plate into the fireplace. *Who exactly did that big hairy brute think he was?* Her jaw clenched so hard it felt locked in place. Did he think Lady Kathryn Sheffield beneath his dignity to bed?

As she whirled to return to the bedroom, her gaze fell on the trunk...his precious trunk full of secrets. She flew to the dresser and took out the heavily bladed knife he'd used to pry open the one from the shipwreck.

Until now she'd respected his privacy...but not now, not any more. He'd proven he didn't deserve respect or trust.

She knelt, fitted the blade beneath the lock and pried with all her might. The clasp flew open.

"What in hell do you think you're doing?" In three long strides he was beside her, yanking her by an arm to her feet.

"I'm finding out what manner of creature I've slept with!" She spat the words at him. "I'm finding out what kind of brute sleeps with a woman, then, in less than twelve hours, rejects her! And..." She drew a deep breath and continued more slowly, more deliberately as a sudden realization came to her. "What kind of a Scotsman loses his Highland brogue when he's overcome with anger!"

"Damnation, woman!" He released her and strode across the room. Pausing before the hearth he stared down into the flames. The cabin fell silent except for the crackling of the fire. Finally he turned back to her.

"So I'm not a Scotsman." His new voice, educated, English, and cold as ice, shocked her. "But no one in this community will ever believe you. I've been too perfect in my deceit."

Suddenly she was afraid. This being with the cool, cultured English voice was more frightening than the beast had ever been.

"I cannot continue to live under the roof of a man who will not allow me to truly know him!" Summoning every ounce of her courage, she drew herself up proudly before him. "I will pack my trunk and leave immediately. I would be most grateful if you would drive me to the village...to the vicarage or the manse or whatever you call it in this country. Your original plan for my future now appears best."

"I'll harness the team. And donnae touch my trunk agin!" he finished lapsing once more into his Scottish inflection.

****

Damn, damn, damn! He cursed as he threw the harness onto his team and fastened straps and buckles. He'd made a mess of the situation. And it need never have happened. He wasn't some young buck who didn't know his alcohol limit. He'd known he shouldn't have had those last few drinks just before the party ended. But he'd been rankled to the core to see her dancing with the young men of the community, then gracefully performing that sword dance with her skirts flying, the object of their admiration and guilty desires. And she'd been so beautiful. When he'd held her in his arms for that final dance and looked down into her bright, teasing face…

What was the use of trying to reason it away. He backed the horses into the traces and fastened them in place. It couldn't be undone. It was best she was leaving. After the sensations and passions he'd experienced with her in that feather bed, he feared he'd spend every waking moment lusting for a repeat performance if she stayed. He didn't need that aggravation. He'd been content with his way of life before she came. He'd be content with it again once she'd gone.

****

The drive into the village was a silent one. The trunk Hamish had rescued from the beach bumped along in the cargo space. She'd packed her few new possessions along with the container's original contents into it. Hamish, however, had refused to relinquish the jewels to her or tell her where he'd hidden them.

"Ye'll get them back when ye can convince me ye'll be usin' them towards a sensible future," he said. "That does not include embarkin' on the next cargo vessel leavin' the Miramichi with a bunch of randy sailors.

"What will you tell the vicar and his wife?" he asked as they were approaching the manse. "I assume you're not about to give them the truth and reveal your true identity?"

"I shall tell them that my husband is a beast of such unspeakable habits that I can no longer abide living under his roof."

"Wonderful," he muttered. "Whoa."

He reined the team to a halt before the manse verandah, tied the reins, and jumped to the ground.

"Come, Mrs. MacDonald." He held up his hands to lift her down. "Let the tale of my infamy begin."

****

"Mrs. MacDonald, I've brought tea and scones.

May I come in?" the minister's wife asked from outside the bedroom.

"Yes, please." Kate crossed the room and opened the door for Alexandra MacKenzie. "This is most kind of you Mrs. MacKenzie but, really, you don't have to pamper me."

"Oh, but I do, my dear." The woman bustled inside and set the tray on a table. "Leaving your husband must have been a difficult decision for you. If you need someone to confide in, I am here for you. Your words will go no further."

"Thank you, but I think it's best I keep the problems between Mr. MacDonald and me to myself," she smiled wanly. "Perhaps some day we will patch up our differences and then I would feel most disloyal for having discussed our private troubles with a third party."

"As you wish, my dear." Mrs. MacKenzie turned away from the young woman and began to pour tea. "Just rest assured that no matter what it is, I've probably heard much worse in my many years as a minister's wife."

"I appreciate your offer and am confident of your discretion." Kate took the cup she was handed, sipped the tea, then continued, "Still, I'm not prepared..."

She dropped her eyes demurely to the cup, hoping she looked convincingly shy and embarrassed.

"Ah, yes. Men can be such unspeakably demanding creatures." Alexandra MacKenzie took a sip from her cup, placed it on the table, and bustled toward the door. "We have dinner at noon in the Scottish tradition, tea at six. Please feel free to do as you please in the meantime."

After she'd gone, Kate sank down on the narrow bed and gazed out the window at the forest behind the vicarage. She felt lost and alone. She wished the previous night had never happened, that she and Hamish could go back to the way they'd been, friends and companions. No! On second thought, how could she possibly wish away last night when it had been filled with the most wonderful hours of her life.

She arose and began to pace the room. Would she never see Hamish again? What would she do without him? She couldn't expect the vicar and his wife to keep her forever but she could think of no place else to go.

Another thought flashed into her mind, so startling she stopped abruptly, her hands going to her flat stomach. What if she were pregnant? She wasn't Hamish's wife. She wasn't even his intended.

She drew a deep breath and sank down on the edge of the bed. She'd always been resourceful. She'd think of something. In a few weeks, she'd most likely discover there was no wee bairn on the way.

A wave of sadness washed over her. The idea of not having Hamish's child sent her heart sinking. *Irrational woman! Are you daft? You haven't even a plan to care for yourself much less a child.*

She stood up and headed for the door. She'd go for a walk and clear her head of such mad thoughts. Wee bairn, indeed! As if Hamish MacDonald, the Hermit Healer, would welcome such news!

****

Hamish paused in greasing the wheels of his wagon and looked down the trail in the direction of the sound. An ancient buggy pulled by a venerable-looking gray mare was coming into his yard. At the reins was Reverend Alexander MacKenzie.

"Reverend MacKenzie." Hamish straightened up to catch the old horse by the bridle as the clergyman drew to a halt beside him. In the heat of the August day, Hamish was naked to the waist, his chest glistening, his trousers slung low on his narrow hips.

146

I must look the perfect barbarian, he thought. *My appearance will give credence to Kate's tales of my brutishness.*

"Good afternoon, Hamish." The minister mopped his face with a large, white handkerchief as he climbed to the ground. "A warm day, is it not."

"Aye, warm indeed. What can I do fer ye, Reverend? Me wife I trust is well?" He hoped the double meaning in his words were understood by the minister but he doubted it. The Reverend MacKenzie could have no idea how often the Hermit Healer wondered about the actual state of Kate's health since that night in their bed.

"Yes, well and busy, and that is exactly why I've come, Hamish." He squinted up at the big man towering over him in the sunlight. "Perhaps I might water my faithful Dolly before we get down to the details of my visit? Like myself, she's not as young as she once was and I fear this heat is taking a toll upon both of us."

"To be certain, Reverend. I'll take her inta the barn and make her comfortable. Ye go on up ta the house. I'll join ya there directly."

"Thank you, Hamish. I do declare, I find this heat harder to bear than winter's cold."

****

Hamish joined the Reverend MacKenzie on the shady verandah a few minutes later.

The minister was sitting in the rocking chair. He'd removed his broad brimmed black hat and was drying his damp, bald head with his handkerchief.

"I brought ya a cool drink." Hamish handed him a tin dipper of water.

"Most appreciated." Reverend MacKenzie accepted it and took a long drink. With a deep sigh of satisfaction, he returned the pot to Hamish and leaned back in the chair.

Hamish placed it on the verandah floor, picked

up a rumpled shirt he'd abandoned earlier that afternoon, used it to wipe his chest and armpits, then dropped it over his head. It was a soiled, ragged garment.

"Ya must excuse me appearance, Reverend," he said with a wry grin. "I'm no guid at laundry and sewin'."

"If your wife were living with you, you'd not have to concern yourself with such matters." The clergyman looked squarely into the other man's eyes. "And that's the reason for my visit. Hamish, you must mend your ways, abandon whatever distasteful habits that have driven Mrs. MacDonald away, and woo her back. God never intended husband and wife to live apart."

"And would there be some reason why you're comin' ta me now with this advice?"

The minister's carefully chosen words seemed to be leading up to an announcement of some sort. Perhaps there was a babe on the way, perhaps...

"She's decided she no longer wants to live with us." Reverend MacKenzie wiped his face again. "And my wife and I cannot in good conscience allow her to leave."

"Givin' ya trouble, is she?" Hamish slanted a malicious grin at the minister. So it wasn't a pregnancy the little man had come to announce, just Kate being her usual stubborn self. "Och, well, perhaps now ya'll be understandin' the blame for our separation may not entirely be mine."

"No, no, of course she'd not causing us trouble. And the money you've given us more than covers her keep. The point is if she persists in her ambition to move out of the manse my wife and I will no longer be able to keep her under our protection."

"Movin' out?" He felt a jolt in his solar plexus. "Ta where? Niver back ta England?"

"No, no, nothing so distant. She's moving into an

abandoned two-room cabin on the edge of the village. She says she cannot live on our bounty forever...as you instructed, we've told her nothing of your generosity in paying her board. She's planning on opening a school...a much needed commodity I hasten to add...in one room while living in the other. She's already applied to the province for a salary and I've no doubt she'll get it. The government is fervently seeking people to establish such facilities."

"A teacher! I had niver known she had the qualifications."

"She's literate and knows a smattering of mathematics, all that is required in such a basic educational institution."

"A teacher." Hamish repeated, rising slowly from where he'd been sitting on the edge of the verandah and grasped one of its posts, his back to the minister. His tone reflected his amazement.

"A most worthy profession even if one that is not highly esteemed in our society." Reverend MacKenzie continued to wipe his perspiring face. "And while her school will be a great advantage to village society, I would be remiss if I did not encourage the pair of you to try to mend your differences and get back together. Once she accepts the government's coin and contract, she'll be duty bound to carry out a six month commitment. Hamish, you must stop her before she's gone beyond the boundaries of your marriage in this manner!"

"I'm sorry, Reverend." Hamish turned back to the man leaning imploringly toward him. "I cannae make her come back ta me. She left of her own free will and she must return the same way. I appreciate yer comin' ta me with this intelligence but there's nothing' I can do. I trust ye've come ta know Kate well in the time she's been livin' with ye and therefore ya know the strength of her will. Tell her I wish her much success."

"Very well." With a defeated sigh, Alexander MacKenzie arose, put his hat back on his head, and stuffed his handkerchief into his pocket. "If you'll kindly fetch my Doll, I'll be on my way."

"Hold on chust one minute."

Hamish turned and strode into the cabin. When he returned he thrust a small leather pouch into the minister's hand.

"A small anonymous contribution to help set up this school of hers," he said.

Reverend MacKenzie opened it and peered inside.

"Hamish, this is most generous!" he breathed. "But can you spare it?" His gaze roamed over the rudimentary farm buildings.

"Oh, aye. Our needs air simple so we've not much ta spend it on, now that we're alone, isn't that the truth, Pilot, me lad?" He patted the big dog by his side and the animal wagged his tail. "Now let me get yer mare, Reverend. I reckon as how this heat will be bringin' on a thunderstorm afore long and I'd like ta know yo were safe at home when it hits."

****

Hamish finished his barn chores and paused to feed Calvin and Clyde each a carrot.

"Good lads," he said giving them both a slap on the rump. "Good lads."

He paused and leaned against the barn wall, watching the big animals settling comfortably in their box stalls for the night. Pilot came up and nuzzled his hand.

"There you are, my fine fellow," he spoke to the dog. "Finally decided to come home, did you? How is Black Beauty? Any signs of her about to become mother to your little ones? I swear, there's nothing more restless than an expectant father."

The words made him pause and squint out into the setting sun. Kate had been gone nearly three weeks and he found himself again wondering.

A horse galloping into his yard distracted him.

"Hamish." Andrew Currie pulled his mount to a halt and swung to the ground. He handed the Healer a piece of paper. "I was just in the village and George Loggie gave me this notice. It's from Fredericton. It seems we all have to go to the provincial capital to register our land grants with the provincial government or risk losing them. We're to go as soon as possible."

Hamish took the sheet of paper and read it.

"Damn government paper work!" he muttered. "Don't those fools in Fredericton realize it's the height of the hayin' season!"

"Realize but don't care is more like." Andrew climbed back onto his horse and swung it about. "They'd be only too happy to confiscate our lands and sell them off to the highest bidder. I'll be heading out next week, Hamish. What about you?"

"Tomorrow," he said, an idea flashing into his mind. "I'll be on me way at first light. Will ye see ta me stock, Andrew?"

"Do you even have to ask, Hamish man? Of course. We'll see you when you get back."

His neighbour touched his heels to his horse's side and he galloped away.

****

Hamish arose early the next morning, did up his barn work in record time, then headed for the pool in the woods. He bathed, then donned the shirt he'd laundered the previous evening, tied his hair back in a queue, and trimmed his beard.

As he saddled the Lad, he paused to rub one boot against the back of his leg, then the other. He'd polished them but hay dust was already dulling the shine.

"What am I expecting?" he asked the stallion. "I as much as told her I didn't want her, that our night

151

together had been nothing more than a drunken mistake on my part. No woman in her right mind would even consider coming back to a man after he'd made such a statement.Unless…"

He didn't voice the possibility. It was the one thing that might make Kate return to him, to consent to share his life. And yet did he really want her that way, to come back to him only because he'd trapped her into a pregnancy?

He led the Lad out of the barn, closed the door firmly, and swung into the saddle.

"Come along, Pilot. We're off to face the moment of truth."

He put his heels to the horse's sides and sent him at a gallop out of the dooryard.

****

"Miss, miss, there's a man in the schoolyard…a big man riding a big black horse with a creature that looks like a bear by his side!" The young lad burst into the small classroom, his eyes goggling. "He's asking for you."

Kate felt as if her heart stopped, then burst into a frantic beating. Hamish.

Had he come to beg her to come back to him? And what would she do if he had? Lord knew she wanted nothing more than to return to the little farm she'd come to regard as their home with him. She knew she loved Hamish MacDonald and always would. Still the sting of his denial after that wonderful night of love making remained rooted in her soul, telling her with brutal frankness that he didn't want her and never would.

"Miss? What shall I tell him?" The child was staring up, eyes round and bright. "He's the man they call the Hermit Healer, Johnny Larson says. He says the Healer saved his mother from dying of the fever last winter."

"Tell him to come in." She smoothed her skirts

and patted the neat bun she'd made of her hair. She knew she looked every inch the prim and proper school mistress and wondered what he'd think of the transformation.

"Yes, Miss."

"Oh, and Gordon? You and the other students will please remain outside until we complete our interview."

"Yes, Miss." He turned and bolted outdoors to relay the message.

****

"Good afternoon, Mrs. MacDonald." He made no attempt at his faulty Highland dialect.

He entered the room, paused and crossed his arms on his broad chest. He was an overwhelming giant in the small schoolroom.

She felt a smile tugging at her lips as she saw he'd made an attempt to look civilized without entirely giving in to it. Had he come courting she wondered, her heart hammering at her ribs. And what was she going to do if he had?

"It appears you're making a success." He glanced around at the benches along the walls, the neat piles of slates and books, the blackboard, and her own desk and chair at the far end of the room.

"I'm trying." She couldn't repress a small sigh. "But a fair number of the children, the boys especially, can see little benefit in learning words and numbers."

"You must tell them how it will keep a dishonest merchant from cheating them, how it will open the world to them through books and newspapers."

"Perhaps in time they'll come to appreciate those facts. I can but hope."

"Yes."

An awkward pause followed.

"Why did you come?" Her voice, soft in the quiet room with the babble of children playing in the background, quavered.

"To make sure you're well." He drew a deep breath. "I'm on my way to Fredericton to register the deed to my farm and…" He paused.

"And?" Kate felt as if she couldn't breathe. Was he going to ask her to come back to the farm? Was that reason he'd put an obvious effort, no matter how slight, into his appearance?

"I thought I should ask…should see…if there were any lasting effects of our night of…intimacy."

"If you're asking if I'm pregnant, you'll be as relieved as I to discover such is not the case." She drew herself up proudly and fought to keep the disappointment and anger welling in her breast from overflowing. Her students were just outside the door. She must not lose control.

"Ah, well then, good."

"Good indeed. You may ride off to register your deed secure in the knowledge there's no heir apparent on the way to inherit your holdings once you've departed this life." She hoped the bitter words would wound him as he'd just wounded her.

"I'll be on my way then." He spoke calmly, without emotion. He started toward the door, paused, and turned back. "Pilot would like to see you. He's in the yard playing with the children."

"Please bring him in. I've missed him."

"But not me or our home?" His penetrating blue eyes caught her and held her in their gaze.

"There can be no home where there's no trust, where there's a trunkful of secrets in one corner."

The moment the words were out of her mouth she realized what a hypocrite she was. In another corner of that same house, until she'd taken her leave, had been the trunk he'd salvaged from the ship wreck, full of her secrets.

"You're right," he said. "I'll fetch Pilot."

He turned and left the room.

****

Kate stood in the doorway of the schoolroom and watched him ride away. In her chest was a heaviness she tried to attribute to the fresh greens she'd eaten for her midday meal. As the children began to file back inside, she drew a deep breath and fought to control the feeling of emptiness threatening to consume.

When she'd told him she wasn't with child, she thought she'd detected the slightest note of disappointment in the word. Or had she simply been hoping? Yes, that had to be it. She'd imagined it because she'd been hoping he'd wanted her to be pregnant with his child, hoping he would then have a reason to ask her to marry him.

But is that what she really wanted? She wondered as she instructed the children to continue with their sums. Surely she didn't want to trap him into marriage. And he'd never once said he loved her, not even during their one memorable night together.

Perhaps he'd even take up with a tavern wench in the capital and once again pleasure himself.

"Miss, I can't fathom this sum." A small student tugged at her dress.

"Come up to my desk, Timothy." She suppressed a sigh and smiled down at the child. "I'll be glad to help you."

****

That night as she lay in bed, tossing and turning, unable to find sleep no matter how she rearranged herself and her bedding, a thought suddenly occurred to her. With Hamish in Fredericton his cabin would be at her disposal. She could go to the farm the next day and examine the contents of that mysterious trunk. The idea brought a smug little smile to her lips. She would borrow Reverend MacKenzie's horse and buggy on the subterfuge that she wanted to collect a few things she'd forgotten from the cabin.

****

That afternoon after the students had departed for home, Kate hurried to the manse, climbed into the buggy Reverend MacKenzie had ready, and drove off down the wagon road to Hamish's farm.

She halted Dolly in the dooryard, tied the mare to a hitching post, and went up the steps to the verandah. The quietness of the place set her nerves jangling as she untied the rope holding the door shut. Once inside she gazed about, a feeling of homecoming sliding over as softly as a warm summer breeze. She drew a deep breath of the familiar smell of ashes on the hearth, of the still-fresh scent of the boards from the new bedroom and knew that the little cabin and Hamish MacDonald would forever be home.

Struggling to dismiss the hopeless knowledge, she turned toward the shadowy corner where he'd housed the trunk. It was gone! Only an imprint on the earthen floor indicated the place where it had sat. Where could it be? He hadn't taken it with him. All he'd carried on his journey had been a bedroll and a pair of saddle bags.

But, of course, it made sense he wouldn't leave his trove of secrets in a cabin with only a knotted rope to keep intruders out she thought as she sank down onto the chair she'd come to think of as hers. But where, where, where? Somewhere it wouldn't look out of place or inspire curiosity. She thought hard.

The ice house! Covered with a thin layer of sawdust it would resemble nothing more curious than another block of ice. She scrambled to her feet, grabbed a thick knife from the dresser, and rushed out of the cabin.

Chapter Nine

Another rope secured the door of the ice house but it only took her seconds to undo the knots and ease it open. Inside, she paused to allow her eyes to become accustomed to the gloom. As they did, she saw a larger than normal block covered with sawdust in a far corner.

"Yes!" she breathed and gathering up her skirts scrambled over to it. Brushing aside the chaff, she saw it was the trunk. Reaching into her pocket she drew out the knife and inserted it beneath the lock. It was stronger than she had anticipated and it took a number of tries before it began to yield to her prying. When it gave, she paused, her heart pounding, her mouth suddenly dry. Then cautiously she raised the lid.

On top inside was the black bag he'd fetched for medical emergencies. She opened it gingerly and wasn't surprised to find a collection of instruments such as a doctor might use and an assortment of bottles and vials containing unknown substances.

Beneath the valise lay a collection of frock coats, fine breeches, shirts, nightshirts, and neck cloths so elegant and obviously costly they made her breath catch in her throat. So he hadn't always been a poor man.

Beneath them she found a collection of heavy, leather-bound volumes. Medical books, she discovered, after she'd examined the first two. Satisfied that they were all of a similar type, she moved them aside. On the bottom a leather pouch lay tucked against one corner.

Her hands shook as she lifted it, arose, and carried it out into the sunlight beyond the door.

Inside was a single paper. Opening it, Kate felt a small gasp escape her lips.

The last will and testament of Dr. James Donnelly, farmer in His Majesty's colony of New Brunswick, dated May 17, 1815.

"I, Dr. James Donnelly, known in the province of New Brunswick as Hamish MacDonald, do hereby swear as God is my witness, that I did not kill Lord Paul Blackwell. His death was an accident. He attacked me when he found me in his fiancé's bedchamber. He was violently inebriated and when I pushed him away, he fell against the mantle, struck his head and died instantly. Neither am I guilty of attacking and raping Lady Margaret. I do confess that she and I were lovers but both willingly and with full knowledge of the wrongfulness of our actions. I am guilty of fornication but never of the rape and murder of which I stand accused. Lady Margaret chose to make me the scapegoat for her sins and while I do not pretend to hold myself innocent of my part in the affair, I would never betray one whom I once professed to love simply to save a reputation that does not, in honesty, deserve saving."

There was a space, then written in another and fresher ink, the epistle continued:

"I believed that in coming to the colonies and burying myself on a backwoods farm, I could live out my days as a hermit with the powers to help alleviate the suffering of my neighbors. I thought to live alone to the end of my days, the punishment for my sins. Then she arrived, washed up from the surf like a mermaid or some other mythical creature, a magic

creature who, I believe, has the power to save my tarnished soul with her compassion and courage.

My Kate has come into my life as a gift but how can I ask her to share my life, a life that must always be lived within the shadow of the noose? I will, however, bequeath to her all my worldly goods. I was not a poor man in England and I managed to bring a decent bit of my wealth with me. It's hidden behind the large brown stone in the far left upper corner of the hearth along with the bill of sale for this farm. When I am gone and this paper is found, let this, my last wish be honored.

Signed this fifteenth day of July in the year of our Lord, 1820. Dr. James Donnelly/Hamish MacDonald"

Kate allowed her hands holding the paper to fall slowly into her lap. Tears trickled down her cheeks.

"Hamish, oh Hamish, I love you!" She breathed the words as she looked up into the leaves of the maple tree above her. "Did you think the fact that you were betrayed by a faithless woman could change that? I shall be waiting when you return from Fredericton, ready and willing to become your wife, just as soon as the Reverend MacKenzie can find a moment to marry us...if you'll have me."

She got up and went back into the ice house to return the paper and the remainder of the trunk's contents to their original place. She must not let him know she'd invaded his privacy. She must wait until he was ready to divulge his secrets to her of his own free will.

Curiosity, however, plagued her sufficiently to inspire her to go the large brown stone in the fireplace and prize it out. Hidden behind it was a sack full of so many gold coins it took her breath away. And, wrapped in a cloth, the jewels he'd taken from her on the day of her thwarted escape attempt.

She could easily take all of it, leave the hiding place exposed and let him, on his return, think he'd been robbed. She could throw things about the cabin, make a large mess, as if thieves had torn it apart searching. He'd never suspect she'd found that will.

But she couldn't. She didn't want to. How could she rob the man who'd written the words she'd just read, who was leaving her all his worldly wealth? A man who'd saved her life. The man she loved.

Carefully she replace the stone and smoothed dust over the area to hide its being disturbed.

As she drove slowly back to the village, she couldn't help wondering about the mysterious Lady Margaret. She must be a very beautiful woman to have inspired two men to fight over her. And she *was* a lady.

Hamish, in his former life as Dr. James Donnelly, must have been a man of position to have interested such a woman.

She looked down at her plain gray dress and felt dull and shabby as she recalled all the unflattering positions and states of dress in which he'd seen her. Surely he'd never carried Lady Margaret to the privy or bought her a chamber pot as a gift.

But, then, she thought as she drew herself up proudly, she'd wager Lady Margaret had never plucked a partridge for his supper or washed his drawers or slammed a barn door in front of his stampeding team.

As for appearances...she cast her mind back to her own trunk, the one Hamish had found on the beach and which she'd taken with her to the manse and then to the schoolhouse.

It contained gowns that could perhaps be restored. She remembered a riding costume of a lovely shade of green. Quite possibly she could have it decent by the time Hamish returned from Fredericton.

"Go along there, Dolly," she flapped the reins over the old mare's back and sent her forward at a shambling trot. "I have sewing to do."

****

"Good morning, sir. How may I help you?" George Loggie, the village store keeper addressed the newcomer.

Kate paused in perusing the roll of green ribbon to glance at the man.

Tall, slender, and dressed in the latest fashion, he strode toward the counter with a confidence she found arrogant, a riding quirt in his gloved hand.

"Good morning to you, my good man." He addressed George Loggie. "My name is Gerard Elliot and I've come to your village seeking a woman."

"A wife, a bride, sir? We've precious few available young ladies of marriageable age in these parts. They're usually snapped up the moment they come of age or step off a ship."

"No, my good man, not a bride for myself. Another man's bride who has gone missing." He leaned a hip against the plank counter and began to pluck off his kid gloves one finger at a time. "She left England in early March of this year aboard a ship called the Avon Queen on her way to Jamaica where she was to marry a wealthy plantation owner. Recently her family in England has learned her ship was wrecked along the coast not far from this village. And while they've been informed there were no survivors, her family has dispatched me to make a final effort to find her. You see, her future husband had paid a considerable sum for her and now he'll be demanding it be returned. Sadly, her family has already used the payment to cover their debts so, as you might imagine, they're desperate to find this girl and send her on her way."

Near the back of the store, Kate's fingers froze on the piece of green ribbon. *No! Not now. Please,*

161

dear God, not now.

"I'm afraid the story you've heard is true, sir." The store keeper placed beefy hands on the counter and looked the newcomer in the eye. "There's been nothing but wreckage and bodies washed ashore from the Avon Queen. Perhaps it's as well the young lady didn't survive. What kind of family sells a child to pay their debts," he finished, bitterness coloring his words.

"My duty is not to judge the Sheffields, sir. There's a decent reward offered for her recovery...not money, mind you, but Sir William's stud, one of the finest stallions in the country. I'm a sporting man, you see, with a couple of prime fillies stabled at Young's Mews in Newmarket. Acquiring that animal to breed with them would produce foals that could put me at the very top of the racing game. If there's even the most remote possibility that Lady Kathryn survived that wreck, I intend to find her. Then it will be back to jolly old England to collect my four-legged gem."

He paused and let his gaze roam over the store, allowing it at last to fasten on Kate's back. "How about you, young lady? Have you seen any new women hereabouts?"

"No." She turned slowly to face him. "I'm Mrs. Hamish MacDonald, the local school mistress. I've no knowledge of any such person. And if I did, I'd not be turning her over to be sold into a dastardly marriage to some brute of a planter." She looked meaningfully at George Loggie.

The store keeper paused a moment, his eyes widening as he caught her meaning, then continued, "None of us would, Mrs. MacDonald. Indeed, none of us would."

"Ah ha! A lady of spirit. And just how long have you been Mrs. Hamish MacDonald, school mistress of this parish?" Gerard Elliot swaggered closer to stare down at her with penetrating eyes so brown they appeared black.

"A year." She glanced at George Loggie who winked conspiratorially behind Gerard Elliot's broad clothed shoulders.

"A pity. I was hoping perhaps you were she in disguise. Although I never had the good fortune to meet the lady, I have seen a portrait of her countenance and there are similarities...hair colour, shape of face. However, madam, you are much more comely. Or perhaps it's just good, healthy living that has brought such a bloom to your cheeks." His lips quirked in a smile that did not reach his eyes. He paused a moment longer, giving her a head to toe perusal, then touched his quirt to his hat, and strode out of the store.

"A London dandy if ever there was one!" George Loggie muttered contemptuously. "I swear, I think he would have been willing to snap you up as a substitute for this Lady Kathryn if he thought he could get away with it. Mind you lock your door, Mrs. MacDonald. There's a rotten smell to that fellow no matter how fancy he dresses and colognes himself."

"Thank you, Mr. Loggie." The cold hand of fear gripping her, she fled the store and headed for the schoolhouse. She'd forgotten the green ribbon.

Hamish, oh, Hamish, please come back soon, she begged silently.

****

Kate waved to the children as they headed down the trail toward their homes the following afternoon, then turned and walked briskly back inside the schoolhouse. She's seen no more of Gerard Elliot and she was beginning to hope he'd given up his quest and gone on his way.

It had been a hot, humid day and now heavy, black clouds were moving in announcing a thunder storm. She gathered up the books and slates, erased the blackboard, and swept the floor. As the first clap of thunder rolled into the schoolroom, she closed the windows, shut the door and headed into her small living quarters at the back.

"Well, Mrs. MacDonald, is it?" His voice made her whirl as he stepped from behind its door and swaggered toward her. "My, you are looking lovely today." He slapped his riding quirt into the palm of his gloved hand. "That Jamaican planter will be well pleased."

"You must be mad!" Catching his intent, she backed away, her heart banging. "I'm not the woman you're seeking! And if you abduct me, my husband will hunt you to the ends of the earth. I warn you, he's a dangerous man!"

"Your *estranged* husband," he said leering at her. "I spent the past twenty-four hours gathering village gossip about him and you. It seems a mighty coincidence that you appeared as this hermit's wife shortly after the wreck of the Avon Queen. Some people were not so circumspect as your shopkeeper friend and talked quite freely about their joy in their Healer's recent marriage to a woman of mystery."

"What if I told you I'm not Lady Kathryn Sheffield? What if I told you I was her lady's maid and my name is Rose Jones?" She was breathing hard, her thoughts darting about the room in hopes of remembering some object with which to defend herself.

"And what if I told you I was the Duke of York?" he sneered. "I've seen a portrait of Lady Kathryn by a rather dubious artist and you resemble that likeness decently enough."

"Kidnapping is a hanging offense!" She was backing away from him. "I'd consider the consequences of what you're about to do."

"In this county where the law consists of a

distant military and a frequently drunken constable, I feel perfectly safe."

"No!" She whirled and made a run for the outside door.

He caught her by an arm and flung her against the wall with such force it knocked the breath from her body. With a gasp she crumpled to the floor. By the time she came to her senses, she'd been secured in a blanket, tied into a bundle, and thrown over the back of a waiting horse.

She spent the rest of the day tied to a tree deep in the woods. Eliot sat leering at her, triumphant in his prize. There was no reasoning with him. He was hell-bent on returning her to England for his reward.

When darkness fell, he bound a cloth over her mouth, rolled her once more into a blanket, threw her across his horse and started off through the trees.

Shortly she was aware of the animal's hooves echoing hollowly on planks and then its unsteady steps as it was led upward...a boarding plank, she guessed...until it stopped and stamped nervously on yet another wooden surface...a ship's deck?

"So you've got your package, Mr. Elliot," she heard a male voice chuckle. "Now will you be wanting to share a cabin with it or will you be seeking separate accommodations?"

"Oh, separate, most definitely separate, Captain," Elliot replied jovially. "This is one package that must arrive in England as unsullied as possible. I want nothing untoward that might cause any delay in my getting my well-deserved reward."

"Oh, aye. You'll not be forgettin' my slice of the booty, now will ye, sir? This old ship needs repairs and I'm countin' on your generosity for my bit in this venture to make those possible."

"Never fear, Captain. You'll be well and truly paid both for your services and your discretion. Now lead on. I want to get this parcel stowed as soon as possible."

Kate felt hands about her waist and the next moment she was slung over a shoulder like a sack of meal and carried down a ladder. At its bottom she was dumped to her feet. As she tried to regain her balance, the blanket was pulled away, the gag taken from her mouth, and she saw she was in a small, dirty ship's cabin with a bunk built into one wall and a two-foot space by its side. A stained mattress with an equally soiled pillow were the only amenities. She shuddered as a rat scuttled from beneath the bed and out the door.

"Not to your taste, my lady?" Elliot removed her bonds and gave her a shove so that she fell onto the foul bedding. "Well, not to worry. Once we're out to sea, I'll allow you the freedom of the deck. You may watch New Brunswick with your backwoods farm and your beastly husband fade forever from your sight."

****

The following morning, he unlocked her cabin door and grabbing her by an arm, propelled her up onto the deck. As he threw her against the rail, she saw a thin line of green receding into the distance.

"That's the last you'll see of New Brunswick," he sneered. "Take a good look."

He turned and walked away, hailing the Captain who stood on the quarter deck. "You've got her well underway, Captain. How about a sharpener? I've some fine Scotch whiskey in my cabin."

The word Scotch was like an arrow shot through her heart. Tears slid down Kate's face. Spray from the plunging bow swept back to mask them and she was glad. She'd never let that miserable lout who'd kidnapped her see her cry.

She wiped away spray and tears with cold

fingers and felt her heart plummet with every dip of the ship's massive bow.

Gerard Elliot couldn't be right. This couldn't be the last she'd ever see of the country she'd come to love. This couldn't be her final farewell to the man who meant more to her than life itself.

She began to sing softly the lovers' lament they'd once sung together.

"Oh, ye'll take the high road
And I'll take the low road
And I'll be in Scotland afore ye.
For me and my true love
Will never meet again..."

She couldn't go on. Memories of his deep, throaty laughter, his crooked grin, his lilting Highland brogue that had comforted and reassured her on that dreadful night that now seemed ages ago, his healing hands, his eyes as blue as a summer's sky, his great strength and even greater gentleness.

She thought about his kisses that had the power to arouse her to the heights of passion, of the way his hands had slid smoothly over her body, of the way he'd made her feel she was the most beautiful, desirable woman in the world. And suddenly she screamed. Screamed her frustration and throbbing loss into the wind that didn't care and kept ceaselessly pushing her further and further away from the man she loved.

****

Back in New Brunswick Hamish rode away from Fredericton, a plan of action in his mind and a smile on his lips. In the provincial capital he'd shown officials the bill of sale stating one Hamish MacDonald had purchased one hundred acres of land and several buildings from one Josiah

Manderson on July 10, 1815. That had been all the personal identification required.

Next he'd been questioned about his farm, the number of acres under cultivation, his stock, his plans for the future. All well and good he'd been assured after he'd given them this information; however, the government preferred land holders be married men who'd be adding to the human population as well.

Hamish had been quick with the reassurance that he was a recently married man. Ah, that was much better the bespectacled bureaucrat had nodded as he signed the deed. Hamish MacDonald and his wife Kathryn were now fully registered legal owners of the one hundred acre farm indicated on the provincial survey map. As the ink dried on the document, he realized the fullness of its possibilities. Hamish had left the government offices, the papers in his breast pocket, confidence in his soul, and overwhelming anticipation in his heart.

With his holdings officially registered in the name of Hamish MacDonald he felt secure in his identity. No one would ever suspect his past and he could proceed to build a new life in this new land with the amazing woman named Kate. No longer would the shadows of disgrace and the gallows haunt him. Today, with the signing of those papers, he'd been reborn a free man. There was but one wrong he had yet to right and he planned to set about it the moment he arrived back in Pine.

He'd been a fool to fall into bed with Kate in a drunken fit of passion he thought as he headed north toward Pine. He should have wooed her properly, then asked her to be his wife, legally and in the eyes of God. That's the way a man was supposed to treat the woman he loved. And he knew he loved Kate. Slowly but surely she'd wiped his desire for Lady Margaret from his mind until now he couldn't imagine sharing his life with anyone but his strong, beautiful little Kate.

His thoughts went back to the previous evening in a Fredericton tavern where he'd decided to stay for the night. He'd been savoring a glass of whiskey when one of the serving girls had approached him.

"Ye're all alone, sir," she said, her ample bosom revealed by her plunging dress front. "There's no need for such loneliness. The landlord tells me ya have engaged one of his best rooms for the night. I wouldn't be taking offense if ya were to invite me to join ya there."

Seated at a table, he looked up at her. Once, as a randy young lad, he would have been tempted. Nay, more than tempted. Willing and eager. But not any more. Not since Kate.

"Thank ye, mistress." He saluted her with his glass. "But I am the happily married man. But I'd not be agin buyin' ye a drink of this fine malt."

The woman, with a contemptuous look, had swung away to ply her trade on a more willing customer. He'd grinned as he'd watched her go. *Damn it, Lady Kathryn, you've reformed me.*

Now he rubbed a hand thoughtfully down his beard and wondered if she'd accept him as he was or if he dared shave off some of this growth and make himself more humanly attractive. Somehow he didn't think she'd care.

Even though his first night with her had been hazed in a whiskey mist he remembered how wonderful she'd felt in his arms, how eagerly she'd come to him in every way.

She'd deserved better than a liquor-soaked lout for such an occasion. And, by God, he'd see that she did on the next occasion.

"Come on, Lad." He clucked to the horse. "We have to get to Pine. I have some serious courting to do." The horse broke into a lope and Pilot followed suite.

****

"Reverend MacKenzie?" Hamish strode into the small church and addressed the man standing at the pulpit praying. "Yer guid wife said I'd find ye here. She said ya'd tell me about me wife. I've been by the schoolhouse and she's no there. Where iss she, man?" Impatience mingled with concern to make his voice rise and echo in the little chapel.

"Have a seat, my boy." The reverend indicated a place on the front bench.

"Nay, nay. I've no the time for talkin'. I must see me wife immediately."

The clergyman looked up at the big, bearded man standing before him and drew a deep breath.

"I'm afraid she's gone missing, Hamish," he said, his facial muscles flinching.

"Missing?!" The word was a hiss of disbelief in the silence of the church. "What da ya mean, missing? The woman couldn't chust vanish inta the air!"

"No, no, that she couldn't." Reverend MacKenzie put a steadying hand on his companion's arm. "We believe she may have been kidnapped, spirited away by a man who came from England three days ago seeking a Lady Kathryn Sheffield, a passenger on the Avon Queen. He seemed to think your Kate resembled her. The following day she failed to be present when the children arrived for school."

"Sweet Jesus! Kidnapped! But surely you...the people...organized a search. How far could a man unfamiliar with this country get away with a woman prisoner? Did he have horses? Did he...?"

"He had only a single horse as near as we can determine but a ship left the wharf at moonrise on the evening before we discovered her missing. It was bound for England. There was no way we could follow."

170

Hamish waited to hear no more. He turned and strode out of the church, leaped onto his horse, and rode at full gallop to the wharf. As he reined to a halt on its planks, a thick grey fog was drifting in to obscure the river and the ships riding at anchor.

His breath was coming fast and hard, his heart banging at his ribs as he peered out into the mist. Somewhere out there Kate, his Kate, was bound for England, a prisoner.

And he could no more show his face in that country than he could fly. Not if he wanted to live to tell her he loved her.

Suddenly he heard her crying out his name. From somewhere out there in the fog and mist, she was calling him, begging him to come to her.

Frustration and pain wracking his body, he threw back his head and emitted a great roar that echoed out into the night and made both his horse and dog flinch. He swung the stallion about and sent him at a mad dash toward the tavern.

****

"Hamish, man, perhaps you shouldn't be drinking so much." Caleb Haines, the barkeeper admonished as Hamish downed his fourth dram. "What if someone needs you? I've never known you to be a drinking man."

"Ye've never known me ta have chust lost me wife," he muttered his head bowed over the bar.

"Aye, well, we're all terrible sorry about that. If there was anything we could do, Hamish, you know we would."

"None of ye took the trouble ta keep my Kate safe while I was away, now did ye?" He raised his head, turned to the patrons and bellowed. "Ye heard there was a man in town lookin' for a woman, a newly arrived woman. Ye might have had the brains ta suspect he might think my Kate was her!"

"We're right sorry, Hamish. We never thought

171

that London dandy seeking a reward of a prime stud meant to kidnap your wife," Andrew Currie tried to protest.

"Whit?" Hamish drew himself up to his full height and squared his shoulders. The men backed away. "Ye mean this bastard was lookin' ta trade me wife for a bit of horse flesh?"

"He said he'd be collecting the animal at Newmarket as soon as he delivered the young woman he was seeking to her family," Andrew Currie struggled out the words. "He was in here the day before Mrs. MacDonald disappeared stating such was his hope and plan."

"Damn ye all ta hell!" Hamish threw his tankard against the hearth and bellowed like an enraged bull. "I've spent five years of me life tryin' ta help ye, mendin' yer broken bones and birthin' yer bairns and yet when me Kate needed yer help, ye weren't there fer her!"

He turned and strode out of the tavern. The customers and barkeep heard him thundering away, yelling at his horse.

"What'll we do without him?" A man finally spoke in the ensuing silence. "My wife is near due. If Hamish isn't there to help her..."

"Don't worry." Caleb Haines drew a deep breath and went to sweep up the mess on the hearth. "Hamish MacDonald is a good man. He won't let any of us down no matter how much he blames us for allowing his wife's kidnapping. Right now he's angry and in a lot of pain but he'll come out of it, mark my words."

"But he's right," Andrew Currie said, slowly looking around at the others in the room. "We should have suspected that bastard would go after Kate. We should have kept an eye on her."

"You don't think that bounty hunter could have been right?" Leam Fraser came forward and leaned on the bar. "We did first find Mrs. MacDonald living at Hamish's farm shortly after that ship wreck."

"You mean Hamish's Kate really is that lady Elliot was seeking?" Neil Currie's tone was incredulous. "But the story is that they met in Scotland where Hamish was a ghillie and she was a lady and that he came to this country to make a life for them before she joined him."

"That's just it." Caleb Haines rubbed his hands on his apron. "It's a story. We have no way of knowing if it's true. Perhaps Kate MacDonald was a sole survivor of the shipwreck; perhaps Hamish rescued her and nursed her back to health. Perhaps..."

"Perhaps she never was his wife." Another man chimed in. "We'd have known if Reverend MacKenzie married them in a village this size."

Silence fell.

"Well, it little matters to me." Caleb Haines spoke finally. "Hamish is right fond of her and they seemed to fit well together. It's up to us to support him in his grief."

****

Far off out on the Atlantic, Kate sat on a crude bed, clutching its edge as the ship rolled over waves that swept it ever further and further from the man she loved.

During her early hours of captivity, she'd railed and screamed and cursed at her captors all to no avail. Now that she'd had time to think, she was coming to believe that had been entirely the wrong thing to do. She smoothed back her tangled hair and brushed dirt from her rumpled dress. Approaching Gerard Elliot with pleas to be returned to Hamish would fall on deaf ears she knew. But what about the captain? Hamish had kept Lady Kathryn's jewels when he'd taken her to the manse. He'd said he didn't want her using them run off on some mad adventure, that he'd return them to her once she had a sensible plan for her future firmly in mind.

What if she promised the Captain a share of those jewels? She had no idea what Gerard Elliot had given the man in return for taking part in an abduction but surely it couldn't be equal to all those emeralds, rubies, and diamonds.

As a plan took shape in her mind, she arose and went cautiously up onto the deck. It was dark, probably near midnight she guessed, and the captain always took the air on the quarter deck with the helmsman around that hour. She could speak to him alone, without fear of Gerard Elliot putting in an appearance.

She emerged onto the deck to find the ship rolling smoothly forward through the waves before a stiff breeze and its captain standing as she'd expected beside the helmsman at the rear.

Being careful not to lose her footing, she walked cautiously toward him.

"Captain, a word if I may?" she called up to him from the bottom of the ladder leading to the elevated deck.

"You shouldn't be about alone at this hour, mistress." His words reassured her and solidified her resolve to approach him with her proposal.

"I believe you're right," she smiled, hoping he could see her in the darkness. "But I must speak to you privately and this seems to be the only time I might find you relatively alone. I assure you, it's a matter of grave importance."

"Oh, aye?" He moved to the top of the ladder to look down at her, a grizzled old salt.

"Please. If you'll just hear me out, I promise I'll not say a word about your part in my…unexpected voyage." She waved a hand in the direction of the helmsman to emphasize his listening presence.

"Very well." He came down the ladder to join

her. "Come to my quarters. Sometimes ships can have ears."

"Captain," she began once they were seated in his cabin. "I have a proposition to make. If you will abandon Mr. Elliot and his plan, if you will agree to see me on my way back to New Brunswick the moment we arrive in England, I'm prepared to give you my jewels, a substantial collection of diamonds, rubies, and emeralds when next you dock in Miramichi. My husband has them hidden but he'll gladly exchange them for my safe return. Think what you could do with such wealth! I can't help but notice your ship is in need of refurbishing." She glanced meaningfully around at the shabby, dirty cabin. "And I'm sure there's some lady ashore who'd appreciate a diamond necklace."

For a moment he paused and stared piercingly at her.

"And who's to say you'd keep your word once I'd seen to your escape? I might never see hide nor hair of those pretty baubles."

"I'm a woman of honor, sir." She drew herself up proudly. "I give you my word as a lady."

"Do you now? And just what lady might that be?'

"Lady Kathryn Sheffield." She drew herself haughtily. "My word has never been doubted."

"If you're speaking the truth, it's a tempting offer." He arose and went to pour himself a drink from a bottle on a table. When he turned and raised it her direction, she shook her head. "But, you see, I could hang for my part in this affair if Mr. Elliot suspected I was planning to deceive him and retaliated by putting the blame on me. He's a gentleman and I'm the captain of a timber dougher, a tramp ship. Who do you think would be believed? And kidnapping is a hanging offense."

"Why did you volunteer to participate in it?"

"You see the reason all about you. This old ship

needs a lot of work, I have a wife and four children at home, and I'm not getting any younger. He offered me a tidy sum for a bit of work that mainly involved keeping my mouth shut."

"But you called kidnapping a heinous crime. Surely being a father yourself you can appreciate what the loss of a child can mean."

"For certain, girl. And that's one reason why I allowed myself to be talked into it. You see, taking you back to your father is hardly the same as holding you for ransom with the threat of death or injury hanging over you. It's not really kidnapping at all when you look at like that."

"What if I told you the man to whom I'm being returned isn't my father, that he's a brute who attacked me, who'll probably do again the moment he realized Gerard Elliot has brought him the wrong woman?"

"Ah, now there you just ruined your case." The Captain turned on her, faded blue eyes suddenly turning hard. "I was ready to believe you about those jewels but now you're trying to tell me that you aren't Lady Kathryn Sheffield, that Mr. Elliot has stolen the wrong woman. If he did and you have the lady's jewels, girl, you're trying to impersonate her and nothing more than a common thief. You deserve whatever fate awaits you. Now be off with you. Back to your cabin and let me hear no more of your daft lies."

Back in her cabin, Kate sank down onto her stained bed and covered her face with her hands. She'd played her best card and lost. Worse than lost. She may have branded herself as a thief and impersonator.

She could only wonder what Gerard Elliot would do if the Captain told him what she'd done.

****

"Well, well, so you're a thief posing as Lady

Kathryn, are you?" Gerard Elliot shoved open the door of her cabin and leered in at her. "You *are* desperate not to be sent off to your intended in the Caribbean, aren't you. However, had I known your so-called husband had secreted away your jewels, I wouldn't have spent our day together on land in New Brunswick sitting in the woods with you fighting off whining hoards of insects. However, water over the bridge. Your father is paying well for your return and if I ever chance to return to the colonies, I'll be sure to ferret out the man you were living with and invent some tale that will induce him to hand them over to me.

"However, for the remainder of this voyage, I think it's best I secure you in place. You're a pretty thing and you may well seduce one or more of the sailors to take your part. We can't have you inciting a mutiny, now can we?"

With that he slammed the door and Kate heard him securing it with a bar. Her heart plummeted. She'd never see Hamish again.

Was this then her punishment for impersonating a lady, for declaring her jewels as her own, and attempting to use them in her attempts to escape? If so, it was indeed a harsh one.

****

Kate had never been so filthy in her life. For over three weeks Gerard Elliot had kept her a prisoner in her cabin, allowing only a gruff, old sailor under his supervision to bring her food and empty her slop bucket. He hadn't allowed her any water to bath or any other amenities that would have made her days tolerable.

Then had come the cry that land had been sighted. Kate didn't know if she was relieved or appalled. She'd be freed from this stinking prison but what she'd face on land made her stomach roil, her head swim.

When Gerard Elliot finally came for her, she preceded him up the ladder to the deck struggling to sustain her composure and ready herself for what lay ahead.

****

"Fix her up for me, madame," her captor told the woman in the elegant shop to which he took her immediately on disembarking. "I'm willing to pay handsomely for her transformation into a clean, sweet-smelling, fashionably dressed lady."

"We will try, monsieur," the finely groomed, expensively gowned lady replied, wrinkling her pert nose. "It will take time."

"Time is exactly what must not be wasted in this instance," he snapped. "She's part of a bargain I want to see fulfilled as quickly as possible. I'll call back for her in two hours."

****

"Here she is, Sir William. Your daughter." Gerard Elliot drew Kate dressed in a silk gown and beribboned bonnet into the library at Sheffield Park. Madame Nadine had worked her magic and had left no evidence of the dirty, bedraggled young woman who'd been shepherded into her establishment four hours earlier. "I said I'd find her for you and I did. Now I'll be taking delivery of that excellent stallion."

The corpulent man sitting by the fire grunted and turned to peer around the side of his wing chair. With a resounding bellow he bolted to his feet, his eyes goggling.

"You idiot! This isn't my daughter! It's her lady's maid, Rose Jones!"

Chapter Ten

"It cannot be!" Elliot turned his gaze from the angry aristocrat to the young woman by his side. "That portrait...her face and hair...even you must admit, Sir William, there is a resemblance!"

"That portrait flattered my daughter beyond reason! She is...was...nowhere near as comely as this girl! Why do you think I had to marry her off to a Jamaican planter who was willing to take her unmet! Get out of here and never darken my door again!"

"But, sir, our agreement...the stallion..."

"Get out, you idiot! Get out before I call the constable on you! And take that creature with you!"

"Oh, no! You may not give me the horse but you'll not foist some serving girl on me!"

Elliot gave Kate's arm a final, painful twist, then turned and strode out of the room.

For a few moments the room was silent except for the crackling of the log fire and Sir William's heavy breathing. Kate felt nausea gathering in the pit of her stomach as she faced the man who'd brutally attacked her six months earlier.

"So you've returned." Finally he spoke. "Well, if you're thinking to stir up more trouble between my good lady and me..."

"That is the furthest thing from my mind." She squared her shoulders and faced him. "All I want is passage back to New Brunswick."

"Oh, you do, do you?" He expelled his breath in a gush Kate recognized as relief. "We'll have to think about it. But first I assume you know my daughter's fate? I'd be obliged if you'd share it with me."

"The Avon Queen was wrecked in a storm off the coast of New Brunswick." Kate looked up at him and tried to think of him as man who'd lost his daughter. It was the only way she could control the outrage flaming inside. "I believe I am the sole survivor. Lady Kathryn, to the best of my knowledge, perished when the ship sank."

"Damnation! How am I to reply to Kensington?" Sir William slammed his hand down on the arm of his chair. "I've already used the money he paid for Kathryn to cover my debts. And how will I explain your return to Lady Anna? She believes I banished you for good." He paused a moment, then slowly turned his small, greedy eyes on Kate. "But maybe, just maybe you can take my daughter's place. Kensington has seen only a copy of the portrait Elliot mentioned. You bear a close enough resemblance to Lady Kathryn to pass for her." He lowered his voice and narrowed his eyes. "In fact he'd be doing better. You're a sight more comely. What do you say, girl? Kensington is a rich man. You'd have every physical comfort you could fancy. A much better life than you're destined to have as a maid servant."

"You must be mad!" Kate drew herself up proudly. "I will not impersonate Lady Kathryn to clear away your debts! At any rate…" She pulled in a deep breath. "I'm already married to a man in New Brunswick, the man who rescued me from the shipwreck. His name is Hamish MacDonald, a farmer. I insist you put me on the next ship back to him and pay my passage. Otherwise I'll have you charged with abduction!"

For a moment he stared at her. Then he burst out laughing.

"Good God, you resemble my mouse of a

daughter less and less! Brazen bitch! Pay your passage to some backwoods farm in the colonies after you refuse to honor my request! Get out of my sight before I throw a few bits of the family silver in a sack and accuse you of pilfering them! That will get you passage...passage to a criminal colony in Australia!"

A subtle knock at the door sounded and the butler entered.

"Sir Henry Dunn, Sir William. He says you had an appointment to meet with him?"

"Ah, yes." Annoyance coloring his tone, Sir William waved his hand. "Show him in. Perhaps *he* can help me out of this conundrum that idiot Elliot has gotten me into. And mind--" He swung on her again. "You keep your mouth shut. I'll do the talking."

A moment later a tall, well dressed, barrel-chested man was shown into the library. Kate shrank back into the shadow of a tall chair, hoping to avoid further notice. She had no idea who Sir Henry might be or what further trouble he could bring to her.

"William." The gray-haired newcomer spoke warmly and held out a hand. "What can I do for you? Your summons seemed urgent, therefore I didn't spare the horses to get down here."

"It seems I have even greater need of your services than when I first sent for you, Harry. Come, sit by the fire. Benson." He hailed the butler standing in the doorway. "Pour Sir Henry a large brandy. He'll need fortification to deal with this mess."

****

Five minutes later Sir Henry stared over at his client as he finished relating the story of Kate's kidnapping by Gerard Elliot.

"Good God, man! You authorized an abduction?

Actually offered a reward for it? I regard myself as a more than passable barrister but even at that, I find myself stalemated by this affair!"

"I thought it was my daughter the fool would be bringing!" he bellowed. "Now I have to get rid of this creature quickly...before my lady wife returns on the morrow. She had taken an unreasonable dislike to the chit before she sailed with our daughter. She must not find her returned. And since the daft creatures refused to go to Jamaica in my daughter's stead..."

"Good God, William, have you taken leave of your senses!" Sir Henry stared at his client. "If she'd agreed, at the very least, you're committing fraud. I will not bother to go into the other charges."

"Then what am I to do with her?" Sir William arose and began to pace. "I cannot allow Anna to find her here. My wife's father may be deaf and nearly blind but a bad word from old Lord Henly and I'll be ruined. I'll lose my seat in Parliament, I'll..."

"So Anna caught you with this young woman, did she?" Sir Henry's eyes narrowed. "Well, then, William, perhaps you deserve whatever Lady Anna has in store for you."

"Dear God, man!" Sweating profusely, Sir William paused to wipe his corpulent face with a wide, white handkerchief. "I swear before God I never harmed the wench. Anna caught us in an innocent embrace in the kitchen. The poor creature had been frightened by a mouse and..."

"Very well, William." Sir Henry heaved a deep sigh as he arose. "I'll help you out this once provided--" he turned to Kate, "--you didn't actually harm her?"

Kate realized he was asking her. She hesitated, then shook her head.

"Come here, girl." Sir Henry spoke directly to Kate this time.

She squared her shoulders and walked with all the dignity she could muster to stand before the lawyer.

"You claim to be the wife of one Hamish MacDonald, a farmer in New Brunswick, do you?" he asked and Kate noted his voice was firm and calm. Perhaps, just perhaps here was a man she could reason with, could convince that she must be returned to the colonies.

"I do not claim to be, I am," she said proudly. "And I demand to be returned to my home and husband.

"I see." He looked at her gravely. "If you were, would you be willing to forget all about this...unfortunate incident?"

"I might." Although her heart was beginning to pound with hope, she managed to remain cool and aloof. Then a mad plan gushed into her mind. "And if your services as an attorney were to be put at my disposal."

"What!" Sir William exploded. "Are you insane, girl? Harry is the most renowned barrister in England! Do you think he's about to work for the likes of you?"

"It is my price for expunging your kidnapping and other misdeeds from my memory." She thrust out her chin defiantly.

"Just what would be the nature of the case you'd have me undertake, young lady?" Sir Henry was looking at her, amusement and respect beginning to twinkle in his eyes.

"I'd have you look into a case involving my husband, sir. I'd have you clear his good name." She realized she was taking a huge risk but she felt this would probably be the only opportunity either of them would have to prove him innocent of the charge of murder. "However, I will speak no further of it until you have agreed to take on the assignment and we may discuss the matter confidentially."

"Good God, girl! We won't be blackmailed! We won't..." Sir William was on his feet, facing her, his corpulent face getting redder and redder with each word.

"Sit down, William." Sir Henry waved his client back into his chair. "I think, under the circumstances, you have no choice but to give in to her demands. I have a feeling she's a woman of her word and once the two conditions she's stated have been fulfilled, she'll never again mention the unfortunate affair of her abduction and..." he paused and looked at Kate, "...other misdeeds, is that not correct, young woman?"

"I will swear upon the Holy Bible."

"Very well." Sir William plopped back down into his wing chair, breathing hard. "But take the wretched creature away with you, Harry. I'll not have such a conniving witch under my roof a moment longer!"

"Or when Anna returns?" Sir Henry arose, set his brandy glass aside and headed for the door. "Come along, my girl. You may companion my wife, Lady Emma, while we sort this out. I think your bravado and adventurous spirit will amuse her no end."

****

"Sir Henry, I have a story to tell you." Kate drew a deep breath as Sir Henry's elegant carriage carried them through the foggy streets of London.

"I'm listening," he said settling himself back comfortably on the padded seat. "I feel certain it will be a fascinating tale."

She began with her being shipped off to Jamaica as Lady Kathryn Sheffield's lady's maid and ended with the story of how Elliot Gerard had taken her to a fashion house on their arrival in England to have her bathed and fittingly dressed to meet Sir William.

"He had provided no clean clothing or opportunity to bathe during the entire voyage," she concluded. "And gave me barely enough food to exist. The man is a common criminal, a kidnapper."

"He definitely is, my dear." Sir Henry heaved a great sigh. "Unfortunately his would be an impossible case to prosecute. You have no witnesses...that ship's captain would swear you came voluntarily, not wanting to get himself in the way of criminal charges for abetting an abduction and no one else witnessed anything that would secure your case. I'm afraid Elliot Gerard will forever go unpunished. But perhaps I can help you in the matter of your husband."

****

"My dear, may I present the former Miss Rose Jones, lately Mrs. Hamish MacDonald, newly arrived most reluctantly from the colonies. These days she answers to the name of Kate."

The woman who had been standing staring out the long window into the autumn gardens of the fine London house to which Sir Henry had taken Kate turned to face the pair. Kate felt her breath suck in abruptly. Lady Emma was an auburn-haired beauty at least twenty years Sir Henry's junior. Bright brown eyes sparkled as she faced the new arrivals.

"Welcome, my dear." She immediately became a gracious hostess. "What a great journey you must have had." She reached for the bell rope. "We'll have tea immediately. I'm sure you can welcome a bit of nourishment. And you, my dear." With a soft rustle of satin, she advanced to her husband, planted a kiss on his cheek, and led him to a chair by the drawing room fire. "You've had a long day. Come and rest. I'll fetch your slippers."

Astonished, Kate watched as the beauty guided the middle-aged man to a chair, urged him into it and knelt to remove his shoes. In all her years in service she'd never known the lady of the house to behave in such an openly affectionate, wifely manner.

"Now, Emma, you must stop spoiling me." Sir Henry admonished but his smile told Kate he was enjoying the ministrations of his beautiful wife. "Kate will be thinking I treat you as a servant."

"Judging by the keenness of her eye, I'd say Mrs. MacDonald is perfectly capable of discerning between servitude and loving care." Lady Emma finished sliding his feet into a pair of comfortable-looking carpet slippers.

"There now, isn't that better?" She arose and beamed fondly down at her husband. Then she turned to Kate. "Mrs. MacDonald, come sit here between us, near the fire. It's been a sallow day and I'm sure you could do with a little warmth and cheer."

"Thank you, Lady Emma." Kate sank gratefully into the proffered chair. The fire felt good as she stretched her cold hands out to its warmth.

"Now that we are comfortable, I will enlighten you with regards to this remarkable young woman's story as she told it to me on the journey here...that is, if I may, my dear?" He looked over at Kate. "I'd ask you to retell the tale only your countenance informs me you'd much rather rest. However, feel free to interrupt if I get any details incorrect."

"Of course, Sir Henry." Kate acquiesced to his suggestion. She was weary and wanted only to let her feet and hands grow warm before the log fire.

****

As Sir Henry finished telling his wife the story of Kate's adventures and of Hamish's wrongful conviction, a maid servant arrived with a tea tray heavily laden with a pot of tea, cups, saucers, cakes, and scones. Kate who hadn't seen such fine food in weeks or eaten that day heard her stomach rumble.

She could barely wait for Lady Emma to pour each of them a cup of steaming brew and indicate she was to help herself from the bounty before them.

"Imagine our being separated under such deplorable conditions as these two young people, my dear." Lady Emma spoke to her husband as Kate sank her teeth into the first feathery-light buttered scone. "That thought alone should be sufficient to inspire you to make your very best effort on their behalf."

"Have no fear, my dearest." Sir Henry arose from his chair. "I will spare no effort to see her husband's name cleared and herself safely on her way back to him with the happy news."

Delighted beyond words, Kate could only smile her joy at the couple.

****

Kate was at breakfast the following morning in the long, gleaming dining room when Lady Emma entered. She was dressed in an elegant green silk dressing gown richly trimmed with delicate lace. Her long, auburn hair was tied back with a white ribbon. She looked so youthful Kate found herself again wondering how such a lovely, young women could have married the stout, middle-aged barrister.

"Good morning, my lady." Kate started to rise but Lady Emma waved her back into her chair.

"Sit, Kate. When we're alone together we'll be Kate and Emma. I wasn't always a lady, you know. I got the title when I married Harry. But," she continued as she sank into her chair at the end of the table. "You mustn't think that was why I became his wife. I married Harry because I love him."

"Of course, my lady...Emma." Kate felt a hot blush rising up her cheeks. Lady Emma had guessed her impertinent thoughts.

"I understand your wondering about us. Indeed, most of London did. They didn't recognize that love does not depend upon appearance or age, you see. Enduring love depends on what is inside a person. And Harry has the kindest, bravest heart I've ever known. Now enough of me. You must tell me about this Hamish MacDonald who has won *your* love. Does he have a kind and brave heart as well?"

"Indeed he does. Everyone in the community respects and admires him. They call him the Hermit Healer. I was with him when he delivered our neighbor's son. It was a breech birth. Mother and child might well have died had not Hamish been there to work his magic. The couple named their boy James which I believe is the English form of Hamish. And then, of course, there was the incident with the bandits..."

Her voice trailed off and she blushed. "Forgive me. I'm sure you don't want to hear such tales."

"You must love him very much." Lady Emma smiled. "And soon you'll be able to give him back his life as he once gave you back your own. Harry is a magnificent barrister. Not another man in England can equal him in matters of the law." Her voice filled with pride as she finished speaking.

"I'm afraid to hope." Kate looked down at her plate. "I'm sure I could wish for no better representative but it seems such an impossible case."

"Trust my Harry." Lady Emma signaled to a servant to bring her breakfast. "He succeeds where other lawyers despair. Now let us finish our meal and dress. I have a desire to go out in the carriage this morning and I'd be most grateful for your company."

She stopped abruptly.

"But how thoughtless of me! You must want to visit your parents! Please, take my carriage. Hampton will drive you wherever you wish to go.

"I'm afraid visiting my parents is no longer

possible." Kate drew a deep, quivering breath and felt sadness break over her. "My parents died of a fever just as I was about to embark for Jamaica with Lady Kathryn. As tenants, they left me nothing. Their farm reverted to Sir William." She paused and blinked back tears.

"My dear, I am sorry." Lady Emma's words were soft with sincere sympathy.

"Perhaps Sir William unwittingly saved my life." Kate forced a wane smile. "If I'd still been living on the farm with my parents, I might have died as well. Life is full of strange twists and turns, is it not."

****

An hour later they were seated in Lady Emma's elegant carriage and driving away from the mansion. Shortly the carriage turned away from the fashionable section of London and headed toward the docks. Astonished at this choice of venue Kate nevertheless remained silent. She was living on Sir William's bounty and she wasn't about to jeopardize being in the good graces of his adored wife.

The carriage paused before a ramshackle, soot-stained stone building. Several dirty children came rushing up to greet them. Kate knew that normally a lady like Emma would have her coachman chase them away. She was therefore surprised when her companion flicked a hand in his direction and he climbed down. Kate watched as he rounded to the back of the carriage and removed several boxes she'd noticed being loaded aboard when they'd gotten into the vehicle earlier. These he handed into the eager, grubby little hands.

"Mind you takes 'em direct to your ma!" he admonished as they darted off.

"My nieces and nephews," Lady Emma astonished Kate by explaining. "Those are my sister's children. She refuses to accept help from me so I've sworn my nieces and nephews to secrecy about the boxes. They're to tell her they come from their father, a useless bit of a sailor who deserted them years ago. She allows herself to be deluded into believing the tale, half because she's in desperate need and half because she wants to believe in the goodness of a man not fit to wipe her boots.

"To Madame Blanchard's, Hampton," she ordered the coachman and immediately he climbed back onto his seat and drove off. "Now, suppose you tell me who you really are, Kate MacDonald."

"As you already know, I was...am Rose Jones, lady's maid to Lady Kathryn Sheffield. I was sent out with her when her father arranged her marriage to a wealthy Jamaican planter in exchange for money. Our ship foundered off the coast of New Brunswick and I, the sole survivor, was rescued by Hamish MacDonald."

"Yes, I already know those details. I would like to know how you came into Lady Kathryn's service."

Kate hesitated.

"Surely you can't be shy about telling me, having just seen where I came from."

Kate hesitated again, then began, her gaze on her gloved hands. "As I've told you, I was a farmer's daughter on the Sheffield Estate. My mother was a Scotswoman from the Highlands. Her accent was pure and sweet. Hamish's didn't ring true.

"Sir William often rode past our farm...more frequently as I became a young woman. One day when I was sixteen he came to our cottage while my father was in the village at a livestock auction. Sir William wanted me to come into his home as lady's maid to his daughter, the Lady Kathryn. No one could have been more surprised than I was. I didn't want to go. I loved my life on the farm with my parents. I was their only child.

"Sir William took my mother aside and when she returned to our cottage, she told me he'd threatened to take away our farm and leave us destitute if I refused. She was in such distress that I packed my few belongings and went with him before my father returned. My father was a proud man and I knew he'd never allow me to be forced into servitude. I also knew I couldn't allow him and my mother to be forced from the only home they'd ever had."

She paused and looked up at Lady Emma. "Lady Kathryn was an entirely obnoxious young woman two years my junior. From the outset she seemed bent on making my life a horror. She told her mother I was lazy and useless, that I habitually ruined her gowns with my carelessness, and that I flirted and worse with the grooms."

"What a perfectly terrible creature!" Lady Emma laid a sympathetic hand over Kate's. "Sadly, I've met that type of little witch myself. Please continue, my dear."

"One afternoon when his wife and daughter went to take tea at a neighboring estate, he came into Lady Kathryn's bed chamber where I was working on her clothing. He..."

Kate broke off and looked down at her hands tightly clasped in her lap.

"He attacked you." Lady Emma breathed and put a gloved hand over hers. "Sadly, not an uncommon tale where beautiful maid servants and lecherous master are concerned. Kate." She spoke softly. "Did he succeed?"

"No, I was only battered and bruised." She coughed, then continued, "God was with me. Lady Kathryn had become ill. She and her mother returned early. They arrived just as he ripped my bodice."

"Wonderful!" Lady Emma clapped her hands and laughed. "I could wish no greater penance for such a beast. Tell me--" She calmed her mirth and spoke softly again, "What was his lady wife's reaction?"

"At first she stood stock still, gaping. Then she flew at him like an enraged feline." Kate suddenly chuckled as she recalled the melodrama that had followed. "They toppled to the floor together and only after repeated admonitions and outright physical intervention by Lady Kathryn could they be parted. Lady Anna's hairpiece was hanging by a few strands and Sir William's neck cloth was dangling like a hangman's noose from his wife's efforts to strangle him with it. Remembering it now, I must say it is amusing."

"And the consequence? There had to be consequences."

"Oh, yes." Kate looked out into the dirty, bustling street through which they were passing and longed for the fresh, green beauty of New Brunswick. "Lady Kathryn had been affianced to a wealthy Jamaican planter. She was to leave the following week and I had been praying to be allowed to return to my parents.

"The incident destroyed those hopes. Lady Kathryn's elderly nanny had been supposed to go with her as chaperone and later to care for any children that would result from her marriage. Now Lady Anna decreed I'd travel with Lady Kathryn in her stead. If I refused, my parents would be forced from their farm. She had no idea it was the same threat her philandering husband has used to get me into their manor or that both my mother and father would die before I left. I actually went willingly after that. I wanted to get away from servitude at the manor and most definitely Sir William. The prospect of a new life and new adventures in the New World appealed to me. And that's how I ended up shipwrecked in New Brunswick and rescued by Hamish."

"You speak well for the professed daughter of a tenant farmer." Lady Emma adjusted her bonnet and glanced at her companion.

"My father was the son of a clergyman." Kate drew a deep breath and continued. "All his vicar parent had to leave him were the results of diligent home tutoring and several stacks of books. My father schooled me using those volumes."

"And your mother? How did they meet, this vicar's son and a Highland lassie?"

"As a young man my father joined the army. His regiment was sent to the Highlands to quell a suspected plot for an uprising. He met my mother, fell in love, and when he was released from service, went back to the Highlands and married her.

"My grandfather had been vicar on the estate that is now Sir William's. My father applied to Sir William and received the tenancy of a small farm. It wasn't an especially good farm. The house was an ancient cottage, the land poor but my parents managed to eke out a living and be happy."

"I was a scullery maid in mi'lord's manor house." Lady Emma startled Kate with her opening revelation. "One afternoon when I was alone in the kitchens, he attacked me. I grabbed a poker from the hearth and hit him where it would hurt most."

"Oh, my!" Kate's hand flew to cover her mouth.

"Oh, my, indeed." Lady Emma allowed a sardonic little smile to tip her lips. "He staggered away, cursing me. An hour later the constables came and carried me off to prison. I'd stolen valuable silver plate they said. It had been found under my bed I was told. It wasn't difficult to imagine how it got there. I was in the dock about to be sentenced to transportation when Harry saw me."

She paused and turned back to Kate. "Something in his eyes as he looked up at me gave me hope. I have never been certain of what he did but three days later I was released into his custody. A week later we were married."

"And you've obviously not regretted your decision." Kate watched for her reaction.

"Not for a moment. Oh, I admit what I felt for Harry at first was gratitude. But he's a kind, truly decent man as well as a brilliant one. It wasn't long before I came to love him. But," she continued with a little chuckle. "It couldn't have been easy for him, turning a sow's ear like me into a silk purse. He hired dress makers and hair stylist and women who taught me manners and deportment as he struggled to refine the serving girl he'd fallen in love with.

"I worked hard. I longed to make Harry proud of me." She sighed. "I hope I've succeeded to some degree but there are days when I have quite deplorable lapses."

"I think you've succeeded wonderfully," Kate smiled. "He fairly glows each time he looks at you."

"Harry sees me with his heart." She smiled absently down at her gloved hands. "Society, however, took its time to accept me. At first they even tried to ostracize him for what they saw as his unfortunate choice of a wife."

She looked up and stuck out her chin. "He knew they couldn't continue to shun him. They needed his brilliant legal mind more than he needed their priggish approval. Before long, invitations began to arrive addressed to Sir Henry and his lady."

"I am happy for you." Kate touched Emma's arm. "You are spending your life with the man you love and who loves you as well. I cannot imagine a greater joy."

"And you shall know it, too." Emma smiled at her. "Harry will have your beloved Hamish cleared of charges within hours just as he did me and you will be on your way back to New Brunswick with the joyous news."

"Yes." The word lacked conviction as Kate once more lowered her gaze to her clasped hands. Perhaps no matter what she did, Dr. James Donnelly could never love Rose Jones, daughter of a tenant farmer and a poor Highland girl.

"Now, come along." Lady Emma adjusted her bonnet as the carriage drew to a stop. "Enough reminiscing for one morning. Here is Madame Blanchard's establishment. She's one of the finest dress makers in the city. I am buying you a decent wardrobe. You can't companion me about London without looking the part and I won't hear a single word of protest."

****

"Well, my dear, I trust you've brought us good news." Lady Emma made her way downstairs to greet her husband, Kate close on her heels when he returned to the manor that evening.

"Alas, no, I'm sorry to say." He handed his hat, coat, and stick to the footman who'd answered the door and looked up at the pair with a weary sigh. "Come into the drawing room, the pair of you, and I'll explain the situation."

Feeling ill, Kate followed the couple into the room at the foot of the stairs and, at Sir Henry's indication, shut the door after them. She could barely wait until Lady Emma had been seated and Sir Henry had poured himself a glass of sherry. He couldn't have failed! Sir Henry was one of the country's best barristers.

"It is like this." Sir Henry sat down in a chair by the fire across from his wife and the sentence was a weary sigh. "I went to see Lord Blackwell this afternoon. I had thought to contact him through his attorney but decided the direct approach in such a delicate matter best. He received me most graciously until he learned of my mission.

"At that point he turned on me like a cornered

cur, demanding I apologize for uttering such malicious gossip about his dead brother and Lady Blackwell. He went so far as to snatch up a poker from the hearth and brandish it in my direction before he realized what he was doing."

"Good heavens, my dear!" Lady Emma started. "I trust you weren't injured."

"Certainly not. Lord Blackwell may be hasty but he's no fool. The next instant he was apologizing and entreating me to have a seat and share a glass of port with him.

"Over that drink he told me his version of what happened that night five years ago." He paused and turned to Kate. "Come, child, don't stand there in the shadows. Take a seat here on the bench by the fire. This tale concerns you most of all."

"Thank you, sir." Kate accepted gladly. Her knees had grown weak and she felt she had much more of a disappointing nature yet to hear.

"It seems that five years ago a brilliant young doctor trained at Edinburgh University and newly returned from the battlefields of France was enlisted by the present Lord Blackwell's father who was in ill health to care for him and the people on his lands which, I might remark, are considerable. This young doctor named James Donnelly was reputedly one of the best that fine medical school had graduated.

"Dr. Donnelly had been serving the elder Lord Blackwell for several months when Lady Margaret Belfour, the fiancée of Paul, the eldest son of the house, came to stay. Her mother had died many years previous and with the death of her father she was left alone and impoverished due her parent's gambling debts. She and Paul were to be married that autumn.

"Lady Margaret was, according to Lord John Blackwell, the present master of the estate and her husband, a magnificently beautiful and vivacious woman who dressed in the height of fashion. Every style-conscious lady in London copied her coiffure, gowns, and bonnets. Moreover she sang like an angel and rode in the hunt like the best man in the field. In short she fascinated and charmed everyone she met...which unfortunately included Dr. James Donnelly."

Kate felt a sick feeling engulf her at Sir Henry's description of the woman who'd won and broken Hamish's heart. Images of herself washing his underwear, milking his cow, and plucking a partridge dashed into her mind and she felt shabby and crude. She gave herself an inward shake and picked up Sir Henry's story again.

"My dear..." Sir Henry turned to her, his face wrinkling. "Are you quite sure you want to hear all this?"

"I must know the truth, Sir Henry." She raised her gaze to meet his.

"My dear." Lady Emma reached out and put a hand over hers, her eyes deepening with sympathy.

"Well, it seems Lady Margaret became fascinated by the robust young doctor while Paul Blackwell preferred to share his time in gaming clubs and with ladies of doubtful virtue. The two conditions coinciding..." Sir Harry paused to take a sip of port.

"Dreadful man!" Lady Emma remarked sharply.

"My dear, she had accepted the betrothal freely and with full knowledge of the character of her betrothed. Whether she cared more for Paul Blackwell's ability to save her from a life of poverty than the man himself is a good question. At any rate, one evening Paul returned home early from a night of debauchery. He'd been drinking heavily and stumbled directly into his fiancée's rooms unannounced."

Again the barrister paused but this time he

glanced at Kate.

"And found Hamish...James with her." A sharp pain infected Kate's chest as she mouthed the words softly, her gaze falling to her hands clasped tightly in her lap.

"Yes. A fight ensued. When servants burst into the room, they found the doctor standing over Paul. He was lying on the stone hearth, dead."

"But surely Lady Margaret told them Hamish was simply defending himself against the attack of a jealous, drunken man!" Kate grasped at a straw of fact.

"Unfortunately she chose to tell quite another tale." Sir Henry shook his gray head. "She said the doctor had come to examine her for a sore throat and tried to force himself upon her. Dr. Donnelly, upon hearing the accusation, fled through a window. The following morning charges of rape and murder were laid against him and he became a fugitive."

"Lies, all lies!" Kate leaped to her feet, her eyes bright with unshed tears. "Hamish is a good, decent man!"

"My dear, please." Lady Emma stood and took the young woman by the shoulders. "I know this has all come as a great shock to you but sometimes we do not truly understand even those closest to us. Perhaps not rape but fornication with another man's fiancé and then murder...terrible offences, you must agree."

"It wasn't like that!" Kate cried. "He and Lady Margaret were lovers, I don't deny, but when Paul Blackwell burst in upon them, *he* attacked Hamish. In the struggle, Hamish pushed him away from him. Paul Blackwell stumbled and hit his head on the stone fireplace. He died instantly and accidentally. Lady Margaret witnessed all of it! She has only to tell the truth and Hamish will be free!"

"She's not about to do that." Sir Henry arose and

went to pour himself another glass of port. "She's now married to Lord John, the current master of the Blackwell estate. To admit to having been a willing lover to a doctor, a man she considered a servant on the estate, would be most disadvantageous for her."

"But did you see her? Did you talk to the lady herself?" Kate whirled to face Sir Henry desperately. "Perhaps if you talked to her..."

"My dear, that is quite impossible. Lady Margaret is ill. Her husband and doctors don't expect her to live more than a fortnight. Lord Blackwell is not about to allow anyone to question her about those horrendous events."

Kate paused, drew a deep breath, and thought hard.

"But don't you see," she continued finally. "It's all the more important that someone question her now, that she tells the truth before she takes it to the grave with her."

"Sir John will not allow anyone aside from family and necessary servants near her bedside." Sir Henry exhaled. "It's most regrettable. Your husband deserves to be cleared of these abominable charges. Fortunately he is deep in the colonies and, after all these years, it's unlikely he'll be discovered."

"But he's a gifted doctor! What if he wants to do more than work in the backwoods of North America? What if he wants to come back to England and practice here? He will never have that freedom of choice if Lady Margaret does not tell her story."

Sir Henry looked down into her distressed face and drew a deep breath. "I'm afraid I've done all I can in this matter. I'll finance your passage back to New Brunswick and you can go on with your life as if none of this ever happened. I think that's best."

"Please, no. At least not just yet." She stifled the shakiness in her voice. "Hamish saved my life. I want to do as much for him."

"But what can you possibly do, child?" Lady Emma came to take her hand. "Of course you're welcome to stay on with us as long as you choose but I don't really see how that will solve anything. If Harry couldn't convince Lord Blackwell to allow him an interview with his wife, what makes you think he'll permit you to conduct one?"

"Where there's a will, there's always a way." Kate squared her shoulders. "I am determined to find it."

"Of course. Take all the time in the world, my dear." Sir Henry leaned back in his chair with a sigh. "But perhaps you'd like to know James's...er...Hamish's background. I did glean most of it today from Lord Blackwell and reading between the lines, as it were, I think I got the gist of the truth. Are you interested or would you prefer he remain an intriguing mystery?"

"I should like to know." Kate sat down opposite him, ready to listen. "Please."

"Very well." Sir Henry took the glass of port Lady Emma handed him, waited until his wife was seated, then began.

"James Donnelly was the son of the gamekeeper on the Blackwell estate. His mother died when he was young and his father became disinterested in the boy. The young lad, however, showed an amazing ability to work with injured livestock. The old Lord Blackwell appreciated his cleverness and took the boy to be educated at the manor house with his own two sons...sons who I gather were a disappointment to him." He paused and sipped his port before continuing.

"When it came time to send the boys off to university, Lord Blackwell decided to send young James off to Edinburgh to become a doctor. He thought having a trained physician about the estate would be good for both man and beast."

"So that was where he picked up that faulty Highland brogue." Kate felt a smile tipping her lips.

"I assume so. He shared rooms with a Highlander. When he finished his studies, war was raging in France and he enlisted in the army. Lord Blackwell was at first furious, seeing it as wasting the money he'd spent on the lad's education. But when James returned, covered with glory for his bravery in treating troops at the front, he forgave him and welcomed him back to the estate as its physician. And the rest--" He looked meaningfully at Kate, "I believe you know."

"But what of his father? He must have been devastated when his son was accused of those heinous crimes on the very estate where he works."

"His father died when James was in the first year of his studies in Edinburgh." Sir Henry set his glass aside and looked over at her. "He's quite alone in the world."

"That is no longer the case." Kate got up and squared her shoulders. "I shall not rest until I see him a free man."

"Nor I." Lady Emma went to her side and slipped her arm about the younger woman's waist. "So you see, my dear, Dr. James Donnelly is as good as exonerated."

****

Two days later Kate returned to Sir Henry's house, her face bright. She handed her cape to the waiting maid and rushed into the morning room where Lady Emma sat answering correspondence.

"Good morning, my dear." She looked up from her writing, a smile brightening her face. "I trust you've enjoyed your morning outing. Did Hampton take you on a pleasant drive? I'm sorry I couldn't accompany you but, as you can see, letters must be answered, invitations accepted or declined."

"I understand, Emma." Kate strode across the

room, glanced out the window, then walked back again, pulling off her gloves as she moved.

"What is it, child?" Lady Emma swiveled on her chair to face the younger woman. "Please, come, sit by me before you wear a path in the carpet."

"Forgive me." Kate did as she was bidden, her face flushed and anxious. "I've had an eventful morning, one of which I fear you may not entirely approve. However, if the desired results of these past few hours are satisfactorily obtained, I will need not only your help but also all the daring and disdain for decorum you can muster."

"Good heavens, child! You're startling me. However--" She arose and walked to the window, her dress swaying gracefully over the carpet. "As you may already suspect, I'm not a woman to shy away from a bit of adventure." She swung back to face the woman who was watching her anxiously. "Life around here has been incredibly dull this past summer. I could do with a bit of excitement before we are forced to launch into the endless round of dinners and soirees of the Yuletide season. Come, tell me about this adventure upon which we are about to embark."

Chapter Eleven

"Lady Jane Fairchild to see Lady Blackwell." Lady Emma, enveloped in widow's weeds complete with long, face-concealing veil, thrust her card into the footman's hand and drew herself up haughtily. Behind her Kate, demurely arrayed in the drab gray of a lady's companion, clutched the case holding the all-important document. An elegant carriage drawn by a pair of matched grays waited at the curb.

"Lady Blackwell is unwell, Ma'am." The footman bowed to her. "She is not receiving visitors."

"She will see me." Lady Emma stepped boldly into the foyer of the country mansion and tapped her gold-tipped stick imperiously on the floor. "I am her oldest and dearest friend."

The footman paused as a tall, dignified-looking man in a perfectly fitted dark suit appeared out of a doorway to his left.

"What seems to be the problem, Sinclair?" he asked.

"This here lady--" The younger man lapsed into his street parlance, uncomfortable in the presence the new comer. "Says she's Lady Blackwell's best friend, Mr. Bordon, sir. She says, bein' as who she is, Lady Blackwell will be willin' ta see her."

"Bordon, is it?" Lady Emma stepped toward him, shoulders back, her nose in the air. "Well, Bordon, I insist you take me to my friend at once or, not only will Sir John hear of your belligerence, but I will also request your dismissal."

Bordon took the card they'd had especially

crafted for the occasion from Sinclair's hand and stared down at it. Kate held her breath.

"Lady Fairchild." He looked up and cast a deep bow. "I'm sure my lady will see you. I'll just go and check with her nurse-companion..."

"No need for that." Lady Emma tapped her stick again. "You'll show us the way and we'll decide the extent of our visit once we see the invalid."

"But my lady..."

"No buts about it. Lead on, my good man."

The butler hesitated, then with a resigned sigh, turned toward the wide expanse of stairs leading to a gallery above them. "Follow me, please, my lady." He paused half way up as Kate began to follow. "Your maid may wait for you in the kitchen. Sinclair will show her the way."

"Certainly not! I'd be lost without my MacDonald. Now make haste. I understand Lady Blackwell's days are numbered."

****

The vast room furnished with large, dark pieces made the person laying in the wide bed appear startlingly small. As Kate and Lady Emma entered, a woman wearing a black dress and white apron got up from a chair by the bed and stepped forward.

"What is the meaning of this, Bordon?" she hissed. Her graying hair caught back into a bun with not a single curl or loose strand accentuated a stern, sallow face.

"This is Lady Jane Fairchild, Lady Margaret's girlhood friend. She insisted..."

"Who is it, Wilkins?" A barely audible voice asked from the bed. It broke off in a fit of coughing.

"Now see what you've done!" The woman turned and hurried back to her charge. "No one, my lady," she said stooping to raise her patient and offer her a drink. "They're leaving. Nothing to trouble yourself about."

"No!" Lady Margaret weakly thrust the cup aside. "I heard Lady Fairchild's name. Jane, is that you? Come closer that I might see you."

Kate felt a great lump of fear rise in her throat as Lady Emma adjusted her veil and advanced to the bed.

"Jane!" A trembling, wasted hand stretched out and Lady Emma caught it in her black gloved one. "It's been years. I shall..." Again a short bout of coughing before she was able to continue. "Never forget the fun we had as girls running wild about your father's estate, riding your horses..."

Staring down at the woman in the bed, Kate found the jealously she'd felt melting like snow in the sun. It was hard to imagine the sad bit of skin-covered bones laying before her, dark hair laced with gray, as a beautiful, vibrant woman who'd inspired men to fight over her; indeed, to die for her.

"Maggie, how it grieves me to see you thus." Lady Emma spoke in a whisper that could have been almost anyone's voice. "I've wanted to come but Jeffrey has been ill. He passed away last month."

"I didn't know," the labored voice rasped. "No one tells me anything anymore. Afraid of upsetting me. As if one more awful fact could matter. It won't be long before I join your Jeffrey."

"No, Maggie, never say that." Lady Emma encased the skeletal hand between hers. "But I must speak to you alone on a matter of great importance. Will you allow it?"

"It must be of great importance to bring you all this way after so many years. Wilkins, Bordon, leave us and take Lady Jane's servant with you. We will speak in private."

"If you please, Maggie I would prefer that Kate stay with us. Shortly you'll understand why."

"Very well. Wilkins, shut the door after the pair of you. And mind you keep your ears away from the panel."

After the servants had gone, Lady Emma slowly raised her veil. The woman in the bed emitted a sharp gasp.

"You're not Jane Fairchild!" she breathed and struggled to reach the bell rope to summon the servants.

"Please." Lady Emma put out a restraining hand and stopped her efforts. "No, I'm not. I am Lady Emma Dunn. My husband is the famous barrister Sir Henry Dunn. And this--" She turned to indicate Kate, "--Is Mrs. James Donnelly."

"James' wife?" Brown eyes blinked wide. "James is alive and married...to this girl?"

"Yes. They were married in the colonies. They love each other very much," Lady Emma said and Kate felt a twinge of shame. She didn't know that Hamish loved her and they definitely weren't married. "Now they need your help. You must give us your sworn statement of what happened on the night Paul Blackwell died. You must tell the truth...that James Donnelly never forced himself on you, that you were his willing lover and that Paul Blackwell met his death as the result of a fall, an unfortunate accident."

"Are you mad!" Gasping in outrage, Lady Margaret rolled her head from side to side. "I am Lady Margaret Blackwell, a respected member of society. I will not admit to having taken as a lover a rude young army doctor fresh from the battle fields of France! What will John think? What will he do?"

"Very little at this point." Lady Emma signaled Kate and she drew a paper and writing materials from the bag she carried. Her hands trembled. What would happen if Lady Emma failed to bring off the plan they'd formulated? Would they perhaps be arrested for impersonation, for gaining entrance to a great house by fraud? Would even Sir Henry's considerable skills be enough to save them?

"Lady Margaret, it's no secret you've but a short time to live. Taking the truth about what happened all those years ago to the grave will not profit you. We don't wish to create a public scandal, simply make it possible for James to come out of hiding. I believe you once loved him very much." Lady Emma's voice became soft and cajoling. "If you did, I beg you, please, please do this thing which means so much to him now. We've written out the course of events as they truly occurred that fateful night. I will read them to you. Then all that is required is that you sign before witnesses...Kate, myself and... your nurse. I should like to have a truly impartial witness. She does not have to read the document, only say she saw you sign it."

"James." His name was a sigh as she closed her eyes, a faint smile on her pale lips. "Is he still as handsome as ever? Does he still ride like the wind? And are his eyes as blue as a summer's sky? Does he still sing a stirring tenor?"

"Yes, all those things." Kate stepped forward and spoke softly. "And he remembers you most fondly. You'll always be his first love." She felt impelled to offer the sick woman at least a bit of kindness even if she suspected it was a lie.

"Does he indeed?" She opened her eyes and Kate was startled as she saw a flash of something hard and cold snap into them as her smile metamorphosed into sneer.

"And does he still ape a Highland brogue as well as ever?" She further startled Kate by chuckling hoarsely. "Ah, the fun we had, pretending he was a marauding Scottish chieftain and I, an innocent English maid." She chuckled again, a sound that held more menace than mirth, then broke off into another fit of coughing. When she regained control of herself she wiggled bone-thin fingers feebly toward the document.

"Oh, very well. Give it here. I'll sign. James and I had some good times together...in this very bed, as a matter of fact. Remember that, my girl, each time he makes love to you. As he thrills and excites you, remember who tutored a crude young doctor in the arts of love." Her tone changed abruptly. "Call Wilkins back inside and let us get to the business of it. Bring Bordon as well." She broke into a fit of coughing.

When she finally regained herself, her wasted countenance twisted into an expression of such malice Kate felt her breath catch. "It will be good for John to know," she wheezed. "He's been a failure as a husband and has made my life unbearable with his demands for rules and decorum. I'd like him to know he was outclassed long before our wedding night by a man as virile and earthy as he is weak and impotent."

A few moments later as her nurse supported her and a disgruntled butler looked on, she took the proffered pen and scratched a straggling signature across the bottom of the document they'd brought. Kate breathed a sigh of relief when she'd finished and Wilkins was adding her name to it.

What a vindictive woman, she thought, looking down at the dying Lady Margaret Blackwell. She's never known true love in her life or she would not now be going to her grave with bitterness as her only companion. Hamish had been fortunate he'd never married her no matter how besotted he'd been with her beauty and vitality. But would he ever be able to put her memory aside and look at Kate with love?

****

"Thank you, Lady Margaret." Kate, the signed document in her hand, moved to the side of the bed as Lady Emma, Wilkins, and Bordon turned away and spoke softly, sincerely. "This means a great deal to Hamish and me."

"Hamish!" she scoffed. "How like James to choose a barbaric name as an alias. You say you live on a backwoods farm?"

"Yes, my lady. He farms and works as a physician. He's known as the Hermit Healer."

"So he's achieved his dream, has he!" she struggled for breath. "He always wanted to work among the peasants. Well, now he can wallow for the rest of his life among them with a serving wench as his companion. Get out of my sight, girl! Do you think I want James' whore to be the last person I cast my eyes upon in this life!"

She began to cough and choke. Wilkins thrust Kate aside and bent over her patient.

"Come, Kate. We've achieved our purpose." Lady Emma took Kate by an arm and led her out of the sick room. "There's nothing we can do for the woman except leave her in peace. At least we've cleared her conscience."

****

"I hope that wasn't too distressing for you, Kate." Lady Emma turned to her as they drove away from Blackwell Hall.

"If you mean was I distressed by Lady Margaret's descriptions and comments about how she and Hamish made love, the answer is yes." Kate let a small, sardonic smile kink her lips. "I take comfort in the fact that even if Lady Margaret were not grievously ill, he'd never love or desire her again. She betrayed him much too cruelly and completely."

"So you will be returning to him without prejudice?" Lady Emma smiled. "Good. We must all forgive our husbands their foolish pasts. Do you know Harry once had a mistress who seduced him out of a diamond tiara and one of his best horses? And he's reputedly London's most clever barrister!

"That," she continued with a sly smile. "Was, of

course, before he met me and became capable of recognizing a good woman. Faster, Hampton!" Chuckling, she tapped on the roof of the carriage. "We must get home and book a passage to New Brunswick immediately!"

****

Alone in his cabin in New Brunswick, Dr. James Donnelly sat at the plank table, his hand clutched about a flask of whiskey. He'd been sipping at it for an hour and was beginning to feel it in his limbs as a languidness spread over him.

"Perhaps we'll just take a nap, Pilot." He looked down at the dog that stared up at him. "I know we've farming to do but I've no desire to get at it. Maybe later..."

"Mr. MacDonald, Mr. MacDonald!" He started as he heard a horse galloping up to the cabin. A moment later the door burst open and the young man who'd mentioned his expectant wife in tavern several weeks earlier burst inside. "It's Abby, me wife, sir! It's her time. Ye've got ta come! It's our first and I'm afeart!"

"Cannae ye fetch old Jenny? She did midwifin' afore I arrived." He tried to think logically through the whiskey haze. He wasn't in any condition to deliver a child.

"She's too auld now. Her hands shake somethin' fierce. Please, Mr. MacDonald!"

Hamish thought a moment, then looked up at the desperate lad before him.

"Do ye know how ta make coffee...strong, black, hot coffee?" he asked.

"Aye. I was cook's boy on a ship afore I settled here."

"Then ye'd best get ta it while I clean meself up." Hamish got unsteadily to his feet. "I'll chust be takin' a quick wash in the pond while you brew it up." He grabbed a shirt from a peg on the wall, then strode toward the door. "And remember, make it so strong a spoon will stand in it, ye hear?"

****

At the pond he stripped and waded into the cold water. He yelped and gathered up handfuls to splash over his face and head as he went deeper until he could no longer touch bottom and had to tread water. An image of Kate bathing in this same pond filled his mind and a great moan escaped him. Where was she, that creature from the sea, the mermaid he'd carried back to his cabin all those weeks ago, the woman he'd come to love?

For a few moments he swam in circles, sometimes ducking his head beneath the surface in an effort to clear away the whiskey cloud, trying to re-centre himself. He couldn't continue like this, seeking oblivion in drink night after night to ease the pain. He'd been a fool and allowed himself to lose the best thing that had ever come into his life; that didn't mean he had a right to deny his services to his community.

He, Hamish MacDonald nee James Donnelly, had to regain control of himself and get back to work, no matter how his heart ached.

With a single long stroke he touched bottom, stood up, and waded ashore. He'd come to this country as Hamish MacDonald, a man who'd become known as the Hermit Healer and that's exactly what he would be once again. He would not allow drink to get the better of him when he had a job to do.

As he pulled clothes on he knew one thing for certain. No woman would ever again mean to him what his Kate did.

****

"You did what?" Sir Henry goggled at the pair as Lady Emma and Kate faced him in his library late that afternoon. "Dear God, Emma, do you not realize in what jeopardy you placed yourself and this girl?

Do you not realize the repercussions of your mad scheme! I'm amazed Sir John Blackwell isn't pounding at our door this very minute with a constable!"

"I doubt you have anything to fear, my dear." Lady Emma touched the paper he was holding in his hands. "If you were forced to produce this document, Lord Blackwell would face far greater embarrassment than you."

"But impersonating Lady Jane Fairchild..."

"Simply to gain access. Once we were in Lady Margaret's presence, I revealed our true identity."

"Dear, dear." Sir Henry sat down in his favorite chair by the fire, adjusted his spectacles on his nose, and began to peruse the document. "It all seems in perfect order," he commented a few minutes later looking up at the pair standing before him. "I had no idea, Emma, that you'd taken sufficient interest in my law books as to be capable of formulating such a statement."

"I haven't. Your clerk Mr. Witherspoon obliged us. You really must recompense him for his diligent work, my dear." Lady Emma smiled coyly at her husband.

"You corrupted my clerk! Woman, are there no lengths to which you will not go to achieve your desired ends?"

"Not when love is involved, my darling." Lady Emma moved to stand behind his chair and slip her arms about his neck.

"Hrumph!" Sir Henry cleared his throat and pretended to be unaffected by his wife's actions. "Well, I guess I can excuse you this one time. But promise me, Emma, you will never do anything of the kind again."

"Oh, you are too harsh surely, my love." Lady Emma straightened up and swirled around to stand before him. "Would you have me become as dull as all those boring women with whom I'm forced to socialize on your behalf? Or would you prefer me to remain the dashing, daring woman you fell in love with and married?" She cast him a devilishly teasing glance beneath lowered lashes.

After a slight pause, he burst out laughing. "Oh, the latter of course. Although I fear someday your dashing and daring will see us both transported."

"Very well." Lady Emma clapped her hands. "Now we must secure passage for Kate on the first available ship to New Brunswick. She must take this all-important document to her beloved. Come, come, Henry, make haste. This is no time to doze by your fire."

****

"Ye've made a great mistake, laddie."

"What?" Hamish MacDonald jerked awake on the hard chair and blinked the sleep from his eyes as he looked down at his patient laying on the rough bed beside him.

"I said ye've made a huge mistake." The old man's words were a rasping whisper but Hamish knew exactly what he'd said.

"In what way, Callum?" he asked. "I've tried ta do me best for ye."

"Aye, that ye have, lad, but it's not me or me care I'm talkin' about. It's..." He paused to catch his failing breath.

"Rest, Callum. If me mistake doesn't involve yer care, it can be of little importance at the moment." Hamish placed a cool, wet cloth on the old man's fevered forehead and spoke softly.

"It does matter...and most of all, at this moment. Hamish, you and I both know I won't have many more."

"Verrae well, Callum. If ye must."

"It's about the wee lass, yer wee lassie, the one what got taken away." The old man looked up at

Hamish through watery, faded blue eyes. "Ye've got ta go after her, Hamish, and no mistake about it. If ye donnae…"

He was gasping and Hamish longed to make him stop but he knew such an attempt would only distress the dying old man further.

"If ye donnae, ye'll end up like me…a lonely old bachelor who's wasted his life and who'll leave no one to mourn him or carry on once he's gone. I know. I once let a lass leave this farm many years ago. We had a foolish quarrel, I cannae even remember what it was about. But she left and took a ship back ta Scotland. Hamish, that ship sank and took with it the woman I loved with all me heart. If I'd only gone after her, stopped her afore she could board that ship…"

He was breathing hard now, his words barely audible.

"But Kate was kidnapped, abducted."

"Such facts donnae matter, laddie." The old man caught at Hamish's hand imploringly. "All that matters is that ye git her back. Git…her…back…"

His eyes closed and, with a sigh, he sank into his pillow. Hamish waited, then felt for the pulse he knew he wouldn't find.

Reverently he drew the blanket over the old man's wrinkled face and arose. He ached from his long vigil at Callum MacLean's bedside less than two hours after he'd delivered Abby Jennings of a lovely baby girl but he didn't for a moment regret either duty. The old man had no family and, due his cantankerous nature, few friends. No one had known why the old Scotsman had chosen to hermit himself away on his dilapidated farm, why he always seemed so out of sorts. Now Hamish knew.

He walked outside into the dawn of a new day and paused on the sagging verandah to suck in a lungful of fresh, clear air and stretch some of the stiffness from his joints. It had been a long night of struggling to save the life of the old man inside the crude log structure behind him. He clutched a porch post, threw back his head, and bellowed out the frustration of his loss, of his sense of failure.

Then, exhausted he sank down onto the steps, clutching his head in his hands. He knew he couldn't save every life. Callum MacLean had been old and ill and weak but it was hard to bear the loss alone.

He looked back at the cabin. Callum MacLean had been a curmudgeon who'd lived out his life in isolated bitterness. Was that what he, Dr. James Donnelly, wanted for himself?

Slowly, sliding over him alike a soft, gentle shadow, the answer came. He'd go to England and find her. No risk was too great if it could quell the gut-wrenching ache in his heart and soul. Better to die now than face long, empty years without his Kate, the woman who held his heart and happiness in her hand.

He buried Callum Maclean behind his cabin, said a prayer over him, then went to feed the dead man's hens and shabby old horse. He'd come back later and take the animals to the Currie farm.

With renewed vigor, he mounted the Lad who'd been waiting patiently at the hitching post. A half hour later he galloped into Pine and left the stallion in Patty's care at the livery stable, then he strode up the street to find George Loggie just opening up his mercantile.

"Tell me everything you can remember about Gerard Elliot," he demanded. "Every single word he uttered."

****

Two days later Hamish drew a deep breath and headed up the gangplank of a timber drougher bound for England. Pilot, on a leash, trotted by his side.

****

"Good-bye, my dear." Lady Emma kissed Kate lightly on both cheeks, then waved farewell as the younger woman climbed into the carriage. The driver clucked to the horses and they trotted off toward the docks and the ship waiting to take her back to New Brunswick.

Chapter Twelve

Hamish stood at the rail and watched the irregular gray line that was land growing thicker on the horizon. Within the day, he'd be landing in Portsmouth and before that time, crucial decisions had to be made. Would he search for Kate hirsute as he was or risk removing at least a part of the growth? With his hair and beard trimmed he would garner more respect than arrayed as the beast he presently appeared. But would someone recognize him? Hardly likely after five years. Surely his alleged crime had been largely forgotten and people were not going about the streets searching for the infamous Dr. James Donnelly.

"A bit of trim, Pilot," he said turning to the dog by his side. "Yes, definitely a trim."

****

The next morning Hamish was in Newmarket at Young's Mews, the stable Gerard Elliot had mentioned to George Loggie. The head groom followed the well-dressed, bearded man about, watching as he critically looked over first one horse, then another.

"What exactly would ye be lookin' for, sir?" he inquired finally. "Perhaps I can assist you by pointin' out a likely one."

"I've been told one Mr. Gerard Elliot who stables a pair of fillies here is about to acquire an excellent stud. I'm looking for such an animal myself. I thought we might do business. Do you know when Mr. Elliot is due to visit his mares?"

"Why, sir, he should be along any minute if ye've a mind to wait." The groom flashed a leering grin. "But he didn't get that stallion ye're referrin' to. Seems the deal he had with Sir William Sheffield fell through. Now all he's got to do his breedin' is old Jack here." He pointed to a box stall nearby. "Aye, he was right fit to be tied when he come back without that stud."

"This deal...do you know anything about it?" Hamish bent and examined a hoof.

"Aye. Mr. Elliot was to fetch back Sir William's daughter, her that was supposed lost in a shipwreck off North America somewhere." The groom paused and chuckled. "Seems as how Mr. Elliot fetched back the wrong young lady. Sir William was right peeved, from all reports. Threatened Mr. Elliot for his mistake. I get all the latest gossip from Sheffield Hall, sir, seein' as my Becky is in service at Sir William's estate."

"And just who was the young lady Mr. Elliot fetched in error?" Hamish felt his heart beat rising to a pounding tattoo.

"Oh, it were Rose Jones, Lady Kathryn's lady's maid." The groom chuckled, shaking his grizzled head. "Becky knows her well. Said Rose was always good at apin' her betters. Small wonder Mr. Elliot was fooled. That Rose Jones is a real actress, my Becky says."

"Oh, aye?" Hamish felt a grin tugging at his lips. "Quite a character, is this Mistress Rose Jones?"

"For certain sure, sir. Before Sir William shipped her off to Jamaica with his daughter who was to marry a planter on that island, Rose could mimic with the best of 'em what was professionals on the stage my Becky declared."

"And would your Becky know what became of the young lady Mr. Elliot brought back by mistake?" Hamish put aside his amusement and looked squarely at the groom.

"Aye." The man suddenly put off by the intensity of Hamish's penetrating stare backed off a step. "Sir William sent her off...with his barrister, Sir Henry Dunn. Becky says Sir William was afeard the girl would say she'd been kidnapped on his orders."

"Thank you." Hamish dug into a pocket and took coins. "Here, my good man. Share these with your Becky. Now, if you don't mind, I'll just take a seat over there and wait for Mr. Elliot to arrive."

****

"I wish to see Sir Henry Dunn." Hamish stood on the doorstep of the London manor and faced the austere butler with a look that brooked no denial.

"Sir Henry is not in residence at the moment, sir." Jenkins drew himself haughtily up to his full height and faced the strange newcomer who looked like a wild man wearing the well-tailored clothing of an excellent London haberdashery. "Perhaps if you leave your card..."

"Is the carriage here yet, Jenkins?" Lady Emma came down the stairs into the foyer, concentrating on pulling on her gloves. When she looked up and saw the big, bearded man standing on the threshold she stopped short.

"Dr. Donnelly?"

"Whom do I have the honor of addressing, madam?" He avoided her question.

"Lady Emma Dunn, wife of Sir Henry Dunn and a dear friend of one truly amazing woman named Kate MacDonald." She advanced to the bottom of the staircase. "I ask again, are you Dr. James Donnelly, known in the colonies as Hamish MacDonald the Hermit Healer?"

"Yes." He risked the admission.

"Come in, Doctor." Lady Emma turned and headed into a room to the left of the staircase. "Jenkins, cancel the carriage. Ask Manners to bring

219

tea into the drawing room. Come along, Doctor, we have much to discuss."

He followed her across the elegant foyer and into a room furnished in the height of taste.

"A fine home, Lady Emma," he commented looking about.

"Thank you. I decorated it after I married Harry. He had a bachelor's taste and interest in living quarters. Do sit down, Doctor," she continued seating herself by the window. "I believe we have much to discuss."

****

A half hour later when Lady Emma, over tea, had finished telling Hamish the story of Kate's adventures he leaned back in the comfortable wing chair by the fire and emitted a soft groan.

"So I've missed her."

"She wanted to make haste back to New Brunswick. She longed to inform you that charges against you no longer exist." Lady Emma smiled at his impatience. "Don't be distressed. I'm sure my husband can secure passage for you on the next ship. He has connections in the shipping community."

"I will be grateful. And even more so if you'd do me another service."

"If I can, Doctor." Lady Emma looked across at him.

"I have something that belonged to the late and genuine Lady Kathryn Sheffield. At my lodgings I have a packet that contains her jewels rescued from the Avon Queen. I'd planned to return them myself and tell her father his daughter would have no further use for them. However, now that I've been delighted to hear Kate isn't Lady Kathryn, I'm wondering if either you or your husband would take them to him for me. I have a small piece of work I must complete before I leave England and time is of the essence. I don't want Kate to get too far ahead of me."

"Certainly. I'm sure Harry will be glad to do you the service. He is Sir William's barrister so it will be no imposition."

"Thank you. Now I must set about the task I mentioned. If you'll excuse me, Lady Emma, I'll attend to it immediately."

****

The following morning Gerard Elliot woke with a raging headache to the rocking motion of a ship rolling over the waves. Darkness surrounded him and as his head began to clear he realized he was in the hold of a vessel at sea. Stumbling to his feet, he groped for an exit but encountered only the solid planking of a ship's hull.

Desperate, he yelled. The force made his head pound even more furiously and he slumped to the floor and vomited. *Shanghaied*, he thought as he retched. But when and why?

When he'd managed to regain control of himself, he drew a deep breath and tried to recall how he'd come to be in such a deplorable situation. The last he remembered was drinking in a Newmarket ale house with a big brute of man with a thick, dark beard and long curling hair. He'd been well-dressed and generous in purchasing ale. The man had claimed to be a horse dealer, someone who could help him get a magnificent stud newly arrived from Ireland. Gerard Elliot vaguely recalled trying to strike a deal for this wonderful stallion and then nothing. Until he woke up in this dank, dark hole.

He did not grasp the irony of he himself being transported closely on the heels of his abduction of the woman he'd believed to be Lady Kathryn Sheffield. He would never associate the horse dealer in the ale house with the man who'd been accepted as her husband in New Brunswick.

****

"Mrs. MacDonald!" George Loggie looked up from measuring flour into bags, his eyes widening. "The Lord be praised! I feared we'd never see you again. Where have you been? How did you manage to come back to us? Are you well?"

"It's a long story." She smiled at him. "You're looking well, Mr. Loggie."

"And you also, Missus." The shop keeper's surprise was slowly diminishing but he continued to stare at her in amazement.

"Mr. Loggie, I wonder if I could ask you a great favor?" She continued to smile as she approached the counter and laid her reticule upon it.

"Anything, Mrs. MacDonald, anything."

"Could you find someone to drive me out to our farm? I want to get home as soon as possible."

"Of course, only..." His voice trailed off for a moment, then resumed, "Well, you see, Mrs. MacDonald, ma'am, Hamish isn't there. He left last week for England."

Kate felt as if she'd been struck by a stone. "Are you quite sure, Mr. Loggie? Hamish had always said he'd never return to the Old Country."

"I'm sure. He went searching for you."

"For me?"

"He's a man in love, Mrs. MacDonald." George Loggie smiled. "There isn't an ocean too wide or deep to keep a man with the look of determination I saw on his face from finding the woman of his heart."

He loves me. The words burst like a song in her heart.

"Will you still be wanting that drive out to the farm?" The shopkeeper brought her out of her joyous thoughts. "Your schoolhouse is still available or I'm sure the MacKenzies would be happy to offer you hospitality."

"Thank you but I'll go out to the farm," she said. "I've come home. I'll wait for Hamish there."

"I'll take you, Mrs. MacDonald." Leam Fraser stepped into the store in time to hear the last exchanges. "But perhaps you'd best come back to our farm for the night. Hamish has been gone for nearly a month. I fear your house may have run to neglect."

"A bit of dust and a few cobwebs won't deter me, Mr. Fraser. I just want to lie in our own bed tonight."

"Well, of course you do." George Loggie gave the younger man a nod. "You've had a long ocean voyage and after such, there's no place quite like home. Leam, collect Mrs. MacDonald's luggage from the dock and then see her safely out to her farm, that's a good lad."

****

Kate stood on the verandah and waved good-bye as Leam and his wagon disappeared into the gathering autumn twilight. Then, with a sigh, she turned back into the silent house. Leam had lighted a fire on the hearth and checked all the outbuildings for tramps or intruders. He'd departed promising as she'd requested to have the Currie brothers bring Hamish's animals back in the morning. But tonight she was alone in the silence with only her memories and hope to sustain her.

She looked at the narrow bed against the back wall she'd occupied on first arriving at the cabin. Its rumpled covers told her it been recently slept in. Had he felt lonely in their bedroom? She ran a hand over the crumpled pillow and smiled a little sadly.

She lighted a candle, placed it inside a lantern, and made her way into the bedroom. The portmanteau supplied by Lady Emma containing the few items of clothing she'd collected during her brief stay at Sir Harry's home stood beside the big, feather-mattressed bed, the same big feather-mattressed bed where she'd lain with Hamish, where she'd enjoyed the most wonderful night of her life, where she'd discovered she loved the man she'd once termed a beast with all her heart and soul.

It had remained exactly as she'd left it. Her surmise gained veracity about his sleeping in the outer room.

As she placed the lantern on the chest of drawers he'd bought for her, its light fell on her trunk shoved into a corner. The last time she'd seen it, it had been in her quarters at the schoolhouse. Hamish must have fetched it back to the farm after her abduction.

She felt her heartbeat increase as she ran a hand over its battered top. He had intended for her to return to the farm. At least, he must have hoped she would.

Another thought struck her. Hastily she raised the lid and knelt to inspect its contents. One glance assured her nothing had been touched. No one, especially not a man, could have replaced everything exactly as she'd left it. He'd respected her privacy as she hadn't respected his.

She closed the lid, a hot flush suffusing her cheeks. Just more evidence that he was a gentleman of honor and she was no lady.

And now he'd gone back to England. At first she'd been ready to accept George Loggie's explanation that Hamish had gone to find her. Now doubts began to crowd into her mind.

The storekeeper had no idea about Hamish's troubled past. Perhaps he'd gone to clear his name so that he might be able to live there once again. He couldn't have known Lady Margaret was dying. Perhaps he'd hoped to renew their relationship once he'd freed himself of criminal charges.

She heaved a great sigh as she began to undress for bed. Her only consolation came from the fact that he would not now be risking his life.

But what if he decided that he would prefer to

resume practice in England even though Lady Margaret would no longer be there for him? What if he were weary of being a backwoods healer and farmer?

She placed the lantern on the dresser and sank down on the edge of the bed. If he never came back, would she be capable of running this farm on her own? Without passage money to England, she would have to try. If she failed she could always go back to teaching school.

****

Andrew and Neil Currie brought the cow, her calf, the team of Clydesdales, the black stallion, and the chickens back to the farm in the morning. They also brought a pretty little sorrel mare with a white star on her face.

"Hamish's team and the Lad aren't suited for a lady," Neil explained after he'd turned the animal lose in the pasture. "But you'll be needing a good little horse to pull the buggy, and ride, so we brought Fancy. She's too light for work around our farm. I can't think why I bought her in the first place." He avoided Kate's eyes and she was struck by the suspicion the young man might have purchased the lovely little animal with the idea of giving it to her. "I named her Fancy because I fancied her."

He looked meaningfully at Kate.

"And this here--" He broke the mood and strode to the wagon to gather up a small, squirming black creature from behind the seat. "Is Pilot's son from that litter he sired at our farm. I reckon he'll turn out to be every bit as good a dog as his father. He'll keep you company. Hamish took Pilot with him."

"Thank you." Kate felt overwhelmed by the young man's generosity, disturbed by his obvious admiration. "I'll pay you for these animals just as soon as I get on my feet."

"That you will not, Mrs. MacDonald." Neil's

words and expression brooked no further argument. "We've been paid many times over by Hamish through the fine work he's done for our families over the years. Whatever we can give you will never half repay his work."

"That's correct." Andrew Currie returned from putting the cow and her calf out into the pasture. "And we'll be over regular as clockwork to help out." Then, as he saw Kate's belligerent expression, hastened on, "But just until you get on your feet, mind."

"And Hamish comes back." She spoke with more conviction than she felt.

"Yes, until Hamish comes back." The two men exchanged glances, then Andrew turned and, leading the Clydesdales, went into the barn.

Neil started to follow his brother, then hesitated and turned back to Kate.

"Mrs. MacDonald?" He looked at her, then quickly lowered his gaze to his boots.

"Yes?" She smiled.

"If there's ever anything *I* can do..." A flush spread over his freckled face.

"Thank you, Neil." She spoke gently, understanding. "That's kind of you."

"I mean, if Hamish doesn't come back..." He managed to meet her gaze straightforwardly.

"He will," she replied softly. "He has to. I love him, Neil."

"Yes, ma'am." The two words reeked with disappointment as he turned to follow his brother into the barn.

She watched him disappear inside the building. Raised as she'd been on an English tenant farm, she'd make a suitable wife for a good, steady country lad such as Neil Currie.

With a sigh, Kate stepped inside the cabin, closed the door and leaned against it. As she look around the cold, deserted room, she wondered if Hamish or James or whatever he chose to call himself, freed of the charges against him, would choose another, someone more suited to his social class.

Her heart feeling like a stone, she went to the hearth and began to lay kindling inside its cold entrance. She remembered watching him stripped to the waist, his muscular body glistening with sweat as he'd swung the ax with a smooth, rhythmic motion and an ease that emphasized his virility and power one hot June day.

She gave a sharp mental shake and returned to her task. She'd never told him she wasn't a lady. Perhaps he wouldn't learn the truth in England and would return still under that misapprehension.

She'd have to tell him the truth and hope and pray that Dr. James Donnelly would love her enough to forgive her.

****

Kate was endeavoring to saddle the mare the next morning when the puppy she'd named Jet began to bark. Turning she saw Marie emerging from behind the cabin. She walked slowly, her distended belly stretching her buckskin dress.

"Healer's woman." She spoke carefully. "It is good to see you returned."

"Thank you, Marie. It is good to be back." Kate came around the back of the mare and smiled at the native woman. "You're learning English and very nicely. You'll have to teach me your language now that I've come back to stay."

"You are having trouble with the horse?" Marie asked looking at the saddle askew on the animal's back.

"It's been some time since I saddled a horse," she admitted. "And Fancy is not cooperating."

"Let me help." Marie moved carefully to the

animal's head and began to talk softly to her in her own tongue.

Almost instantly the mare quieted and stood still.

"Now," Marie instructed holding the animal lightly by the bridle.

Cautiously Kate stepped forward, straightened the saddle, and drew the girth tight.

"Thank you, Marie," she breathed stepping back. "You must teach me your secret for quieting her."

"Speak softly, rub her neck so," she demonstrated. Suddenly she clutched her middle, her face contracting.

"Marie, what is it?" Kate was instantly by her side, her arm about her.

"My little one. I fear it comes early." She held her belly and grimaced. "That is why I came to this farm. I knew something was wrong. I hoped the Healer would have returned. I do not want my husband to know I am not carrying his child well. I do not want to lose the son of my husband."

"Come." Kate urged her toward the cabin. "I am the healer's wife. Perhaps I can help."

****

As Marie lay on the bed in the cabin, Kate discovered the truth. Another breech birth.

"Your time has come early, has it not?" she asked the sweating, stoic woman. "You are not due for several weeks?"

She nodded. "Please, I do not want to lose the child of my husband."

"I'll do all that I can." Kate rolled up her sleeves. "First I must fetch water from the well."

****

As evening descended over the little wilderness farm, Kate washed her arms and hands. Then she rolled down her sleeves and smiled at Marie and her twin boys ensconced in the bed where once she'd spent that glorious night with Hamish.

"Thank you, healer's wife." Marie smiled up at her. "Without you, I would have died. My husband's sons would have died. We owe you a great debt."

"You've already paid me more than my fair share, Marie." She smiled down at her. "You were the first woman to offer me friendship in this new land, the first to bring me presents."

"Woman, what has...?" Kate swung to see Paul standing in the bedroom door, musket in hand. Then he saw Marie, a baby in each of her arms, and his eyes goggled.

"Woman." His voice softened as he moved to the bed and knelt beside the trio. "Woman, what have you done?"

"I have given you two sons, my husband," she beamed up at him as he gently lowered first one, then the other bit of blankets that held them to look upon each of them. "The healer's wife saved both them and me from death."

He looked up at Kate, his expression still incredulous. "You made this miracle?"

"You and Marie made the miracle," she smiled. "I only helped it to its conclusion. Now I'll leave you alone. I'm sure you want to spend the night with your family, Paul."

She left the bedroom closing the door behind her.

****

Bessie the cow wasn't cooperating. She swished her tail and shifted her hind quarters in a slow, deliberate manner that was annoying Kate to the bone. She had so much farm work to do. She didn't have time to waste with a belligerent cow.

"Hold still, Bess, there's a good girl." She tried to sooth the restless bovine. "You'll be sorry if you don't let me take your milk."

"Slow and easy, lass, slow and easy."

Kate swung to see a tall, handsome, fashionably dressed man standing in silhouette in the sunlight streaming in through the open barn door. It couldn't be. But it had to be. That voice could belong to no other. Her heart leapt with such joy she thought for a moment she'd lose consciousness.

As she sat mesmerized on her milking stool he advanced into the barn's shadowy interior. His clean shaven face was one of the handsomest she'd ever seen, his black curling hair fashionably cut about his ears. He wore an elegant riding costume and his boots gleamed with polish. The only things familiar about him were his faulty Highland brogue and his blue eyes, those wonderful blue eyes that could see right down into her soul. Beside him the big, black dog pranced on his leash, whining in joy.

"Hamish?" The word was an incredulous whisper. "Hamish MacDonald?"

"Aye, Hamish MacDonald, the Hermit Healer, and yer intended…if ye'll have me."

"Oh, Hamish!" Gazing at him in awe-struck disbelief, she rose slowly to her feet.

"Ah, lass, donnae just stand there gapin'. Come ta me. Ya've already saved me life. Now come and save my soul." His words shifted back to English inflection as he held out his arms.

"Hamish." His name was a soft breath as she ran into his embrace. His appearance might be that of a stranger but his arms, his words, his eyes were those of the man she loved.

"Welcome home, Healer." Paul was grinning as he stepped into the barn and extended his hand.

"Thank ye." Hamish released Pilot but kept his left arm about Kate as he accepted his friend's greeting and returned to the accent by which he was known in this country. "It iss verrae guid ta be here."

"You can banish that oh-so poor Highland

accent," Kate teased as she fended off Pilot's overjoyed greeting. "You never were verrae guid at it anyway."

"Donnae mock me, woman," he chuckled. "I did me verrae best."

"She has done her very best for my family and me as well." Paul grinned at the couple. "She has helped Marie present me with a pair of fine sons."

"What!" Hamish looked down at her, his eyes widening. "What have you done now, woman?"

"Marie was visiting when she went into labor," Kate explained. "I discovered, thanks to your teaching, that the first was to be a breeched birth and set about to remedy it as you demonstrated with Lizzy. After that, all went well. Marie was wonderful."

"Good God, woman! You are a marvel. First you restore my reputation and good name and now you take over my duties as resident healer. What next!"

"How do you know...?" she began, eyes widening in surprise.

"I had a most informative interview with Lady Emma Dunn." He was grinning widely. "She told me of your escapade. It seems that in Lady Emma you encountered a woman as adventurous as yourself. Fortunately all went well and you both didn't end up in prison."

"I hardly think there was any danger of that, sir." She cocked her head to one side and gave him a sly smile. "I doubt that there's a law enforcement officer in the whole of England who'd lay hands on Lady Emma Dunn."

"Still you took a great risk on my behalf and now I'm asking you take another."

"I've no idea what you're talking about, sir." She cast him a coquettish sideways glance. "What would you have me do?"

"Marry me, Kate," he breathed against her hair.

"Marry me this day. I cannot bear another day without you. I've already convinced Reverend MacKenzie that there is no need to post the bans since, in the eyes of this community; we've been man and wife for months. He'll marry us this afternoon at the manse with his wife and George Loggie as witnesses."

She hesitated and he drew her away from him to look down into her face.

"What is it? Surely I haven't completely misread you? Surely..."

"Hamish...James, I'm confused." She gazed up at him, emerald eyes wide. "You look and sound so very different. Like someone I don't know."

"The trappings may have changed but--" He drew her back into his arms and murmured into her ear, "--the man beneath hasnae and I've no the time ta wait for ye to get know a suit of clothes."

She felt a chuckle bubbling up inside as he lapsed back into his faulty Highland brogue and she caught the implications of his words.

"It's not a suit of clothing I'll be marrying, my fine lad," she stood on tiptoe to whisper in his ear. "It's the man beneath." Then she pushed him out to arm's length and winked up at him. "Aye, I'll marry ye, laddie, and be proud ta."

She grew serious as she reached up to touch his smoothly shaven cheek. "But first I must tell you something. Then you must decide if you wish to pursue your suit. Hamish, I'm no more a titled lady than you are a backwoods beast. My real name is Rose Jones, daughter to a Highland lass named Iona Cameron and Joshua Jones, tenant farmer on Sir William Sheffield's estate."

"There's no need to explain." He put a finger gently to her lips and smiled down into her distressed expression. "Lady Emma, in the course telling the tale of her adventures with you, had to

232

tell me about your past so that I might understand. And it doesn't matter. In fact, I feel fortunate to be getting a wife who knows her way around a farm, who has the brains, courage, and practicality to share the sort of life I've chose to lead. There's only concession I will ask."

"And that would be?"

"That I may always call her Kate, my Kate who came out of the sea to save my heart and spirit."

"Of course. And perhaps I may always call you Hamish?" Her eyes were twinkling. "Dr. James Donnelly sounds so stiff and stuffy."

"Hamish MacDonald the Healer I shall remain." He grinned down upon her. "I doubt I could get our friends and neighbors to begin addressing me otherwise. And since the law states it's the man who marries, not the name, we'll be wed as Hamish and Kate MacDonald...if you agree."

"Of course," she replied, delight beaming out of her expression. Then she sobered as she continued, "If you only knew how much I've longed for this day, how I feared I might never see you again, how I dreaded that, free of the charges against you, you might decide to stay in England and go back to your practice there."

"England holds few attractions without my Kate." He cupped her chin in one hand and raised her face that he could gaze down into it. "And I discovered I had no desire to spend my days catering to rich aristocrats. These people, our neighbors, need me, need us; we've been happy here, haven't we, Kate? This is our home now, isn't it?"

"Yes," she nodded vigorously. "Oh, yes, Hamish. To build a life here with you, to work by your side whether it be as the wife of a farmer or healer is my greatest desire."

"And perhaps mother our children?"

"Especially to mother our children."

"It's good, you both staying with us." Paul who'd been standing in the background grinned. "Perhaps my woman and I will continue to have pairs of babies now that we know you'll be here to help them into the world."

Chuckling, he left the barn.

"I want to marry you this very day," Hamish breathed taking her back into his arms once Paul had gone. "We may have first met on All Fool's Day but there'll be no fooling about when it comes to our being wed. And today is Thanksgiving. That makes it perfect. I know I for one have much to be thankful for."

"Oh, Hamish, we both do. But just look at me! I cannot possibly stand beside you before Reverend MacKenzie."

"I've risen to take charge of the occasion." He released her and stepped back to peruse her from head to toe. "I took the liberty of purchasing something for you to wear for our wedding before I left London. I'd planned to give it to you in the cabin and then enjoy some premarital pleasure watching you donning it. However, with Paul and his family in residence, I fear you'll have to change here in the barn."

"What a presumptuous lad you are!" She put her hands on her hips and slanted him a sly glance. "And a sad waste of money if I'd refused!"

"Ah, but you didn't, did you!" He spun her about, gave her a light shove on the bottom. "Now into that stall yonder and I'll fetch your wedding gown. While you change I'll finish milking poor Bess, harness that fine little mare over yonder. I rode here and while it makes a romantic picture, I hardly fancy taking my bride to her wedding riding pillion."

"I would ride a donkey to be wed to you, Hamish MacDonald, "she said looking up into his face. "Do you think I went to all the trouble to save you from

234

the gallows just to set you free? No, my counterfeit Highland laddie, no indeed. I had others plans for you...and still have."

With a flirtatious flick of her skirts she turned and went into a stall, coyly unbuttoning her faded blue dress as she went.

He glanced toward the cabin, hesitated a moment, then followed her.

"Hamish MacDonald, what do you think you're doing?" she shrieked as he tumbled her back into the straw. "You'll be going to your wedding full of chaff. Lord only knows what Reverend and Mrs. MacKenzie will think."

"I little care, lass." He reverted to his Highland accent. "After all, they think me but a rude Highlander with no better manners than ta tumble his intended afore the fact."

"Ah, but Dr. James Donnelly is a gentleman," she teased running a finger coyly over his lower lip as he lay over her.

"Ye've obviously got a few things to learn about the guid doctor," he chuckled as he peeled her out of her dress.

It was some time before they arose. He brushed straw from his frock coat and trousers, and then went to fetch her wedding gown.

A word about the author...

The award-winning author of nineteen published books, Gail MacMillan is a graduate of Queen's University. Her short stories and articles have appeared in magazines in Canada, the USA, and Europe.

She lives in New Brunswick, Canada, with her husband and three dogs.

Thank you for purchasing
this Wild Rose Press publication.
For other wonderful stories of romance,
please visit our online bookstore at
www.thewildrosepress.com.

For questions or more information
contact us at
info@thewildrosepress.com.

The Wild Rose Press
www.TheWildRosePress.com